Son

Neil Sonnekus

Press

Published by 99% Press,

an imprint of Lasavia Publishing Ltd.

Auckland, New Zealand

www.lasaviapublishing.com

Copyright © Neil Sonnekus, 2023

Cover Design: Daniela Gast

ISBN: 978-1-99-118981-3

For

Rudolph Henry Sonnekus

(1918–2007)

Even the wisest man grows tense
With some sort of violence
Before he can accomplish fate
Know his work or choose his mate.

W.B. Yeats, *Under Ben Bulben*

The Usual Department

The best few moments of my marriage, without a doubt, took place in a divorce lawyer's office. I signed my name on the solid line, walked out of those shadowy chambers and into the loud sunshine of a bustling Johannesburg street. Hawkers were shouting, hooters were blaring and shop radios were throbbing as a crowd of pigeons exploded around my feet. I was a free man.

There was only one rule going forward, if you'll pardon that piece of corporate speak, which was this: no more relationships. None whatsoever. The sole activity I was interested in from now on was good old-fashioned sex, having lost a whole decade to The Ex and her adulterous bastard of a lover, her career. But that was all over now, thank you very much. We were finished. History. Kaput.

I had what may be called a life again, even though it very much resembled the days preceding that particularly bright Monday.

In the mornings I'd get up, ablute, dress and get dragged down Emfuleni Road by what used to be our 'baby', Butch, a mottled mongrel with the look of a killer but the cheerful soul of a suburban florist. Once in the park I'd let him go chase hadedas, squirt his personality all over the place, roll around in avian corpses, and smell each and every available pooch's rectum. After that little constitutional, I'd eat, drink and leave the key on the windowsill (but out of others' sight) for what used to be 'our' domestic worker, the one and only Ms Beauty Motsepe.

This was also a relationship, of course, but it wasn't romantic – or sexual. I was the landowner, she, the worker. But if I controlled the means of production, she controlled the very *atmosphere*, being even more of an expert at casting a mood than I'd been in my scowling, sugary youth. So I made sure that by the time she came in with her emotional baggage I was upstairs and writing my novel about, well, *something*. I wasn't quite sure yet.

After that double dose of living hell, it came as a great relief to go and perform some paid dross at that receptacle of universal misery, otherwise known as the *Daily News*, where all the casualties of the community, city, country, continent and cosmos appeared on my screen in seemingly dead black bytes. Millions died of such horrors as old age and privilege, but we preferred to make it look like more perished of AIDS, mudslides, train crashes, mining disasters, earthquakes, traffic pile-ups, drownings, religious fanaticism, hunger, terror, riots and mainly political incompetence, all of which I coolly cut to size and gave a fitting headline.

I liked my job because it was relatively well paid, populated by lunatics and seldom (or almost never, as modern journalese would have it) followed me home. I was forty-two, suddenly, single and probably depressed, but I was also employed and fairly independent, which most of the world couldn't say and I knew. Most other men my age looked way beyond it, but I was lucky enough to have a body that didn't show the punishment I meted out to it, yet easily responded to any bit of exercise I hurled in its direction. Then again, most of those I compared myself with – not to, note – thought nothing of starting the day with a determined beer, joint or sometimes worse, so that wasn't saying much.

Our working week started on Sunday afternoon and ended on Thursday night, whereupon I now continued cruising for flesh after post-deadline drinks and passed out, unsated, after more post-deadline drinks. But there was no luxury of sleeping in on Friday mornings, for Ms Motsepe still had to work. I'd seen no point in getting someone to clean our mini-mansion five times a week, but The Ex had argued that at least it was creating employment and live-in shelter for one other soul, not to mention food and a rudimentary education for Beauty's three dependents out in the back of beyond. It was an argument only the most hard-hearted bastard, which The Ex had accused me of being anyway, could counter. I had also seen no point in having a pet, which required all kinds of additional commitments, but after most of our neighbours had been robbed and/or assaulted and/or raped and/or murdered – with or without high walls, spiky palisades, razor wire, electronic devices and dodgy-looking security guards – there was a fairly persuasive logic to that bit of reasoning too.

Coming back to Beauty (and it always does), I could usually tell by the way she knocked whether she was in a good mood or not. If she was peeved because I'd forgotten to put the key out the night before, or her kids were giving her grief, or her sister had once again told her that *she* was earning more than Beauty, she almost broke the door down. If she was feeling really sorry for herself, which was often, she knocked so timidly that I could barely hear her, except that I was always half expecting it tensely anyway. I don't know which annoyed me more.

Why couldn't I just give her her own key, she'd asked. Because I'd read and heard of other domestic workers being attacked, then having their keys taken to get to the real target, the wealthier inhabitants of the house. It was a lose-lose situation I'd said in our lingua franca, Afrikaans, which used to annoy The Ex (and please me) intensely. It really wasn't because I didn't trust her. Beauty had pursed her lips and the silence had said it all: the dog was supposed to protect her. But, I'd said, I had also been informed about walls and palisades like ours being scaled, the dogs poisoned, the domestic worker subjected to variations of the above, whereafter it was the houseowner's turn. Her grumble had implied I was thinking of the domestic workers who collaborated with the criminals against their employers and that I suspected her of being one of them. I was ready for that argument too, for if she really wanted to pursue this matter to its very bitter end, she knew I would say – because I had done so before, much to The Ex's chagrin – that if I suspected her of anything, I wouldn't keep her in my employ. Moreover, *I* was the one who was actually paying her, and if she didn't like living in her spacious back room and getting paid more than double the minimum wage our new masters had determined, even though it was less than her bloody *sister* was being paid, she could always go and work somewhere else. Two days of sulking would follow, after which Ms Motsepe would mysteriously cheer up again.

Life was so safe and simple in the new South Africa.

If she let herself in on a Friday morning, of course, I could always go back to sleep. But that never happened because I could hear her washing the dishes downstairs, the volume entirely dependent upon her state of mind. And if I did lie in or pretend to sleep until ten o'clock and then head downstairs for breakfast, that would clash with her coming upstairs with the vacuum cleaner. The last thing I felt like doing was trying to get in and out of the shower with a non-interested party around, and if I pretended to sleep after that it was in an atmosphere of such tolerant disapproval that it wasn't worth it. So I'd wash myself in a daze and see to it that I was dressed and gone by the time Beauty came muttering up the stairs, though we usually ended up shuffling past each other anyway. Worlds apart.

Out in the allegedly free one I would buy myself a breakfast, quickly scan the paper to see that I hadn't committed a sub's worst nightmare – a typo in the headline – and get annoyed by middle-class housewives complaining about their servants. Didn't they have anything *better* to talk about? Then I would rent a movie, have a chat with the shop's knowledgeable proprietor, and go home. By that time Beauty would have finished vacuuming and emoting upstairs, and I could watch the DVD on my computer in the study while she made an almighty racket downstairs. Just as the movie ended, she would take her lunch break and sit in her room for an hour to the very second. I would have lunch too, then go back upstairs and write up the review for the rest of the afternoon and the weekend edition a week hence. By six I would be in the pub, by nine I would like almost everybody, and by one I'd be gliding through the quiet back streets of suburbia to avoid the cops and pass out in a stupor of mostly missed opportunities.

Saturdays I could finally sleep in but didn't because, well, I was getting older. Also, Ms Motsepe would approach the front of the house in her white-and-green church uniform, noisily unlock and relock the gate in the larger electronic one, and head to the main road, where she would catch a minibus taxi to church and spend the rest of the weekend with her fellow workers, both loved and despised. This was the best part of the week. I didn't have to go out shopping with The Ex or stay in fighting with her anymore. In summer, as it was now, I could walk around dick naked and listen to the silence or music *I* liked, and gradually ease myself into the day. Then, after a basic lunch with a bias towards carbs with further alcoholic traffic in mind, I would amble over to my colleagues and pals Jay and Veronica Redland's in the next suburb, just like The Ex and I used to do, but without any of the simmering tension.

Jay came from a province that was supposed to be fully Afrikaans, the Free State, but he was a *soutie*, a redneck, an African pom. Veron, on the other hand, was a firebrand from the Flats – or so I'd assumed.

'Do you think Coloureds only come from the Cape?' she'd challenged me the first time we met.

'No, but most of them do.'

'Well, I'm not most of them.'

'I'm sorry.'

'Okay, but don't do it again,' she'd said.

'Is that a chip I see on your shoulder?'

'Ja, but I've got one on the other shoulder too. I'm a balanced Coloured.'

After which we got on famously.

Jay and I would sit and watch two English soccer teams with three Limey players between them at the most, commenting on how they each earned more than our annual salary a week and, more to the point, who in the office we would like to screw and in what order. Somehow we never tired of that conversation. All of this while drinking up a storm of good cold beer and going outside for a smoke next to their pool at halftime, lest Veron crap all over us for doing so indoors.

'Life in the suburbs,' I would say in the constant sunshine.

'Who said it was going to be easy, bru?'

Later on, he would invite me to stay for a braai with Veron and the girls, and I always accepted. Then we'd get even more trashed, whereupon she would send the kids off to bed, start drinking as well and get particularly bellicose as the evening headed for its social climax. My friend was inclined to get all soppy when he was drunk, and Veron was more than just inclined to give poor old pasty-faced, mealy-tongued Jay a verbal lashing second to none. Contrary to what many people thought, this was not matrimonial or even interracial animosity but sexual foreplay. What it therefore meant was that it was time for me to stumble home from their jacaranda-lined suburb to mine with its plane trees, wondering whether one fragrant night I'd end up on the sidewalk with a knife between my ribs, though I always woke up with a rusted old tanker lodged firmly 'twixt mine ears.

I would lie scowling in the small mansion I had insisted on buying for us in a moment of sexual optimism, when all I'd really wanted was a two-bedroom flat in Rosebank within walking distance of work. The property was so big it could have accommodated two more houses and extended families, like the more practical folk a couple of doors down the road, Indians with whom The Ex had wanted nothing to do. They had not yet cast off the yoke of tradition, she'd maintained somewhat imperiously. Be that as it may, I had obviously belonged to that class of idiots who did what they thought others wanted them to, so I was clearly getting some or other karmic comeback for all my years of alleged bastardy. In summary, all I had to show for my life with The Ex was a mountainous mortgage, a domestic worker who had perfected the art of sulking and a dog that seemed to shit more than it ate.

Yet, just as I was getting used to my new existence and finding it increasingly agreeable, albeit in a numb sort of way, I went to work as innocently as one could on a sweltering mid-week afternoon in southern Africa, which is when I first laid eyes on one Kayla Greenwood. She was rushing headlong to the deputy editor's office and, being a man in the usual department, I was instantly attracted to her. She was about twenty-seven, had straight brown hair and was extremely shapely. She was also quite badly dressed and seemed to have been scratching her face, but she was full of focused energy behind her specs which I, for some or other reason, found a bit of a turn-on. Hell, I'd be a liar to say I didn't know there were porn sites dedicated solely to women who wore glasses. But my head wasn't the only one that was turning and I didn't expect anything to come of it. After all, I was at least fifteen years older than her.

'Who's that?' I nevertheless said to my good friend and fellow sub, Jay.

'Haven't a clue, my bru,' he rap-rhymed.

On Time

The next day was Thursday, meaning that after deadline it was effectively my Friday night, so I obviously started drinking. Friday was therefore my Saturday, so I continued drinking as the rest of the Gentile world joined in. Saturday was thus my Sunday, which meant I had to sober up for the start of my working week, but then I'd never liked feeling excluded from the rest of sinful humanity, so I just continued jubilating with the infidels. The result was that I always started my working week with a hangover. This meant I had to have a little curative drink, a *regmaker*, on Sunday night, just to steady me for the rest of the week. Monday, Tuesday and Wednesday nights could then serve – in theory at least – as my collective, abstemious Sunday night. Mostly.

I mean, I worked in the *media*, for fuck's sake.

But the one little part I omitted, like any subeditor worth his or her office grime, was another kind of relationship. This was the one that happened every Sunday morning, which I didn't just faff, fart, fidget or fritter away in the house which used to belong to The Ex and me. Oh no. While the rest of my friends, colleagues and peers might nurse their hangovers, start abusing themselves afresh, fight with their second spouse or post-marital partner, clash with their children or stepchildren or both, watch sport, less likely partake in it and more probably return home from gambling in one of the former homelands, I would struggle up and drive to Pretoria to visit my old man, who was determined to make it to ninety-three. This had to do with some or other ditty he liked, which he always quoted me and I nevertheless instantly forgot.

The Ex had at first accompanied me but soon tired of the old man's endless repetitions and domineering, one-way conversations – she never did like competition – and I couldn't exactly blame her for that. But why did *I* do it? Why did I go and visit a man who still had some kind of hold over me in the sense that I still couldn't bring myself to smoke in front of him – at my age! Because I had promised my mother I would visit him at least once a week as she lay rotting of cancer a decade previously and, still being a man of words, I had kept them. But that wasn't the only reason why I went to see the old sod. I wanted to know why she had stuck with him, regardless; why she had imposed such a burden upon me; why he had failed to provide yours truly with any guidance whatsoever; why he had been content to be a fingerprints clerk in the South African Police for about a hundred and fifty years after the blasted war; and why there was a part of me that nevertheless admired – let's not even *talk* about love – his intransigence.

Moreover, I resented him because he'd been one of those who had dutifully helped prop up the previous administration his entire working life, though in all fairness he'd despised the Safari Suited mindset that accompanied it. I therefore hated that city as well, even though we hadn't actually lived in it. Instead, I grew up in a squeaky-clean mess called Lyttelton, named after the Colonial Secretary, Alfred, the youngest of twelve children to Mary and George, Fourth Baron Lyttelton. George had had a port named after him in New Zealand, produced three more daughters from his second marriage and, according to Wikipedia, committed suicide by flinging himself down a flight of stairs at the ripe old age of fifty-nine.

His last son, Alfred, was an accomplished sportsman. As a footballer, he'd been an expert dribbler in the days when passing the ball was anathema, and he scored England's lone goal in his only international, which was against Scotland. The score was 3-1. Alfred was also an excellent cricketer in the position of wicketkeeper, playing four Tests against what were probably considered those criminal chaps from Down Under. But he later became involved in politics and favoured indentured Chinese labour to South Africa, opposed Welsh independence, but had an open mind to decentralisation in the colonies and women's suffrage back home. The liberals, again according to that site which derives its name from the Hawaiian word for truth, completely opposed his idea of letting the colonies run themselves. Naturally, the land was untamed, empty and therefore nameless before whites arrived, even though the locals had always called it Mhlahlandlela.

Anyway, the town named after Alfred Lyttelton should never have been a suburb of Pretoria in the first place, since it was over twenty kilometres outside the capital. But some or other bright spark had wanted a satellite that could serve the city's burgeoning civil service and surrounding military complex, and that was that. Lyttelton finally became a municipality in its own right and its road signs were mis-spelled by the mainly Afrikaans clerks who ran it, thinking quite logically that if 'little' was spelled the way it was – which made no sense anyway, since that was not how it sounded – then Lyttelton should too. 'But then the English has [sic] always been a treacherous bunch,' they would say. There was no cinema in that town, no hotel. The only place of entertainment by the time I left for university was an off-the-pavement bar within spitting distance of the railway track, which neatly dissected the valley and therefore town. That was also the year Lyttelton's name was changed, though the central grid and main train station retained the original. That dump was now called Verwoerdburg, named after the milk-white Dutchman who had devised that wonderful bit of social engineering called separate (but grossly unequal) development, otherwise known as apartheid.

'Bastard's probably never even been here,' the old man had said, though it's doubtful Alfred Lyttelton had, either.

In one of his more light-hearted moments the man whose wife and sisters called him Son would name that place Verwurgburg: Strangle City. But even after the African National Congress came into power in 1994 the town still kept that despicable title, and its fancy new shopping mall was called Verwoerdburgstad for quite a while before it was hastily changed to the more politically neutral Centurion Mall, what with a chill wind blowing in from the nearby Union Buildings. Name-changing was clearly a long and arduous business because, by the time The Ex and I got divorced, the mall was still surrounded by Hendrik Verwoerd and John Vorster Drives, the latter named after our very own Nazi terrorist. The mall had been built along the Sesmylspruit, close to where an old girlfriend had lived and we malcontents had spent endless

Chekhovian weekends, devising ways to get out of that town. To achieve that monument to progress, all the houses along the Six Mile Stream had been bought up, demolished and transformed into said mall with cinemas and a couple of generic hotels next to a shallow, man-made lake. And, just to make everyone feel a little more patriotic, an international cricket stadium, named after its sponsor, was thrown into the mix.

The only reason I still went to Lyttelton was to visit my late mother's grave, which happened to be close to that mall, and the old man's living one. I would never put my foot in that town again once he was 'gone', he who had never had a drop of liquor over his lips, nor smoked a cigarette, nor slept with any other woman except Yvonne, my dearly departed mother.

Driving to Lyttelton, I was getting pissed off anew about all the warehouses sprouting up along the highway to Pretoria. When I'd finally returned from varsity, ready to be fêted by the world, there had been a sole thorn tree on a rolling Highveld hill. Then came the Development Bank, which had at least planted indigenous trees to swallow up 'my' lonely acacia, followed by each and every designer-stubbled wanker's idea of what constituted industrial design along the way. If apartheid had had its unfair share of abominable architecture, then the new money was not doing any better. In fact, it was doing worse because it was supposed to know better.

Also, I was working myself into the usual state after making the mistake of telling the old man I would be there at about ten o'clock. By the time I got to his dull, still predominantly white suburb – passing the new hospital in which my mother had breathed her last, then the architecturally brutal Afrikaans high school I had attended, I'm really sorry to say, quite happily – it was half-past eleven. My only consolation was that I had a definite escape route in that I had to leave at the stroke of one o'clock, thereby avoiding an awkward lunch, to get back to the *News* by two for the start of my working week. If the old man had been silent about my years of being a successful but non-income-generating screenwriter, then he was completely supportive about the fact that my current job was work and it had to be done, no matter whether he didn't understand what the hell it was all about. If it felt to me like the last refuge of a complete failure, then for him it was work, it was paid and it was therefore good. Period.

Now he was waiting, as always, at the gates of the only house I had known up to the late age of twenty, when I'd left home for good. It was from the late Fifties and functional in a slightly less aggressive way than my Sixties face-brick school: a three-bedroom house on a quarter of an acre flanked by a smaller, matching block consisting of a washroom, single garage and tiny servant's quarters at the back. Both the roofs were corrugated and from the street the garage complex looked like a soldier's head: a lance-corporal wearing a stiff beret with the washroom's window serving as his visible eye. The old man had co-designed this house and he had paid it off over a very long time and now it was his and the only way he was going to leave it was when he was 'as stiff as a dead man's you know what'. There he stood with his still-full head of fine, silver hair combed straight back above his tanned scowl, his sun moles and broken nose from a police-college scrap. He was dressed as if he was going to some event he wouldn't attend on principle in his polished Hush Puppies, neatly ironed chocolate-brown trousers, green buttoned-up golf shirt and light-brown check jacket. He stood as upright as the only filmmaker who'd ever made any sense to him, Charlie Chaplin, and as defiantly good looking as someone he'd never listened to: Beethoven.

He opened the gates, I hello'ed him as I drove through and down the driveway, past the neatly clipped grass, along the side of the garage, over the vast and obsessively mowed back lawn and under the double canopy that had been installed for Ma's car and mine. As I disembarked, he came through the door connecting the house and the garage, crossing the cement courtyard towards me.

'Howzit, Dad.'

'You're late,' he said, faux friendly.

'I'm sorry,' I said, instantly annoyed.

'I've been standing out there since a quarter to ten.'

'Ja, well ...'

'I've been worried *sick*.'

He showed no interest in the reminder that I'd said I'd be there at 'about' ten o'clock, because *he* had never been late in his life.

I muttered something and he said 'What?'

Physically, this was the only thing wrong with him. While my mother had been alive, I'd suspected that his deafness was selective; now I was convinced of it because he always answered the phone when I called him on Thursday nights after deadline, just to check if he was alright and to say I'd see him on Sunday. Of course, he always answered the phone as if he was about to hit whoever had the audacity to call him so 'bladdy late', meaning just after nine. Then he'd thank me for calling him and God bless me.

'Nothing,' I said.

'And your car's dirty.'

'I must have driven through a puddle last night,' I said pathetically.

'You know, people used to think the Chevy was brand new, after twenty-five years.'

'Ja, you've said so.'

About a million times, I thought. His repetitiousness might well have driven my mother to a permanent solution, because it would most certainly have driven me to divorce, suicide or murder if I'd had to live with him for the half a century she had.

'*Twenty-five* years!'

'How are you, Dad?' I said, offering my hand to the man who, statistically speaking, should have died long before his much younger wife. Ma had confided in me that she was hoping she'd be able to live off his meagre police pension – which would have been further reduced because she was the spouse – for a few years of peace and quiet after he 'went'.

'Hello, my boy,' he said: eighty-eight years of puritanical piss, gall, vinegar and Nestlé's condensed milk rolled into one.

Then he squashed my tender little sub's hand.

A, Like, Cool Night

Now that I was aware of Kayla, we kept on making eye contact across that great open-plan divide that separates the hacks from their saviours. We'd see each other in places like the canteen with its canine-friendly food, the distorting brushed-steel lifts and the less glamorous parking basement, where she might rush by in her second-hand BMW while I fired up my Crouching Kitten, otherwise known as a very seasoned Honda Civic.

It didn't make any sense. She was somewhere near her big-three crisis (in other words, thirty), while I was definitely managing a permanent one in my early forties. She was on the up and up while I was on the fixed sideways with a bias, all things considered, down. She no doubt believed in the corp and the country while I found it hard to even believe in the after-hours' writing I did to relieve the endless tedium of relativity. She radiated an air of positivity while I wore the sour mantle of a recent divorcé. She was probably a good person, when all she had to do was give our opposition paper a call and ask The Ex what kind of creatures ground their serrated legs between my ears.

Or was I imagining things? It had happened before, much to my embarrassment. Maybe she wasn't attracted to me at all. Maybe she was just being friendly, with a dash of sympathy thrown in for my age and all the misanthropes, druggies, piss-cats, cynics, tired chefs, failed writers, broke muzos and vicarious sportsmen who seemed to litter my profession. I couldn't be sure about those looks, which was why I kept things friendly but aloof. The last thing I felt like was making a fool of myself with someone I might have to see every working day thereafter: one of the many lessons I had learnt from The Ex. But after a few more days of visual footsie, we were introduced by good old Jay at an event that was clearly intended to be a little more than just a post-deadline drinks session that Thursday night. (I had made my usual resentful call to the old man). We had gathered on the balcony of a fortress-like building that reeked of mid-Eighties paranoia, but it was a late summer's evening that still had a faint whiff of lemony jasmine battling its way through the metallic carbon monoxide, closer nicotine and rank journalistic sweat. Most of her mousy-coloured hair had fallen away from the clip that was supposed to contain it, and she'd been harassing her face again, her old-fashioned specs slightly greased up. Moreover, a bra strap was protruding from under an ample orange tank top, and her brand-new black Kenyan kikoi seemed on the verge of falling to her scuffed brown sandals at any moment.

All she had on her side, really, was youth.

Of course, we men were not allowed to dress so sparingly. We *had* to wear collars, even though we never got to work with the public. But at least we'd moved beyond that sartorial atrocity, that corporate noose, the necktie. So I generally wore brown boots, black jeans and freshly ironed white shirts ('thank you, Beauty'), which I flattered myself carried a head sparking with subversion. Jay, on the other hand, showed his deep and abiding regard for management by wearing old red Converse sneakers, ripped blue Levi's and a Liverpool supporter's jersey which, if the suits really wanted to get technical about it, sported a collar – even if it was made of canvas. In winter he deigned to wear one of his father's sick-green suit jackets that dated to roughly around the time of the Rinderpest. The reason he got away with this, of course, was that he was so bloody good and fast at what he did that he was indispensable.

'And this is Len Bezuidenhout,' he said, getting to the point where everybody was his good old chum.

She looked me directly in the eyes with her steady, framed ones but had a damp handshake.

'Hi Len.'

'Haven't I seen you somewhere before?' I mocked, having had a couple of beers to stir up the me I preferred.

'I, like, doubt it,' she gamely said.

'So what, as we in Joburg so subtly say, do you do?'

This, of course, was a stupid giveaway because it could mean I knew she wasn't from the Highveld and had therefore made discreet enquiries about her.

'I'm one of the, like, new political reporters,' she replied, not giving anything away either.

I knew that too, but couldn't tell her I, *like*, knew.

'And you?' she said, alive.

'What about me?' I said, noticing her fingertips held the bubbly glass with the concentrated pressure of an alcoholic in training.

'What do you, like, do?' she said rather earnestly.

'Oh, I work in hell.'

'What do you …?'

'I fix other people's copy.'

'Ah,' she said blankly.

The editor cleared his throat loudly and said he would like to welcome two new additions – 'not editions,' he added, eliciting polite if not sincere grins – to our editorial team.

The first was Kayla Greenwood, freshly arrived from the Mother City, who most of the men tried hard not to show they were assessing sexually, making the air all the more charged. The other was a 'fellow comrade', a bald-shaven Edward Motshekga. I had seen this strutting peacock in passing but hadn't thought for one second he might be a journalist; he certainly wasn't dressed like one. He was wearing a Gucci suit, a designer T-shirt, a gold necklace that would have covered my monthly drinking bill, and those fashionable crocodile-leather boots with long, pointy toes that made him walk as if he was traversing a field of doves' eggs.

I watched the older, more regular political reporters and picked up expressions of detached disapproval from the last remaining whitey to ones of dead-eyed patience among the darkies, who'd seen similar poseurs come and go before the likes of Motshekga. But the times they were a-changing. Fast.

Towards the end of the evening, Edward and a vertically challenged, obsequious prat called Jack Weisz spoke to Kayla. Weisz was another piece of work in his nouveau-colonial uniform of tasselled, well-polished brown shoelets, grey flannel trousers, a navy-blue, double-breasted jacket, a white shirt, and a maroon cravat and matching pocket kerchief to complement his florid phiz. To complete the picture, he sported a billowing coif to give the remaining hairs 'body' and, just to show that he had once been a hip music critic back in the Eighties, Bono specs. He had worked his way up from junior reporter to arts editor to freebie general and, finally, deputy head of that department which always gets it budget cut first: human fucking resources. But if he and Edward looked all pally-pally, then their expensive deodorants were invisibly battling for racial and corporate dominance while they laughed and chatted with Kayla. More odiously, they were smoking fat cigars, fingering their Johnnie Walker Blacks and talking to her in such a manner that they might as well have been ejaculating on to her – let's be kind here – black skirt.

On Youth

The old man was waiting at the gates of 123 Harry Smith Avenue, named after that colonial cradle snatcher who had given the order to shoot Hintsa, the paramount chief of the Xhosa nation, who was then decapitated. We greeted each other as I drove through, down, past, over and parked out back. Beyond the bay I saw that one of the trees, which had survived his scythe after Ma had died, was carrying fruit. So I got out and helped myself to a fig as he came through the door, over the cement courtyard and across the lawn towards me. The fig was as decadently swollen and sweet as ever, and the old man said he would put some in a bag for me.

'Don't worry,' I said, giving him my left hand to crush, since the fingers of my right were too sticky

'You know,' he said, 'when I grew up we had figs, avocados, mangoes, *bunches* of bananas. All in our garden, all growing wild. We had a whole *acre* of garden.'

'Good,' I said, elongating the word in that Afro-Afrikaans way of filling up space, seeing a low, spread-out house surrounded by orchards and monkey-vine forest in the place we'd gone to every holiday since time immemorial. 'That's probably why you're still so healthy.'

'Not only that,' he said, as I started body-languaging us towards the courtyard. 'It's because I've never smoked, drunk or slept with other women.'

'So you've said,' I muttered. About nine-hundred thousand times, I thought.

'What?'

'Shall we have some coffee?'

'*Good* idea,' he said as we stepped on to the courtyard, which was semi-surrounded by the main bedroom's one wall, the small back stoep which led into the kitchen, and that back part of the garage complex that used to be the servant's quarters, which then became my teenage bedroom and was now a dusty storeroom. Under a shortened gutter was a grey 45-gallon drum to catch the rain water and about a thousand cigarette butts, which as a teenager I'd known nothing about, honestly. To complete the picture, there were two white wire chairs and a matching table that always had bits of cardboard under its legs because, like so many of Joburg's coffee bars, it wobbled.

We were about to ascend the three steps on to the stoep when something unusual happened: my cellphone rang. It was Kayla, who hoped I didn't mind her calling me out of the blue like this. 'I'm sure I'll survive,' I said, but she was going away on a job for the week but would be back next Saturday. That's two 'buts' in a single sentence, I thought, but could we possibly go out for a walk then, she continued. Watching the old man go into the washroom on the left and emerge with a vomit-yellow Checkers bag to fill with figs, I responded that I'd have to consult my diary, but that it should be okay: I'd call her if Random House or Hollywood suddenly rang. You never know, she said much too positively for my liking. After enquiring and hearing that she was working on a job with Ed Motshekga, I said good luck. 'See you next Saturday,' she laughed, and rang off.

The old man said he'd put the figs in the car. All I'd wanted was to eat one or two bloody figs, but no, and he told me the car was dirty.

'Maybe I'll wash it after coffee,' I said.

'I'll help you,' he replied.

This was just what I needed after a night of heavy drinking with Jay and Veron as we went up the three steps, past his flimsy security gate and stable door into the kitchen, which still had its original Fifties oven, sink and cupboards. The tiles, shelves and wooden furniture, however, had replaced the old linoleum-covered floor, table and chairs some time since. I'm sure Ma had told me about it, but like so much else it had passed me by in a haze of anti-detail impatience.

One of the objects that had survived her demise, however, was her hefty, fake-marble bust of Beethoven, which had spent years on the rarely used piano in the no-longer-utilised living room, staring way beyond the semi-naked Italian beauty, care of J.H. Lynch, lounging on a misty tree trunk on the opposite wall. But Uncle Ludwig had moved to a kitchen shelf for reasons unknown and always seemed to be looking at me from under his eyebrows, no matter where I stood. Maybe he was accusing me of preferring African music to his pomposity, and I think the only reason why the old man never got rid of him was because he'd paid for it. Ma had never really listened to old Thunderballs (Gé Korsten, yes) and the old man didn't just hate classical music, he hated most music. As for those long-haired rock 'n roll bastards with their reedy voices on *Popshop*, 'They should all be shot.' The only kind of music he liked was the stuff that had rhyming lyrics from the Thirties and Forties, none of which he collected. Now he started telling me that he'd bought himself a coffee mug, decorated with cosmos flowers, at Checkers for two rands ninety-five.

'Oh?' I grunted.

'They're usually *six* ninety-five,' he crowed.

'Hm?' I said, trying to sound positive, thinking of Kayla's musical arse as she walked ahead of me in an open-plan office awash with testosteronal egos and oestrogenic strategists.

'Which mug do you want?'

There was a choice of five cosmos florals and the one I always chose, which had rings around it.

'I'll take this one,' I said for about the eight-hundred-thousandth time.

'*Everybody* likes that one,' he said for the corresponding number of times.

'Really?'

'And I got us some Lemon Creams,'

'Good,' I said, wishing my mother a peaceful rest.

'But, you know,' he said, pouring boiling water onto his one spoon of insipid instant mud and my five spoons of the same, 'someone said to me the other day I should stop taking my coffee with two spoons of sugar *and* two spoons of condensed milk.'

'Dad, you're eighty-eight, you're as healthy as a pig. If you've made it to here, I don't see why you should suddenly change anything.'

'Ja, but I want to make it to ninety-three.'

'I know,' I said, my temples starting to throb.

Bring on the SFX

Back at the office, we had two political obsessions. In the case of foreign affairs, it was that old fruitcake just north of our border, Robert Gabriel Mugabe. In national affairs, it was our Supreme Leader, who was another foreign affair since he spent most of his time overseas anyway. If he wasn't brown-nosing the nut job up north, he was castigating the West at the United Nations. The honeymoon period of Nelson Mandela was over and Comrade Mugabe had started appropriating white-owned farms left, right and centre. In essence, he was telling the world to go and get stuffed in a perfectly – and unintentionally ironic – Oxbridge accent. Everything was the imperialists' fault, which was largely true, but then he was hardly acting in a manner less vicious and expedient than his predecessors. This, however, didn't matter because, like so many left-wingers, he somehow thought criticism was only his to give, not receive.

Obviously we white subs and mainly black editorial thought he was barking mad or just plain impractical, but it wasn't half as cut and dried as that. There were people in the office who became silent when we mouthed off about Uncle Bob, and when he came to the country for some or other convention in which the only decision reached was when to have the next bloody summit or symposium, he was not greeted with boos. He was hailed as a hero of the revolution in a manner that seemed to veer between idolatry and sheer, infantile spite. His speeches were eloquent and made perfect sense to all those ex-exiles who had been schooled in an ideology formulated in the nineteenth century by a European whose philosophy only seemed to work, watered down, in northern European countries like the doubting Dane's old stomping ground. No matter. He was always invited as a matter of protocol by our Supreme Leader, who personally oversaw a mainly black populace dying in their droves thanks to his inaction on AIDS. His greatest transgression, from my point of view, was that he was the most boring little mass murderer I had ever listened to. 'His' people were being raped and murdered at such a rate that, statistically, it made the war in Iraq look like a Women's Auxiliary tea party.

But, as with most things South African, it was all invisible. The violations happened elsewhere, meaning mainly in the townships or on the farms, both of which he as an outsider and theorist knew squat about. Most of the tortured and then murdered farmers were Afrikaners and, because their tribe had previously been the supposedly sole oppressors, they weren't given much ear time by the powers that be, including the English media – us – who tried to convey the impression that we were looking at the bigger picture of building a constitutional et cetera, et cetera. Most white intellectuals had fallen silent or resorted to class analyses, while the black heavies were in a bind because this was what many of them had clamoured for all along. We couldn't expect everything to be perfect immediately. After the Big Bleed we'd have the Big Build, even though it felt like we'd need another three-and-a-half centuries to sort everything out. But our glorious leader's rhetoric was very much the same as in the past: we had to stand together as one nation (with eleven official languages), fight the injustices of the past and the resulting poverty of the present, so that we could have a renaissance for the future. Not a renewal or a rebirth or something truly African, a *Renaissance*. I fantasised about seeing him fall asleep during one of his own speeches, as I tended to, but as far as I was concerned the enemy was still those who abused power, regardless of their skin colour, which was a dangerous thing to say. In fact, it was seen as unbridled racism in those halcyon days of carrot-up-the-arse correctness. You couldn't criticise the new lot, since they had come from the moral high ground, and this is what annoyed them most about the *Daily News*. Somehow they'd expected the so-called liberal, white-owned press to fall over backwards and praise them to high heaven, no matter what they did. The problem was they weren't doing much that was worthy of praise. Sure, they were making all the right noises, even laws, but the people who were supposed to execute those orders were either fired because they were white or appointed because they were related. These leaders of men were screwing their own people more than their fascist predecessors by abusing the principle of *ubuntu* in its most cynical guise. If indeed we are what we are through others, then how can individuals possibly be held responsible for being caught with their fat fingers in the till?

Of course, the *News* was by now owned by blacks, run by blacks and edited by a black man, but they'd all, of course, been co-opted by the white, capitalist pigs. This from socialist comrades who were as obese from the proceeds of our taxes as those clunky, petrol-guzzling 4x4s they drove. They truly hated us for not applying their brand of democracy, which was to defer everything to the Supreme Leader, and I truly liked the fact that they hated us, because we were at the frontline of another battle. There was a passionate debate raging for the soul of South Africa, and we had it at our fingertips – literally. All things considered, our office was a fully functional, integrated and therefore sexy social democracy.

But the likes of Edward Motshekga and Kayla Greenwood bothered me; they were unknown quantities. Now she had invited me out for a chat, in broad daylight on a summery Saturday afternoon, so it didn't appear to be any kind of sexual come-on. And I needed sex. Badly. Or maybe she first wanted to check me out. Assess me. Maybe this was the modern, liberated way of doing things. I certainly had no idea how to ask someone out. What did you do? Call them up and ask them to go to a movie or eat out with you? Talk about one thing and think about something completely different? Why couldn't you just call someone up and say, 'Hey, would you like to have sex with me tonight?' Surely that's all it boiled down to in the end? The Ex and I had had an argument in the office, continued it in a bar and then got sidelined by sex. After that initial distraction, which lasted about a year, we had only had arguments. Unfortunately, by then we'd also been married. Big mistake.

Kayla wasn't in the Zoo Lake parking lot, so I smoked a cigarette and three of those later she arrived, looking as sartorially challenged as ever.

'You're late,' I said.

'I'm, like, sorry,' she said.

'You could have called.'

She had run out of air time and we started walking as I tried hard to ignore the duck shit, the litter and a pair of conjoined hounds showing what they thought of social decorum.

'How are you otherwise?' I asked.

She was fine and so was I, and I wondered what I could 'do for you, Ms Green Wood?'

'Nothing,' she virtually sang. 'I just wanted to, like, talk.'

'Okay, if you want to talk, please do me a favour. Please try to talk without, like, using that expression the whole time.'

'Sorry.'

'But what, pray, would you just like to talk about? And why with me?'

'I don't know. I just find you kind of interesting.'

'What? Like an old rock in a museum?'

'No,' she said laughing, 'you're funny, and not many South African men are, like – sorry – funny.'

'Have you been out with all of them?'

'No, but all of those I have been out with are …'

'What?'

'Dull.'

'You see, you can use the occasional adjective,' I said as two middle-aged women strode past us, talking simultaneously and held together, respectively, by their Spandex attire. 'But maybe you've been moving in the wrong circles.'

'That's quite possible,' she gamely said.

'Then again,' I said, 'I haven't met too many laugh-a-minute South African women either.'

'Have you been out with all of *them*?' she shot back somewhat annoyingly.

'No, we usually just stayed in,' I replied.

At which point she slapped my arm playfully, almost intimately, as if we were a couple already. I asked her to tell me about herself but she didn't know where to start.

'Well, where did you go to school? Which university did you attend? What do your parents do? Do you have any siblings, friends, hobbies? What kind of music, art and writing do you like? You know, all that stuff that nice, middle-class liberals like ourselves talk about.'

She had gone to upper-middle-class schools in Cape Town and her mother was a businesswoman, her father a retired advertising executive who had started out as a copywriter and had opposed apartheid, 'obviously'. He was a 'witty, creative type, like you'.

'Excuse me, I'm not retired, creative is out to lunch and only some people find me funny.'

'You know what I mean.'

'Siblings?'

'My brother is a really interesting accountant who loves cricket' and her best friend was currently the art director for one of those women's magazines that have models breaking the aquamarine surface in the Seychelles for hair products, toothpaste and tampons.

After school she'd done a Bachelor of Arts at the University of Cape Town, going on the obligatory overseas trip afterwards, working her way around Europe as a barmaid. She had met a French businessman and they had started importing African fabrics to Paris. Business boomed. But the man had been a racist and a sexist and she'd finally dumped him 'after five, um, intense years'. She returned to Africa (not just Cape Town) and did a Bachelor of Commerce while working as a journalist.

'I heard you're doing an MBA now.'

She was, she said, with an emphasis on that great oxymoron: political science.

'Ah, business, politics …'

'You say that as if they smell bad.'

'No, rotten,' I said, warning myself that I was being way too negative for a seducer, but I couldn't help myself, seeing a sleeping tramp half sitting, half lying on a bench beneath a weeping willow.

'Why?'

'Because it's true.'

'But that is what society consists of,' she said, getting ready for an argument.

That explained a lot, I said, which of course she wanted explained.

'Do you think it's working?'

'Yes, I do.'

'Then why are you writing so critically about it?'

'Because it's still in process.'

'That's a real hey-shoo-wow Cape Town expression,' I said.

She wanted to know what I meant, again, as a group of men and boys played cricket on the kikuyu lawn and the women in their saris sat on blankets where the food was, chatting away: the quintessence of what The Ex had rejected.

'I mean I'm tired of things being "in process". Why can't they just *work* for a change? Like now.'

She responded that the country *was* working and I said it wasn't even a work in progress.

'Why do you say that?'

'Because of those things you're probably studying after hours. Stats. And I'm not going to rattle them off here. I'm supposed to be a creative type – oh, and witty – but I'm the only one who seems to be taking them on board.'

'Give me just one example.'

'All right, since you insist and seem to be a woman. How about the fact that fifty rapes are reported every day? And that's just reported.'

'But you have to see the thing in its broader context.'

'Would you personally tell that to a seven-year-old rape victim in the township? "You have to see the thing in its broader context."?'

'We *have* to look at the cause of all of this, no matter how painful it is.'

'I think you're a bit too young and well-off to be that prescriptive.'

'I can't help where I come from, but I can ...'

'Yes, yes, change where you're going to. And what was the cause of all this misery again? Oh yes, apartheid.'

'Obviously.'

'That word again. And I suppose it's all the Afrikaners' fault?'

'Ja,' she said, though not as forcefully, intuiting perhaps that my sarcasm – in tandem with my very Afrikaans surname – was pointed.

'Well, it is and it isn't.'

'Explain?'

'I don't somehow recall hundreds of thousands of English people marching through the streets to protest their comfort, or moving to Soweto to show their solidarity. I don't recall them or their great empire apologising for what their forebears did to Boer women and children – and blacks – in the concentration camps, long before the Holocaust. I don't recall the Anglo Americans of this world setting up nice little family homes for their migrant workers from the homelands and the rest of the continent. And isn't it odd how the Old Mutuals are suddenly delisting and going international? They're taking their money and running. We're more than a decade into a so-called democracy and I don't see our great leader dealing with the present. I just see him exploiting the past for present political capital.'

'But I still have hope for this country,' she lamely capitulated.

'So do I, like I have hope in a cement life jacket.'

'I like that, even if I don't agree with it.'

'How very libertarian of you.'

Now she asked me whether I'd read *Disgrace*, which impressed me because I thought it tied in nicely with our earlier talk about rape. I told her I had and she asked me what I'd thought about it.

'I liked it a lot, if "like" is the word. Maybe "admire" is more accurate. But I don't buy the seduction-stroke-rape of the student. I find his playing her an abstract dance video unbelievably twee, and I find her acquiescence questionable. But then people make so much about how cold the book is that they forget David Lurie actually weeps in it, which is one of the things I liked about the film. We think he's crying in his car, but actually he's getting a blowjob from a prostitute. The point is, it's very difficult to counter Coetzee's thesis that rape is the ruling metaphor for this country. Rape, the living murder of Everywoman, the ...'

It suddenly occurred to me that I was doing one of the many things I didn't like the old man doing, which was rave and dominate a conversation.

'Wait a bit. What did *you* think of the book?'

'I haven't read it yet.'

I burst out laughing and said it was after five and therefore any sub worth his or her office sweat needed a drink.

'But now it's your turn to tell me about you,' she replied.

After we drove to the nearby Jolly Roger in our respective cars, we occupied the balcony, partook steadily of the happy water and watched the late-afternoon sky grow dark purple, then increasingly inky in a way that Steven Spielberg's CGI department would never capture because you can't feel the tug of the wind, nor smell the mine dust being stirred up. But she persisted in wanting to know about me, so I went on a long, self-deprecating rant about how I'd been a spec screenwriter forever, but how my scripts had been too black and/or bad when they were supposed to be all white, and now, a decade into the new dispensation, they still had *characters* in them. This was not what those morons at the South African Broadcasting Cock-up – I beg your pardon Corporation (a bad joke that got her laughing a tad brashly) – wanted. But then there was something in me that would rather get up their psychopathic noses, even if it meant cutting off my own, than clinch the deal. After years of that frustration, I'd been lucky to get a job through an old university connection at the *Daily News* and, apart from subbing, made my grand switch from writing film scripts to star-rated DVD reviews. A few peers had intimated, mostly silently, that I'd sold out or given up by becoming a critic, a sentiment with which I was inclined to agree. But the truth of the matter was that, no matter how badly the papers paid, they did so dead on time, whereas film folk suffered the happy delusion that you had to feel so honoured to be in their exalted profession that they could rip you off to their hearts' content in terms of time and money. So I was fairly comfortable, if not exactly content, writing half-worthy reviews rather than making lousy white-devils-and-black-saints abortions posing as cinema, let alone art.

'So what's your book about?'

'What?'

'I heard you're writing a novel.'

'Everybody believes that, except me. Most of the time I stare at my blank screen, wondering how I'm going to live up to a myth I stupidly created myself.'

'I don't believe that. I think you're secretly writing the Great South African Novel.'

'"Great"? If only I could find something to write about and finish it. That would be great.'

'And your family?'

'What about them?'

'Tell me about them.'

I told her I was an only child, that my mother had died a decade ago and that I went to visit the old man every Sunday. I didn't, however, tell her about my hungover epiphany when I'd last seen him, which was that I would try to tease some kind of narrative out of him, to make my visits bearable. This was partially because I had failed to do so with Ma, to my eternal regret.

'What's he like?'

'He's a World War Two vet, an octogenarian and impossible.'

'Why?'

'He prefers the company of animals to people.'

Now she wanted to know about that too.

'The first time I realised it was when I came back from varsity in the Eastern Cape, fresh from twenty years of future depression.'

'My friend also gets the black dog,' she said.

'Well, this realisation also had to do with a dog.'

'How come?'

'To cut a long story shorter, I inherited a St Bernard and only had enough money for the two of us to get as far as Germiston from Grahamstown. The old man said he would come and fetch us – my mother was overseas at the time – and I didn't sleep on the train that night. For one I was worried about Bella and for two I was worried that she would make a mess in the old man's Valiant.'

'Was he precious about his car?'

'"Was he precious about his car." You didn't *breathe* in that car. It didn't leave the garage if there was a hint of rain or the prospect of a dirt road. My mother hated it almost as much as she hated the Chevy which preceded it. So I was pretty uptight by the time we got to Germiston.'

He had brought an old bedspread, a bowl and a two-litre Coke bottle filled with water. When we got to Tembisa, Bella promptly puked all over the back seat. I thought the old man would lose his rag, but instead he was the milk of human kindness.

'Amazing.'

If only he'd been like that towards Ma, I couldn't help thinking.

'So what kind of dog does your father have?'

'He doesn't. He's still mourning the loss of his previous one,' I said, realising Butch needed to be fed. I could have called Beauty and asked her to do so, but I didn't feel like that weight either. Also, there was a carnal advantage to under-staying your welcome. I said I had to go but I would walk her to her car and halfway there, of course, the skies opened and we ran to her BM in the pounding rain, laughing like crazy.

When we got to her BM, she didn't get in but stood with her back against it and lifted her face to the rain and thunder. I expressed my surprise that, like most Capeys, she wasn't scared of that aerial violence, and she just looked at me through her greasy, rain-speckled specs, her breath more alive than the charged air, her lips as fresh as an apple the old man had once peeled me in a single, Escher-like curve with his steady brown hands.

'Thanks for the chat,' she said, offering me her pale, wet palm.

On Fathers

In the middle of my second-last year at university, I went to visit my girlfriend, Alexandra, in the recently liberated Zimbabwe. It was exhilarating to be in a free country and almost all the whites were happy about the way Mr Mugabe was conducting himself. It felt so good, in fact, that I couldn't wait to get back to my chains, my back room, my little turquoise Olivetti. So I left Alex, came back into prison and landed up at Pretoria Station, where I took the first train of the day, passing the siding of Fountains, stopping at the second station, Kloofzicht, then disembarking at the hard, functional Sportpark. It was a trip the old man had done thousands of times.

I walked up Cantonments Avenue, a section of which had once caved in and swallowed a house, and picked my mother a bunch of flowers. She, who so loved it when her darling son went travelling, as she did. He, who never stood in our way but spent sleepless nights worrying about us, who would never go anywhere else again except to see his sisters in his home town once a year.

Back in the present, the old man looked ready for a fight, standing at the gates, following me to the back. Before he could say anything, however, I said 'Happy birthday for yesterday, Dad' as I closed the Civic's door.

'*Agh,*' he said, as if his eighty-ninth birthday on St Patrick's Day was an irrelevant irritation.

'Come on, Dad. It's a big thing. Most people don't make it to seventy, and if they do, they don't look half as good as you.'

'Do you know why that is?'

I told him exactly why that was so and he replied that we shouldn't really be celebrating *his* birthday.

'What do you mean?' I said for about the seven hundred-thousandth time.

'Because I had *nothing* to do with it. It was my *mother*'s doing. If anyone should be getting a present, it's *her. She's* the one who carried me for nine months and gave birth to me.'

'But she's been dead a long time now, Dad.'

'Ja, and do you know what?'

'No,' I lied, too hungover to offer much resistance.

'I forgot her birthday one year and I'll *never* forgive myself for it.'

'I'm sure she forgave you,' I said.

But he would have none of it and I remarked that he and Nelson Mandela were born in the same year – full of a sub's useless info, I – but he was more interested in regretting forgetting. I wondered what these two very different men would talk about. I imagined that he would probably have the now-retired politician in stitches with his childlike candour, as he often did my friends when they met him for the first time. But then meeting someone once and seeing them regularly for four decades are two very different creatures.

'Here's your present, Dad,' I said, giving him a block of peppermint crisp chocolate.

'You *shouldn't* have,' he said, outraged.

'Why not?'

'Do you know it's my *favourite*?' he said.

'Hell, no.'

'Hey?'

To change the subject, I told him that *he* looked like his mother and *I* looked like mine, which made him slightly weepy, so I suggested we have some coffee.

'*Good* idea,' he said and we crossed the cement courtyard, ascended the trio of steps into the kitchen and went through his coffee-mug-bargain-and-how-many-people-choose-the-mug-with-the-circles-around-it routine.

When I put five spoons of Ricoffy into my mug, he wanted to know what I was doing and I made a mental note of bringing a bottle of my own, better poison next week.

'You'll kill yourself,' he said.

'Shall we go and sit outside?'

'Ja,' he said, and we went out and down the steps and on to the courtyard and sat at the table, which had to be restabilised before we had our bad coffee and crispy Lemon Creams, which I made the mistake of remarking upon.

'Take them home with you.'

'It's okay, Dad.'

'I got a whole lot on special yesterday.'

'It's fine,' I said, wondering whether Kayla had been deliberately leading me on as I surveyed the back lawn, which used to be an orchard. But the old man hated cleaning up the leaves and, after Ma had died, he'd cut down most of the trees. The apricots, peaches, plums, pears and quinces – all gone. The loquat had been given to my mother by 'some man' who sang with her in the opera and it, too, had gone the way of most flora after she'd died. The six trees that remained were two umbrella-like evergreens in the middle of the lawn, a struggling lemon that produced a few fruits for the occasional Vitamin C tea, the fig, and two pines that had grown from seedlings to a pair of giants overshadowing the main bedroom, 'mucking up' the roof with thousands of small, sticky needles. The avocado tree, which had once shadowed a large part of the back lawn and in whose branches I'd smoked my first vile Rothmans, had been chopped down to make way for the parking canopy.

The quarter-acre yard had been veld when he'd bought the property, and he'd dug up numerous jagged rocks from that rich, dolomitic Highveld soil. The smaller ones he'd used to make flower beds, but the larger rocks he'd rolled to the bottom border and arranged along the fence. The massive one in the corner, however, he'd rolled there from the veld when the school opposite us hadn't existed yet. It had taken him the whole night to do so.

Beyond this rocky boundary there was a slight incline and topping it, in all its dumb, generic glory, a grey Vibracrete wall. On the other side of it you could see the neighbours' wide corrugated roof and tall syringa with its poisonous, mustard-yellow pods, excellent ammunition for my catapult in days gone by. Through its branches we could see the Waterkloof Air Force Base hangars in the distance because between us and it there was the Lyttelton valley. Above it all was a sky Jacob Hendrik Pierneef could have painted every day, so large, billowing and varied were its clouds. Gliding through that right now was the underbelly of a Boeing, silent and white, much like a whale, I imagined.

'God, that's beautiful,' the old man said.

'So where does a father fit into a birthday arrangement?' I wondered.

'You know, my father was *on* the ship, *in* Durban harbour, all ready to go to World War One when they pulled him off.'

'Why?' I said, for about the six hundred-thousandth time.

'Because he had a German surname.'

'Right,' I said, visualising a dark oval frame in my Eshowe aunt's living room. The man in the sepia photograph was sitting upright on a cane chair, legs crossed, wearing the khaki uniform and riding boots of a mounted cop. He had a twirly moustache, studio-enhanced ruddy cheeks, his pale brown eyes looking slightly unhinged.

'What was he like?'

'Well, he was a big-game hunter, a sportsman and, boy, did he have a temper? He had a *real* German temper.'

'What do you mean?' I said, wondering what an unreal German temper was like.

'One day I complained that my sisters had more food than me and he got so furious he fell off his chair!'

'What did you do?'

'I went and hid in the orchard.'

'Were you scared of him?'

'Scared? I was *terrified*! He hit me when I was naughty, and I often was …'

'But?'

'Sometimes he just hit me,' he said, as if he'd never thought about it before.

Sex and the Metropole

After deadline on Thursday, I called the old man, who was in a filthy mood. I let him blow off some steam and told him I'd see him on Sunday, for which he thanked me, passionately. Friday and Saturday went much as usual, up to the point where I arrived at Jay and Veron's. He had invited our fellow sub and No. 1 office fantasy over, possibly to match us up. Desiree Purple had bleached hair, large brown eyes, freckles, and the body of a Sixties goddess, the decade in which her parents had conceived her and officially changed their surname from Cohen. She only ever wore tight jeans and bra-less T-shirts and, frankly, it drove us a little mad. The problem was she could get all lovey-dovey with you the one second but then accuse you of stalking her the next. Plus, she had a way of coming up with some really disturbing statements, like: 'This copy is so bad I feel like poking my eyes out with a pencil.' You kept things nice and distant with Des, who was about as 'easy' as dancing barefoot in a field of thorns. Everybody wanted to bed this highly competent sub, but then she was fully aware of it and that might well have been one of the reasons why she would occasionally throw a tantrum worth beholding. She would become incandescent with paranoid rage, which would have her seniors scurrying about and us aroused, guiltily. But it never lasted. You'd think the universe was about to come to an end, yet the next day she'd be as mild and reasonable as a New Zealander I'd once met. When she was on an even keel, she was witty, generous and surprisingly sentimental. When she wasn't, you ran for cover. But we were all relaxed now, helped along by the usual loose juice, and she wanted to know how the writing was going.

'Great,' I said. 'I've started a novel about my father,' I bullshat. 'It opens at a very exotic place.'

Des: 'Where's that?'

Me: 'Germiston station.'

Jay: 'So it's more than just a germ of an idea.'

Des: 'But is it germane to the story?'

Me: 'Well, I do have German roots, according to the old man.'

Des: 'But where's the Scottish angle?'

Veron: (interjecting) What's that got to do with it?

Des: (to Veron) The original Germiston is in Scotland.

Jay: 'Excuse me, are we in *that* play or is this an assegai I see floating before me.'

Veron: (to self and all) 'Fucking subs. You're all the same.'

And so the night proceeded, with Des becoming increasingly drunk, morose and belligerent, but refusing to be a responsible driver and sleep over. She was perfectly sober thank you very much and could drive just fine and she wasn't going to fuck either or both of us. It was her life anyway, did we mind? Veron told her there wasn't going to be any of that while *she* was around and Des said she'd heard Veron was a lesbian anyway, so fuck her too. This got the three of us laughing uncontrollably, whereupon Des cursed us, started her car, reversed down the driveway, and scraped the length of her Conquest on the tree trunk out on the pavement. Then she shot forward down the road and stopped at the crossing with a squeal of tyres. We waited for the sickening impact of steel and shattering glass with gritted teeth, but it didn't happen and we presumed she'd be okay – guiltily.

So I walked home regretfully, restless and aroused, checked that I had enough cash to buy off some cop who wanted to lock me up, got into my car and left poor Butch looking puzzled in the driveway again. I finally ended up driving along Oxford Road, which of course was lined with black prostitutes and the occasional white junkie from Krugersdorp with a long, sad-luck story. I had been there and done that when I'd still been a successful screenwriter (in my head), but these days I was a hocked-up subeditor and just drove past to remind myself that I was still half alive.

Now, however, I saw a woman who might as well have been Naomi Campbell, just taller. She had long legs, smallish breasts and her hair was short and thick, like midnight corn on the cob. She was wearing a white T-shirt, a scrap of cheap brown *sheshwe* cloth and sandals. I decided I wasn't going to take this African queen to some quiet, neurotic spot and let her relieve me: I was going to take her home and treat her properly, or rather as properly as one could. So that's what I did and gave her the requested soft drink, noticing that those luscious legs were actually quite scarred, conjuring up recent images of machetes in Kenya and razor fences at our border.

'You're not South African, are you?' I said, pouring a beer.

'No,' Judith said, not a tenth as confident as Campbell.

'You from Zimbabwe?'

'Hm.'

I was still expecting The Ex to make her livid appearance or Ms Motsepe to suddenly appear and give me one of her withering disapprovals, but they didn't and I told 'Judith' to take off her clothes, which she dutifully did, and stroked those long legs, kissed those cool buttocks, that long back, those small breasts, that dense, smooth skin.

'How many kids do you have?' I asked.

'I have two children.'

'How old are they?' I said, struggling to control my breathing.

'Two and six months.'

The little blighters had drunk her almost flat.

'And the father?'

'He's somewhere in Zambia.'

'Does he at least send you money?'

'Yes,' she lied.

'And Mugabe?'

'We are waiting for him to die.'

'But don't you think his generals might just take over?'

'It will be alright,' Judith said.

'Put a condom on me,' I said, thinking that that more or less summed up my present state of mind.

She did as I told her and relieved my paranoid cock with her abundant mouth as I held her rough, exquisite head and drove her back to town afterwards, giving her double what she had asked for and too guilt-ridden to pick up on the hint that she would like to see me again, no doubt for my sexual prowess and sparkling personality.

Looking forward to oblivion, I was just about to get into bed when my cell rang. It was Kayla, who apologised for calling so late, but would I possibly consider coming to fetch her at the airport. She had no cash and she'd left her wallet at a hotel in the lively metropolis of Port Elizabeth.

'Okay,' I said.

'Are you sure?'

No, I'm just saying so for the hell of it, I thought.

Driving to O.R. Tambo, I thought if you were of a certain persuasion and had a cell number in the old days, it meant you had political credibility in the present. If you didn't have a cell number as in mobile phone, now, you were completely out of touch with the twenty-first century, like the old man. I also thought if our political masters really had a sense of history, they would have left the airport's name exactly as it had been, Jan Smuts, since it was internationally recognised – and he had at least taken a stand against global fascism, letting people like the old man see the world, however reluctantly. But then Oom Jannie was seen as the one who had ordered a massacre at Bulhoek, though the facts suggest the members of the Israelite sect got their just deserts after even the ANC's forerunners had tried to persuade their leader to cease his apocalyptic tripe. Surely if that same party retained Oom Jannie's name, in Mandela's spirit of conciliation, then the need to build another airport with the next dubious leader's name would arrive sooner than later and there'd be a sense of continuity, let alone economic progress? But no, history would start all over with the new elite and that kind of power was intoxicating, as I knew in a manner that was as questionable as theirs.

Arriving at the airport in a mood not entirely void of self-pity, it occurred to me that I was used to taking people to and fetching them from the airport. I *liked* doing it, maybe because I'd been doing it all my life. If it hadn't been The Ex off to Durban then it was the old man and I taking my mother there, endlessly. Good old Len Bezuidenhout, no one would say at my funeral. He was the one who always stayed behind: he was the stayer. A traveller by proxy, was our Len. He liked seeing the distant horizons in other people's eyes, or on the blank pages of his computer screen.

'What do you feel like doing?' I said, once we'd collected Kayla's stuff.

'I'd like to see your house,' she said.

'I could show you my lithographs,' I said. 'Literally.'

So we went to my big, empty house and she and Butch instantly loved each other while I poured us a Grouse, hoping the air freshener I'd dug out hid the smell of used condom. I proceeded to tell her about said lithos, which I'd bought with my credit card, by an artist whose work I not only liked a lot but whom I also thought was going to be the next best thing, aesthetically and financially. All the while I was faintly aware of a rustling sound behind me, but I was too busy delivering my lecture to realise what it was. Once I'd finished telling her why I thought Johann Louw was a genius, I turned around to see what she thought of that, but she had become more interested in finally acquiring a bit of dress sense.

Apart from her spectacles, she was stark naked.

On Hunting

How shall I put this, while driving to Pretoria? I could blame 'Judith', age, drink or pornography, but the short of it was that I couldn't get an erection again. Obviously Kayla had said that was alright, making as if it (the situation) was charming and asked whether she could sleep over. I'd been too slow and embarrassed to say that I still felt as if I was violating The Ex and my space, so I resorted to my old trick and soon had her laughing about my Independent Member of Parliament, which did just what it liked, when it liked, if it liked.

'So do you call him your Imp?'

'And my I.M.P. But right now he's an impi, isn't he?'

'That depends.'

'My God, I'll still make a sub out of you,' I said, impressed that she could see the rich possibilities of talking in the military sense if she meant it in Zulu, or the diminutive sense of it in Afrikaans, if that's what she meant at all.

'Maybe he's just an *impimpi*,' I continued.

'What's that?'

'Don't you remember how township informers used to be doused in petrol and set alight in the mid-Eighties?'

'I was *born* in the Eighties.'

'Sorry. I forgot. Well, those kinds of township informers were called *impimpi*.'

'Oh ...Tell me a story.'

'What?'

'Please tell me a story. I love it when you when you tell stories.'

'Just like that?'

'Ja.'

'I always blank out when someone says tell me a story or a joke. What kind of story do you want to hear?'

'I don't know. How about a love story?'

'Okay... Once upon a time I was sitting in the office and I saw a beautiful woman walk by ...'

'What did you think of the woman?'

'I thought she was very beautiful, very sexy.'

'So why did you do so little to pursue her?'

'What do you mean? I married her.'

'You shit!' she laughed, not entirely convincingly.

'Sorry. The reason why I didn't pursue the other woman was because a) she was much younger than me and therefore I didn't think she'd be interested, b) she was also beautiful and probably had a significant other, and c), I'd just come out of a divorce. I didn't think I could have any more relationships,' I said, leaving the option open in case one was developing here, if only sexually.

'So you're not in any kind of relationship now?'

'No, apart from the master/servant thing with my domestic

worker – 'my' domestic worker – and a different kind with my father.'

'Is the domestic worker pretty?'

'Yes, she is.'

'Have you ever thought of – you know?'

'Fucking her? Yes, once or twice.'

'Why haven't you?'

'Because it would disturb the local economy, and we'd have nothing to talk about. She's got Standard Three. I've got a bad degree.'

'And what kind of relationship do you have with your father?'

'Difficult. We don't have much in common. I mean, his reading matter consists of the Bible, the *Reader's Digest* and *Dennis the Menace.*

'That's so sweet.'

I grunted.

'You seem angry with him.'

I grunted again.

'Why?'

'Long story.'

'I don't mind long stories.'

So I started telling her about my resentment towards him over my mother and was just getting into my stride when I realised she was fast asleep and – hello – the I.M.P. wasn't. Story of my life. And so I spent the rest of the night wrestling sheets and now – hungry, hungover, horny, driving – wondering about my 'failure' to perform at the appropriate time. The more I thought about it, the more I became convinced that the main reason for it was that I'd felt pursued, hunted. I'd had a similar feeling when entering the Skyline in Hillbrow with a friend back in the gay Eighties, finding myself – ha! – making a fine study of a bunch of straight-looking men's Hush Puppies. Was this how women felt all the time? Perused, pursued, visually pawed?

The old man, with his body of a gymnast, had also been perved during his police college days, he'd once told me, but he'd been emphatic about not indulging that angle whatsoever – perhaps too emphatic – whereas I'd been more tolerant; a bit of a tease, even. Now he was standing in his HPs at the gate with his silver hair and I wondered, if his father had hit the living daylights out of him, why had he never lifted his hand to me – not once? It didn't make sense: usually those who were abused became abusers in turn, and I had certainly given him plenty of reasons to give me a deserved thrashing.

'What's that?' he said.

'It's coffee, Dad.'

'But I've *got* coffee.'

'Ja, but this is better coffee,' I said. I, a coffee snob, usually only drank strong, foreign filter coffee, but from now on I would only have Nescafé, a mild improvement on his Ricoffy.

'You should have *told* me,' he said. 'I would have bought you some.'

'You don't have to buy me anything anymore, Dad.'

'But I *want* to,' he said.

I gave him my hand, which he proceeded to demolish and I accepted. Why? Because my mother had always complained about how painful her arthritic hands were and I'd always scornfully dismissed such things, following his lead, so this was payback time. This was my deserved punishment, I thought, and said: 'How have things been?'

'What?'

'Shall we have some coffee?' I said somewhat aggressively, insinuating us towards the kitchen.

'*Good* idea. I've just had some oats.'

'Mm?' I said, trying to sound interested.

'You know, I've probably eaten oats every day of my life since the war.'

'That's probably another reason why you're so healthy,' I said as we entered the kitchen.

'Sometimes I wake up in the middle of the night and I'm starving, so I make myself some Jungle Oats.'

'Why're you hungry in the middle of the night?'

'Because I forget to eat, but most of the time I make a stew with some boerewors, two small cabbages, three carrots, four potatoes and an onion. That lasts me for days.'

'Most of which you used to give to the dog,' I said as I put on the kettle.

I might as well have punched him in the guts.

'Don't even *mention* her.'

'Why not?' I said a little cruelly, seeing his and Ma's dachshund in my mind's eye. The poor thing had died of kidney failure because the old man would pour his sweet, insipid coffee into a saucer, take a few sips, then break half a Lemon Cream into the rest and give it to the dog.

'I still dream of her,' he said.

'And Ma. Do you dream of her?'

'Um, no,' he said, a little taken aback. 'But I think of her. All the time.'

I felt unexpectedly emotional as he told me about his bargain buy and how everyone chose the mug with the circles and would I like to take a packet of Lemon Creams home?

'No thanks, Dad.'

'I got a whole lot on special...'

'Shall we go and sit outside?' I said, my head starting to throb.

So we took the coffee and biscuits went out through the stable door, down the sunny steps and sat on the wire chairs, which needed adjusting again. We watched a Boeing flying overhead and I asked him whether his kind sister in Eshowe and the bossy, beautiful one in Empangeni had called, as they always did. Yes. Once the coffee and Lemon Creams were finished, the mugs had to be washed and dried immediately, and then in a particular way. First, they had to be scrubbed in warm, soapy Sunlight, then rinsed in cooler, soap-less water. After that they had to be given a cursory wipe with a damp rag and then with a dry-as-bone dish cloth. They also had to be packed away, there and then.

We were standing at the sink I'd been sitting on when I'd seen him for the first time after returning from my sole overseas trip to Europe, having taken a year-long break in my so-called studies. I had caught a bus to Pretoria, then the train to Lyttelton via the Fountains, Kloofzicht and Sportpark with the last of my money. My mother was on the phone at the end of the passage when I arrived a week early, as a surprise, and rang off in that voice of hers which got louder when she was happy or stressed. When the old man got home, we'd embraced each other, the only time we ever did so in my adult life. His hair had gone the colour of bone.

'I *never* eat chicken,' he suddenly said. 'Do you know why?'

'No,' I said for about the five hundred-thousandth time.

'Because I had to kill one at least once a week. Every time I'd chop off its head and it would go running around the yard, headless. Blood all over the place,' he said, grimacing.

'Ugh.'

'But then my father used to shoot food for the pot. Often. One day I went out hunting with him in the Amatikulu valley. The trees formed a kind of canopy, so you could see for *miles* under them. And there in the distance stood a kudu. It was a male, and it had huge curly horns. My father told me to be quiet and went down on his knee, taking aim. He was going to kill that beautiful animal...'

'So what happened?'

'I was standing behind him...'

'Ja?' I said, knowing exactly what happened but too hungover to change the course of the conversation.

'I *waved* my arms.'

'Did it run?'

'Yes.'

'What did your father do?'

'He asked me whether I'd frightened it off.'

'What did you say?'

'I said "Yes, I did," almost shitting myself.'

'And?'

'He said, "Let's go home", and never hunted again.'

Food for Africa

Of course, if we were obsessed with the dictator up north and his local pal, then we had our own little dictators right here in the office. While the politicians were seeing just how and where they could screw their own people, we would argue, fret and complain about hyphens, commas, the death of the semi-colon, split infinitives, compound nouns, the use of adjectives, verb-less sentences, upper cases, lower cases, court cases, nutcases and the falling standards of modern journalism in general. In short, we dealt with words, words and more words, and the chief dictator in all of this was another Bob.

Robert Black was a short, bald man with a very big beer belly and he'd almost been a Springbok. He'd been selected for a tour and he'd been injured just before that tour, and his replacement, an Afrikaner, had shone to such an extent that Bob Black was never selected again. He'd continued playing top-flight provincial rugby for a while after that, but the combination of the recurring injury and his disappointment had worn him down so badly that he'd become what all lost souls with a couple of brain cells do when they fail in their dreams and somehow bypass the film industry: he'd become a hard-drinking journalist. Not a sports journalist, mind, a 'real' one. He'd been too educated and English, he'd reasoned, to play with 'those dumb, oversized Dutchmen', even though we all knew that you didn't necessarily have to be short to be a good scrumhalf anymore. He'd been a good court and later crime reporter, but now he was in his late fifties and had become the revise subeditor, and a very good one at that. Chief among his bugbears was 'the leafy suburbs', a cliché that was strictly *verboten*. The only problem was that he had come from an era that felt it necessary to kick every new sub's arse into gear before he and, later, she was properly initiated. If sociologists spoke about the gatekeeping process in the media and academe, then Bob simply said 'You do as I say or you're out, pal.' Come mid-evening, we would be on deadline with some or other scandal about to break and a lawyer standing by. One of us would try to sub the front-page splash while Bob poured himself a beer, loudly called an old police connection to find out if there was any dirt, failing which he'd watch the week's rugby matches at maximum volume online, cursing all the players for being useless, incompetent Dutch arseholes. This did not make it easy to sub a story seamlessly, and Bob had an eagle's eye for clashing tenses or a name spelled in two different ways. Once he'd revised your subbing and changed your brilliant headline, he'd open his second quart of beer, stand up, loosen his belt, unzip his fly, rearrange those furry jewels beneath his gut, belt up again and go on to the balcony for his sole cigarette of the day. Black prided himself on the fact that he only smoked one fag and drank two quarts every twenty-four hours these days, and always went out for a post-deadline steak with his wife on a Thursday night. His wife was quite the babe, had a New Zealand passport and, if the weather wasn't so crap there, he'd emigrate there tomorrow to get away from all these dumb (black) journos and stupid (Afrikaans) crunchies. Bob would say that loud enough so that everyone could hear, knowing he'd reached his ceiling at the paper and all he was really doing now was cruising until his retirement in a few years' time. Unless, of course, upstairs made him a retrenchment offer he couldn't refuse. But don't come to him with arguments like black journalists were actually writing in what was not their first or mother tongue, hey. It wasn't his job to hold their hands – or learn their language in turn – but to challenge their facts, correct their grammar and therefore maintain the *News's* impeccable journalistic standards, which were still going down the slimehole as far as he was concerned. What didn't occur to him, management or possibly even the journalists in question, was that a completely new kind of English could have been born right there, the kind I had found in Njabulo Ndebele's novella *Fools*. The man's use of English was recognisable as set in a uniquely South African township. It was rich, different, inclusive and therefore exciting. Occasionally the odd columnist or guest writer might experiment a little, but generally if they veered too far off Bob's idea of English, which was a kind of neutral, mid-Atlantic mess, they'd be in for the chop. In that sense the 'ultra-left' had a point that the paper was still a white one, for we still 'spoke' in a language that was directly descended from Thomas Pringle through to Robert Black, who didn't give a flying toss about any discourse on the ideological implications of linguistic tone.

Nor did Lesley Makhene, for that matter. It took me quite a while to meet him, because he didn't like being in the office, yet when he was there he would smile at me as if we'd known each other for years, let alone never been introduced. He, too, was short, had a bald head full of creases as deep as the Rift Valley, a permanent frown on his nevertheless beautifully benevolent forehead, an enormous burnt potato for a nose, skew teeth, no neck, a big gut like Black, X-legs and splayed flat feet. As we became friendly through sheer proximity, I gleaned that he had been at the paper since the early Seventies and had therefore seen plenty of change. He'd started as a messenger and stayed thus for ten years, until Black had taught him how to write journalese – 'That man, I owe him my *life!*' – and spent the rest of his career covering the townships. That was what he knew, that's what he liked doing and that's where he liked being. He was a township boykie through and through. He'd covered the '76 students' uprising, the dark Eighties, the vicious early Nineties and the brief honeymoon of liberation before its side-effect, crime, had sprayed its bloody pus like a lanced boil during the early, so-called Noughties of the present. He'd been surpassed by the new lot who had come off the streets, who'd been given some writing lessons by European institutes and were now very high-ups. If they had offices, he had a desk consisting of a messy mountain of old newspapers, an ancient PC screen and a much-fingered keyboard. His partition wall was decorated with a single photocopied press photograph of a beaming Lesley Makhene shaking hands with the tall Bushman himself, Nelson Rolihlahla Mandela. Even when he was at the office, Les was more inclined to hang around the car pool in the basement and talk to those guys or even the security guards – somnolent men who worked twelve-hour shifts and reminded me of the old man's lifetime of meniality. It was down there where he would catch me on his way back from Soweto or maybe a catnap in his exhausted Toyota, one of its windows broken from a smash-

and-grab, wheels filthy from the township dust, innards messy from children's toys and endless chicken-and-chips takeaways.

'How are you, my friend?'

'I'm fine, thanks. I'm Len.'

Les just smiled at me and said: 'Have you got family?'

'No.'

'You've *got* to have family.'

'I'm working on it,' I lied.

'And do you believe in God?'

'No.'

Les burst out laughing, as if he'd just heard the funniest joke in the world, so I started reading his stories with more attention: dry, factual stuff about what actually happened in the townships, all the while implying that life there was as cheap as a used plastic Coke bottle. The next time he caught me down in the basement, he took my hand and walked with me to the Crouching Kitten: the short black man holding the uptight white prick's hand as if he were God only didn't know what.

'You know, me,' said Les, 'I'm a pastor.'

I must have expressed some surprise at this bit of seemingly contradictory information.

'But I've got a problem man, Len,' he said, rolling his r's.

'What's that Les?'

'No man, Len, the women: they thrrrow themselves at me.'

'But you're married. You're ... you're a pastor!'

'Ja,' he said. 'But what can I do?'

And he bursts out laughing.

Les and Bob Black were old school, and Jay, Desiree and I were probably heading that way too. The likes of Motshekga and Greenwood, however, were new school. Their orientation was blatantly political and corporate, respectively, and now that Kayla and I had had an attempt at cellular interaction, we made eye contact in a completely different way. She'd asked me whether we could keep what was 'happening between us strictly between us'. 'Okay,' I'd responded, wondering what was happening between us, relieved that she didn't want to announce it to all and sundry. My colleagues and I had laughed over her copy. Jay had said it was so bad she was clearly meant for management. I'd replied that you got good reporters, good writers, and sometimes both in one person, and neither she nor Motshekga were any of the three.

But she and I did agree to go out to supper that Saturday after two changes of time at a restaurant in Parkhurst, not far from the Jolly Roger. It was one of the few joints that played music at an acceptable volume. That is, soft enough not to intrude but hearable if you wanted to tune into it. Loud music irritated me if it was bad, and most of it was, but distracted me if it was good. After all, how many people could claim to be more interesting than even the vastly overplayed *Four Seasons*? Very few, if any. Yet every Tom, Dick and Thabo wanted to force their idea of whining, thudding good music down your earholes every minute of every day – in malls, supermarkets, restaurants, banks, cars, lifts. If obesity was a way to extend your empty power physically, then loud music was a way to extend your hollow power invisibly. Noise and silence, the only two approaches fascists have to sound, in that order. Noise when they're in power, silence when they have to account for it. The louder the music in a restaurant, the more inclined you are to leave sooner and thus hasten turnover. It was audio rape and it drove me around the twist, as Ma used to say.

Anyway, I couldn't help noticing that Kayla was dressed as skimpily as was legal and tried to ignore my alarm system, which had a woolly theory that the more women showed, the less they performed. We ordered our drinks and a steak and chicken salad, respectively, from a handsome young man called Vusi. Kayla gave him the kind of smile that said she was on his side (from her side of the great divide), but then he didn't seem to mind.

'Bon appétit,' she said.

'Thank you, and the same to you.'

'What are you thinking?'

'I was just thinking about what my old man always says about food,' I lied.

'What does he say?'

'That we're living in the lap of luxury if we can eat out like this.'

'I know,' she said, putting on a momentary spare-a-thought-for-the-starving-masses look.

'Not that he eats out, ever. Maybe it's because he'd known what hunger was during the war.'

'Yes?' she said, glowing.

'We don't know that kind of stuff. I mean, when he got back, he ate a whole pound of butter, just like that.'

'Oh God.'

'Well, I don't know if he has much to do with it.'

'I beg your pardon?'

'Never mind.'

Our drinks arrived via a friendly Vusi and she took a sip of her chardonnay while I took a deep slug of Windhoek.

'Are you going to see your father again tomorrow?'

'Ja, every Sunday.'

'You don't look very happy about it.'

I muttered something about duty and she rather perceptively asked if there was anything about him and me that was similar.

'Not that I can think of,' I said as Vusi brought our dinner and she gave him her personalised smile.

Now she poked a piece of smoked chicken with her fork and put it in her mouth while I sawed into my steak, unable to suppress seeing its sad journey to my bloody plate, yet persisting.

'Tell me about your mother.'

'Well, she didn't have a very good education, having first looked after *her* mother, then her lazy father. Then she married my old man, a fingerprints clerk, and became a dental assistant to supplement his income.'

'Were they compatible?' she asked, listlessly poking around in the rest of her salad, like a chicken.

'Absolutely not. If he never went out, she was outgoing, sociable, which is probably what got her her other job. Friends of theirs had started a travel company and suddenly became fabulously wealthy. So she became a courier for them, travelling all over the globe for about a third of the year, every year.'

'And your father didn't mind?' she asked, having settled into the liquid part of her dinner.

'I don't know if he minded, but he certainly didn't stand in her way. Then again, he probably lay worrying himself sick about her, just as he did and maybe still does with me.'

'That doesn't sound too bad,' she said, taking another sip.

'No, it doesn't. But the most important thing is she had a voice. She could sing. She sang in the local opera chorus. She sang in the church, at weddings, christenings, for the aged.'

'Amazing.'

'When the neurosurgeon called us in and told her she had six weeks to live, she asked him whether she could carry on singing.'

'That's so sad.'

We were finished and I signalled Vusi that we wanted the bill by writing in the air.

'Yes, it is. But somehow she had cobbled together an existence, and I suppose one should be grateful for that. And your parents?'

'They're divorced,' she said as Vusi arrived and gave me the bill, which she insisted on paying. He was slightly embarrassed and she hastened to put him at ease, which I found a tad over-compensatory but, again, he didn't seem to mind and she seemed amused about something as he walked away with her card.

'What's so funny?'

'Other men won't let me pay for them.'

'Why do you think that is?'

'I think they're threatened by the fact that I'm equal to them, even though I still earn much less than them. But just the fact that I'm young *and* doing an MBA seems to, you know ...'

'Intimidate them?'

'Yes.'

'Well, the only reason why I'm not threatened by your forthcoming millions is because I'm secretly hoping that, when I finally get my novel written and published, it's going to become an international bestseller, after which I'm going to be rolling in my own.'

'And if it doesn't?'

'Then I'm just going to carry on being bitter and twisted.'

'That's the other thing I like about you,' she said, putting her arm through mine as we strolled along the postprandial boulevard of Fourth Avenue, distantly aware of the fact that, if we were lucky, we'd only get harassed by needy car guards, many of whom came from the Democratic Republic of Congo, spoke fluent French and could earn more hovering like a conscience than as the engineers and doctors they were qualified as back in the old, alleged heart of darkness. If we weren't lucky, however, we'd get abducted, tortured and/or raped and/or murdered.

'What? The fact that I'm a demon sub?'

'No, you idiot. The fact that you've got a sense of humour.'

I liked her confidence, even though she was already getting repetitive.

'Well, it's one of the few things we older men have going for us.'

'Strange, I don't think of you as being older than me,' she said.

'Thank you. Neither do I, until I look in the mirror and see I'm not twenty-four anymore. And it's actually okay: I still *feel* twenty-four.'

'What were you doing when you were twenty-four?' Kayla said.

'Wandering around Europe, starving, wondering about a song by Neil Young.'

'Who's Neil Young?'

'You don't know who Neil Young is?'

'No. Who is he?'

I gave her a brief biography of the Canadian singer/songwriter and, when I croaked her the refrain from his best-known hit, it rang a bell.

'My father probably listens to him,' she smiled.

'Or maybe Young was sampled on a rap song.'

She didn't want to know about 'Old Man', where the twenty-four-year-old artist talks to and praises his father, but asked instead whether I'd ever smoked dope.

'Hell, no,' I said.

As usual the irony went right over her head, but we did go to my place and did something Jay and I had somehow outgrown. We smoked a joint on the couch and I told her that if she wanted to go into business, she had to know that KwaZulu-Natal's biggest export wasn't sugar cane but marijuana, ganja, dope, dagga. And the stuff from that neck of the woods certainly had a more recognisable brand in certain quarters than Huletts sugar. What was it, she asked.

'Have you never heard of Durban Poison?'

'No,' she said dreamily.

'So why don't you do your MBA thesis on the financial benefits of legalising good old Poison?'

'It's an idea,' she said, stoned, red-eyed.

'You might even give it a medical angle.'

'Could we please not talk about work?'

'Sorry. What would you like to talk about?'

'Nothing,' she said, inviting me to start kissing her, with which I had almost no problem at all, apart from an alarm bell distantly ringing in that fraction of my skull that could be considered rational. And my theory had once again held: the truth of the matter was that Kayla had lain there and seemed to think that opening her legs wide and shouting at what seemed the appropriate moment somehow constituted good, wild, deeply satisfying sex. It hadn't and, after she'd fallen asleep, my natural nocturnalism had kicked in. Others could sleep on the stuff, but all it did for me, combined with the beer and Grouse I'd been consuming, was rev up my already excitable metabolism. I couldn't just leave her there and go and sleep in The Ex and my bed upstairs, so I got two blankets and covered her and tried to sleep on the other couch and finally started dozing off, uncomfortably, whereupon the phone rang.

An older friend of mine's much younger wife was calling from England to say her beloved husband and our good friend, Dick, had just died. Kayla got up and started getting dressed, which turned me on because it was morning and the opposite of the usual jump cut from a dressed porn starlet to a naked one wrapping her *vagina dentata* around some well-hung stud's monster cock. She was very sorry about my friend, had an assignment to do and once again requested that we keep 'this thing' strictly between us.

'Sure,' I said.

On Loss

I tried to doze in after that, but it wasn't working. Maybe I should take Butch for a walk, as The Ex and I used to, so I checked the time and saw that it was, in fact, late. Maybe I had slept a little, after all. But now I could feel guilty about Butch *and* arriving late at the old man's, speeding along, trying to work with the scraps he'd given me. His father had hit him randomly, it seemed, but had then sensed something about his son and stopped hunting. Prod too much, however, and the old man clammed up. He wouldn't say why he thought his father had acted thus, so he was also being a bit of an editor, perhaps even a censor. But where did that leave things as he stood at the gates, checking his watch at arm's length?

'You're late,' he said as I got out of the Crouching Kitten at the back.

'Ja,' I said.

'And you haven't shaven.'

'I don't need to shave, Dad. We don't work with the public. And it's Sunday.'

'I have shaved every *day* of my life, since I was seventeen.'

'Good for you,' I said.

'You'll lose your job.'

'Well then I lose my job,' I snapped.

I saw a flash of the old Beethovian temper for an instant before he asked me whether I would like a cup of coffee and we went through the bargain and mug speeches. He became completely confused about me hauling out my own bottle of coffee, so I reminded him that I'd brought it along the previous week.

'Oh,' he said. 'Shall we go and sit outside?'

So we sat in silence in the early autumn sun and he juddered his left leg and used his left index finger to click his right thumb nail by pulling it back and releasing it, which used to drive Ma nuts in church when we still did that sort of thing. Then, unusually, he asked me what the matter was.

I wondered what his reaction would be if I told him that Diederick Johannes Reineke and I had become friends because a sweet dopehead I'd met on a film set had said we'd get on well. She'd been right and Dick and I had had much more than dagga in common. He was an anthroposophist, an adherent of Rudolf Steiner's way of thinking. He therefore painted and sculpted accordingly, which meant he never used straight lines in his work. Like most teachers, Dick was mildly in love with his own voice, but I only came to appreciate his skills when I tried to read Steiner, whose style of writing – or perhaps that of his genuflecting translators – was awful. Dick made that whole universe come alive. He had given up on teaching and was now an actor, though he didn't quite play the darling game either, so his second wife basically kept home and hearth together as a legal secretary. They had had three children together and he had six in the Cape from a previous marriage. Dick and his new family were always broke and they always had just enough food for them and any stray visitors, but their children were extremely happy. It was another world from the strictly utilitarian, tense one I had grown up in, and I was intrigued by this highly sophisticated form of Christianity, much as I thought some of it was laughable. Dick looked like a German poet from another era, quoted Goethe extensively and looked very tired, but happy, when his wife called to say she was pregnant again. They were anti-contraception and abortion and those spirits who asked to come into this world should be allowed to, and he often spoke about how he'd delivered his children himself and named them after Greek heroes or Biblical characters. Dick was actually a lapsed anthropowhateverist by the time I met him and I picked up, through a fog of coffee and smoke over the years, that he'd been a bit of a messianic character in earlier times. He had left behind the more intense types, all of them reincarnations of great souls like Aristotle's second adviser but never, say, a local piss-cat in Athens, circa 350BC. The point is he could spin an excellent yarn and recite long stretches of *Hamlet* and tell me everything about the man who had, like one of my youthful literary heroes, Herman Hesse, seen straight through Adolf Hitler. Most importantly, he practised his faith in the sense that he was generous to the point of embarrassment. He would literally give you the clothes off his back and didn't exhibit or sell his paintings, good or bad: he gave them away. After 1999, Dick had taken his family to Cape Town and then out of the country, arguing that there was an ugly sensibility afoot. South Africa lacked a unified folk spirit, he'd said, which I'd read as elitism. I had resented that, realising that he'd also been a kind of surrogate father to me, but they moved to Albion anyway and raved about how friendly the locals were. A few years later he got a brain tumour and not even the mistletoe could cure him.

'A friend of mine has just died of the same thing as Ma did,' I said. 'He was only sixty-three.'

'You know,' the old man annoyingly and predictably said, 'we were playing rugby in another town and two men came walking towards me. I knew then and there that my father was dead.'

'How old were you?' I said, absently.

'I was in my third matric year. I was nineteen.'

'How old was he?'

'Forty-eight,' the old man said. 'He'd never liked the idea of converting from horseback to motorbikes. But he'd been called out to a farm in the hills and drove up the dirt road, went round a corner, skidded, and a 1936 Ford Whitehound was coming from the front. His head hit the silver emblem on the bonnet and he died instantly.'

'Do you miss him?'

'I miss him every day of my life.'

'Did he leave you anything?'

'Only a walking stick, which you'll inherit. But do you know what?'

'No, Dad. What?'

'We were supposed to inherit a pen nib factory in Bonn. We're supposed to be multimillionaires.'

'So why aren't we?'

'I don't know,' he said.

'Great.'

That was the end of that and we lapsed into a long, awkward silence in which he clicked his nail and juddered his foot before he said: 'I wish I could win a hundred and ... *twenty*-three million rands.'

'What would you do with it?'

'I'd give most of it to the poor and you, but I'd take the Valiant down to Elgin and fill it with apples.'

'What for?'

'So it can smell like apples, obviously.'

'Right.'

Another juddering, clicking silence. After an unbearable while I said I'd better go and he seemed almost relieved and walked to the front gates as I started up the Civic, reversed to between the wash line and the fence, forward past the garage and on to the driveway, where the old man was standing at the open gates. As I got there, I rolled down my window and was reminded of my mother as he squashed my hand.

'Bye, Dad.'

'Take care,' my boy.

'You too,' I said, and drove off, watching him close the gates in my rear-view mirror.

When I got to the red traffic light, I wondered whether his father had sensed he was going to die and therefore became more lenient towards his son, or whether the old man's son had felt he'd painted his father too negatively prior to that and now wanted to show him in a better light. Or maybe it was just a personal mythology. If not a completely distorted memory. If not downright fiction. I decided it was probably a little of each and that that was fine, but we have to work with what is presented to us, which is no doubt influenced by what we ourselves present. When the lights changed, I turned up towards the hospital and saw that the old man was still standing at the closed gates, as upright and silver-haired as ever.

I couldn't wait to get out of his sight to light a cigarette.

The Leafy Suburbs

Somehow I made it through the rest of that Sunday: driving to work, enduring Bob Black's bigotry, looking forward to one thing and one thing only: sleep. I collapsed into bed and it felt like five minutes had elapsed before Ms Motsepe almost broke the door down. I had forgotten to put the key out for her in my desire for oblivion. She wouldn't even bother to grace my apology with a reply, so I decided to get the hell out of that house. The last thing I felt like was Beauty's pout as she sat at the kitchen table, eating her oats and drinking her sweet tea in staring silence.

So I got dressed and gave The Ex and my 'love child' a look he knew as clearly as if I'd said, 'We're going for a walk, Butch.' He started jumping about like a mutant lamb until I managed to calm him sufficiently to get the choker around his neck. Thus we proceeded down Emfuleni Road, its leaves starting to turn, occasionally see-sawing down to the tarmac, me holding him back or him dragging me along, I wasn't sure. We were giving every locked-up canine a chance to exercise its jaws and lungs, barking up a storm and annoying everyone I knew by sight, nought by name.

Guarding the parking lot at the entrance to the park was Lukas, a giant tub of a man who wore laceless army boots, faded jeans and an unravelling orange jersey beneath his filthy old army coat. He had somehow appropriated the dusty lot as his exclusive domain and made a point of greeting people when they arrived in their dog-laden vehicles, the back seats often curled up from the sun, torn by animal nails and half covered with smelly old blankets. When they returned from their arboreal strolls he'd hover in their vicinity, rubbing his forehead with his thumb, and they would pay him for having been prepared to protect their cars with his very life. I could just see him pursuing would-be thieves down the road with his heavy frame in those loose boots and coat, but never mind: these guilt-ridden contributions presumably kept him fed.

Once in the park there was the usual crowd of dog lovers living out their controlling or nurturing fantasies through their hounds. This literary grand dame with her bossed-about Dalmatian, that intensely friendly man with his wild eyes, army fatigues and two highly strung Dobermans. I passed the environmental hottie admonishing her blood-thirsty bull terrier with its pertly pink gonads, then that old fart with his equally half-dead Lab. Next up was a grim Afrikaans woman with her Alsatian, then the bore with his check shirt and over-energetic border collie and, finally, a shrivelled German raisin with her troop of terrifying Rottweilers.

Circling one or two of the small dams, depending on my mood, was more or less the sum total of my exercise, which nevertheless earned me praise from the quack in terms of that Barnardian pump, the heart. Now we passed the small wetland separating the higher dams from the lower, larger public one. The wetland was drying out and its tall reeds would soon be control-burnt for winter, adding to the hard, dry Highveld beauty of the botanical gardens.

When I got home, Ms Motsepe was having her ten o'clock tea break, so I skulked upstairs and, instead of writing, made a list of requirements for the next exciting item on the day's agenda. I had been too nafi (no ambition, fuck all interest) to go shopping that Saturday and started seeing the old man's point when some idiot wailed that the object of his affection was 'beeyatiful' – over and over. Alright, I thought, I get the picture. She's beautiful. Move on. More importantly, why was this junk being forced down my ears while shopping on a Monday morning? The singer was just about to have a castrato orgasm when he was interrupted by another one of those morons who has a deep and abiding affection for their own voice box, the supermarket DJ. He was telling us, no, loudly enthusing at breakneck speed that there was a bargain for spaghetti meatballs in tomato sauce and we should get ours *now*. Naturally I'd chosen the customer queue that had a credit card hold-up as shoppers in other queues sailed by.

I went home and unpacked my groceries during Ms Motsepe's lunch break and wasn't sure whether I wanted to burst out laughing or crying in that crinkling silence. Something had to give. A yellow leaf had inveigled its way in under the door and into the kitchen, Ms Motsepe's efficient eye notwithstanding. Autumn had arrived in the City of Gold like a mild-mannered man with a very sharp knife. His arguments were extremely persuasive in the broad light of day, but in the small hours of death none of it added up. My life, basically, was a mess. My job thrived on others' misery. I was caught up in yet another unsatisfactory affair, an almost mirror image of my marriage to The Ex on the professional and sexual front. That is, I wasn't getting a lot of sex, thanks to corporate imperatives, but when I did get it, I wasn't exactly inspired to write poetry or anything. Talking of which, I had created an expectation that I was writing something of import when I didn't even know where to start. I had thought I'd have something of value to offer my fellow citizens, a little pleasure amidst the resolute misery, but it didn't seem to have turned out that way. Hopefully I hadn't caused others too much distress, since everything in this country seemed to be measured in degrees of complicity in others' pain. But what was I to *do*? I was too much of a coward or sensualist to commit suicide, and I had more or less outgrown drugs. Alcohol? Been there and still doing it. Religion? Did very little for me. Academe? Too dry and difficult.

You don't have to write or pretend you're writing, I told myself in a moment of lucidity. Go for a drive in the country. You're allowed to. So I locked up, said goodbye to a puzzled Butch, drove down the road and got as far as the botanical gardens' public dam, which had a road running along it and therefore had parking. Water helped, but not much. A Chinese couple, restaurant owners perhaps, were teasing crabs from the muddy bank beneath a yellowing willow. I looked at the radio and thought maybe I'd give the classical station a try, even though it usually gave me nothing but bombast from other centuries while I tried to negotiate the traffic and ignore beggar women rearing their babies on narrow traffic islands next to increasing potholes. But not this time. The host said listen to how full the composer makes four simple string instruments sound. He had already mentioned the maestro's name before I'd tuned in, but I was pretty confident I could work it out anyway. I couldn't. But what I did hear was a thinking, feeling life in all its rich diversity. The piece was as short, fast and catchy as a pop song, driven by an up-down sequence of rapidly building, logical argument, sparking with seriousness, defiance and discipline, then released by satire, laughter, freedom, before returning to order, beauty and a no-nonsense stop. The music was so unbearably beautiful that everything else was bearable again. I could carry on living. Others had religion, drugs, maths, motor cars and shopping lists to stay deluded, but I called the station, got the composer's name – of *course* it was him! – and drove straight to a music shop, where I bought myself the entire collection of the man's quartets. I had something coursing through my veins apart from blood, cholesterol and self-pity again. I no longer cared whether this genius was considered kitsch, overly emotional or out of date. As far as I was concerned the artist had done his work so well, almost two centuries ago, that he'd saved my life right now.

I was listening, of course, to none other than Ludwig van Beethoven.

On Dreams

The rest of the week slowly got better and Kayla and I greeted each other with detached intimacy. She'd be away for the next week on some or other top-secret investigative job, about which Jay was seriously skeptical.

'She needs to first investigate the basics of journalism,' he said. 'You know, the five double-u's and an aitch: the facts, not to mention readability.'

In other words, things were returning to normal. Ms Motsepe was emotionally stable, as was Desiree, and I enjoyed listening to Uncle Ludwig driving home after work at night. I had always only wanted to hear the fast movements of 'classical' music but was now perfectly content to hear the long, slow, melancholic genius of the second quartet's rewritten adagio, always maintaining that dramatic tension, jolting one towards the end. I even saw and reviewed a fairly good film that Friday and, much to my surprise, had a bit of glad-eye with an older woman at the pub before her limping partner rejoined her from the Gents.

Jay and I watched an excellent match the day after and only got mildly drunk. Hell, even Veron was in a good mood. All of which was good and well, but it wasn't solving my primordial problem, which was sex. Still, I felt newly resolved and only slightly hungover when I drove to Pretoria, thinking about what the old man had said about missing his father, and losing him at such a young age. Had I ever missed him? There had been that one night in Crete. My German girlfriend and her entourage of two had left for another town, and I'd sat in an open-air tavern drinking the local rotgut, retsina. There were two car speakers nailed to wooden posts and they were rattling out Young's 'Old Man'. I had gone down some steps and stood there in the middle of the night, the black Mediterranean lapping at my feet. Just over *there* was Africa, I thought, North Africa, where the old man had once been, which he never stopped talking about, and the next thing I knew I had liquid crocodiles running down my cheeks.

At 123 Harry Smith Avenue, we sat down in the courtyard with our usual coffee and Lemon Creams.

'What was school like, Dad?'

'I hated it. I clung to the pillars at the entrance on my first day like my *life* depended on it. I was five years old and I cried like a little baby.'

'And girls?'

Now he shook his head as if this was another one of life's numerous obstacles that had to be endured.

'Some bright spark thought he would put a girl on the bench next to me, but I refused to sit next to her.'

'Why?'

'I can still remember her name. Ethel bladdy Meriwether.'

'Ja, but …'

'I never wanted to be near girls.'

'Why not?'

At which point the phone rang and he continued complaining about Ethel while I got tense about the phone, which was set at its loudest. I finally said the phone was ringing, excused myself, ran into the kitchen, then into the darker passage, down towards myself in the mirror, and was about to pick up the phone when it stopped.

'So you didn't like girls?' I said as I sat down again.

'It's not that I didn't like them. It's just that I wasn't interested in them.'

'What were you interested in?'

'I had colours in rugby, hockey, athletics, gymnastics, cricket…'

'That's amazing.'

'Hm,' he said, while juddering his left leg and clicking his right thumb nail.

'Why did you do matric three times?'

'I couldn't do the maths. I just couldn't.'

One of the few things I recalled about Steiner was that if a pupil didn't understand something it wasn't his or her fault; it was the teacher's.

'And in those days you *had* to do it.'

'No, most other cops just went up to Standard Eight and then joined the force.'

'But you stuck to it.'

'It was hell.'

'Good for you. And after school?'

'I went to police college and broke in horses.'

'You broke in horses?'

'Ja. My father'd taught me. And then I became a PT instructor.

Man, there was a course being offered in Denmark …'

'Yes?'

'We were preparing to go on it. I could become a gymnast and teach phys-ed. I *dreamt* about that course.'

'And then?'

'Then came the bally war.'

'Why'd you volunteer?'

'My station commander said if I didn't go, they'd post me to the Cape.'

'What's so bad about the Cape?'

'I don't like the Cape.'

'But you'd never been there!'

'Man, I wasn't going to the Cape.'

'You married a woman from the Cape.'

'So?'

'And you want to go to Elgin to fill the car up with apples.'

'What's your point?'

'And there I thought you were fighting international fascism.'

'That too. But you know, I must have been the luckiest guy in the war.'

'Why's that?' I said for the four hundred-thousandth time, remembering a faded black-and-white photograph of a man sitting stark naked in the Libyan desert with the Mediterranean behind him, covering his privates and scowling at the photographer who had crept up and tried to surprise this simple man with the temper of a Teuton, the body of a god and the smile of an angel.

'Every day we'd get a ration of water and I kept mine until I had enough for a bath. But someone ratted on me and they wanted to charge me for stealing water, which amounted to treason. They could have shot me.'

'So what happened?'

'My friends explained to them that I'd kept my water so that I could bathe.'

'But why didn't you go on the course after the war, Dad?'

The old man either didn't hear what I'd said or acted as if he didn't hear me, or he wasn't going to answer it, or it was a dead spot, and I somehow couldn't bring myself to ask the question again.

Young Woman Pleads Exhaustion

The week passed in its usual way and I was asked to work on one of those extra jobs that came along in the Hydra-headed corporation. It would take place over Saturday and would help towards paying off the mortgage, avoiding my novel and passing the time. There was only international football that week anyway, so I agreed to co-sub the insert, which dealt with the exciting world of commercial and brand surveys. It was about as interesting as bashing your head against the wall and looking forward to stopping. The only mildly exciting thing that happened was that Kayla phoned and asked whether she could come over after work. 'Sure,' I said, and went back to editing something that did vaguely interest me: a comparison between the English and Afrikaans media's sales, since my ill-educated parents had wisely decided that I needed to be bilingual.

The big difference was that the English media tried to deal

with the broader issues of the day while the Afrikaners reported on its hot, hard facts. The main issue was that the Supreme Leader was trying to centralise power, which didn't exactly make for exciting copy. When he was out of the country and boring others to death, which was most of the time, there was always that reliable old crutch of a quiet day at the newsroom: the vox pop survey. Were whites happier now than during the apartheid years? Yes. Were blacks better off than during the apartheid years? Yes. Another survey, of course, would come up with exactly the opposite results, or variations thereof. A sample of a thousand people spoke for the entire nation of fifty million souls, of whom about ten percent were illegal anyway. People like Judith were streaming to the new United States of Africa. They didn't care how badly they'd be treated – and they were, guilty as charged – there was money here. Given the times, the Afrikaans press usually led with a murder story, always black on white, failing which they featured a sport or celebrity story. The point is their scandals were local and not dependent on the Anglo-American axis of manufactured mundanity. They had plenty of randy stars in both spheres to keep their small but loyal readership buying at a handsome profit. Moreover, they had their well-informed opinion pages and made sure to cater for letters from not-so-little old ladies who increasingly expressed their faith in light of all this darkness. But, most impressively, they featured extensive cultural coverage. If the English press had given up on reviewing things like the theatre and symphony concerts for commercial reasons, then the Afrikaners still took these events seriously. It was a cohesive culture that was taking a lot of strain and we felt it in our office too, since a good portion of us were Afrikaners or half-castes, like yours not so truly.

One such Afrikaner was Albertus Grey, his English surname

notwithstanding. I was just leaving to meet Kayla at home when I saw he was still working. There was nothing unusual about that. Albertus – or Al – was always working: early, late and later. He was our IT man and loved to speak the lingo, which might as well have been Mandarin as far as I was concerned. He knew the technology inside out and he had an incurable disease, which wasn't working; it was talking. Ask or tell him anything, as I did by pointing out the latest farm horror on that day's front page of my other tongue, and you'd end up hearing his life story.

Like the old man, he was a genius at coercing anything towards his tale, which was that he and his wife had had a beautiful house with a swimming pool on the West Rand. But their two-year-old son, Naas, had been mauled by their American pit-bull during a break-in and had died three days later. The pain of that loss had been so severe that they had emigrated to England (his-biological-father-had-been-English-hence-the-surname-and-passport-but-he-had-died-two-years-after-Albertus-was-born-and-this-time-his-mother-married-an-Afrikaner-man-what-a-good-man-he-even-let-Albertus-keep-his-biological-father's-name-and-how-many-people-let-alone-Afrikaners-would-do-that?) and his daughter had excelled at acting. She had also started taking drugs. But the damp cold of Blighty had proven too harsh for these white Africans so they'd returned. They had also lost a lot of money, what with the exchange rate being what it was, so Al was always in the office. He had a permanent screen tan and the few hairs he had left on his head pointed in all directions. He was building a palace for his wife on the West Rand again, and she was driving a Merc again. He had all kinds of technology projects on the side, but the main one concerned a computer-generated story about Naasie, who had been only two when he was mauled by their American pit-bull. He looked so peaceful, you know, lying there. And, man, it had broken Al's heart to blast old Bliksem to kingdom come. Meanwhile, the daughter was occasionally praised, but usually reprimanded on the phone. Albertus Grey was ruling and rearing his nuclear family from the office for all to hear, but he was our IT man and without him we couldn't function. He was one of the chief workhorses in the office. Come to think of it, most of the workhorses in that office were Afrikaners.

Back home Kayla was waiting at the gate and Butch got so excited by her attentions that he didn't know his arse from his eyeballs. She had lost weight and had dark rings under her eyes, pleading exhaustion. She wanted to know whether she could sleep over for the night, just sleep, mind you, 'because I feel safe with you'.

'You don't say.'

'I didn't, like, mean it like that.'

'How *did* you, like, mean it?'

'Sorry. I don't know.'

'When last did you sleep?' I asked.

'Does it matter, Mr Sub Editor?'

'Yes, it does. Didn't your mommy tell you it's bad for your health?'

'Oh, what the hell. Do you feel like a jay?'

So we smoked a pre-rolled joint with a sad Butch watching us from outside, suffering the exclusion blues.

'How's work been?' I said, realising that I didn't want her to sleep upstairs.

'Work? There aren't enough hours in the day. I'm doing a nine-to-five job while people are dying left, right and centre. Then I'm doing an MBA with people scrambling for the top, and then I'm trying to do you,' she said, breaking into a neurotic giggle about her weak little joke.

'Don't think you're too young to burn out, missy.'

'Yeth uncle Len,' she said coquettishly.

'Do you want a drink?'

'I thought you'd never ask.'

So I went into the kitchen and got a bottle of Grouse, two glasses and a bowl of ice and went back to the living room. She was sitting on Judtih's couch, as usual, and wanted to know how the old man was doing. I said he was okay.

'I'd like to meet him.'

'What for?'

'You never stop talking about him.'

'What do you mean?' I said, worried.

'You don't.'

'What else has been happening?' I asked, to get off the subject.

'Ed's been making the most outrageous comments.'

'Ed who?'

'Motshekga.'

'Oh, him. What's he been saying?'

'Well, things like all whites should be driven back into the sea.'

'Has he said this to your face?'

'Yes. But I think it's just drunken talk.'

'That means he means it.'

But no, she had challenged him on it and all he'd meant was that those whites who were still stuck in the past had to leave. How the hell were the likes of him going to determine who was stuck in the past and who not, I asked.

'I don't know,' she giggled.

'Do you think it's funny?'

'Yes, I do. I don't think it's serious.'

'I think it's very serious. I didn't like that prick from the moment I saw him.'

'He's got a gentle side too, you know.'

'So did Joseph Goebbels.'

'Who was he?'

'Jesus, Kayla! You're a political commentator, you're studying for an MBA, but you don't know who Goebbels was, you've never read *Disgrace*, you talk like an American sitcom character...'

'I know,' she said, getting all teary. 'But I'll get there. I'm, like: when do I sleep? I mean, what do you know about Richard Cole's *Six Principles of Developmental Economics*?'

'Nothing. And I'm not sure I want to. But if you convince me he's worth reading and that he writes in English and not Economics, I'll give him a bash. In fact, would you like me to Google him right now?'

'No,' she said, looking vulnerable.

We had reached our first stalemate. I didn't know what to say or do, so I said: 'Can I play you some non-thud-thud music?'

'That'd be ... that would be really nice,' she said, relaxing a little, trying hard not to like anything.

I took out a disc and said I'd been depressed the other day until I heard this. As far as I was concerned it was more rock 'n roll than rock 'n roll and I'd bought the whole set.

'What is it?'

'This particular piece is the first movement of the fourth quartet, which was actually the fifth, because even in the eighteenth and early nineteenth centuries there were commercial considerations.'

I could see I'd lost her, but she was looking at me as if I were the font of all knowledge, as others sometimes did when I (and especially the old man) spun a yarn.

'The piece that got me going again was the second movement of the 13th quartet, the B-flat minor, because it could be a scherzo

– as in mocking – as much as a presto. That is, fast.'

'Please don't shout at me, but who is this?'

'Beethoven. Have you heard of him?'

'Yes,' she said, close to tears again.

'The man who appeals to amateurs and aesthetes alike. And please don't cry. I'm not good with crying people.'

'Okay. Shall we have another jay?' she said.

'Sure, I said. But listen to this. Doesn't it conjure up images of Heidi frolicking over the Alpine grasslands?'

Her look told me she didn't have a clue who Heidi was.

'Won't you please tell me the story of *Disgrace*?'

'Sure, but not while the music is playing. Being a man, I can't concentrate on two things at the same time.'

So I faded the music and told her about the white academic who effectively rapes one of his students. He refuses to apologise for the rape publicly, gets fired and goes to live with his daughter in the Eastern Cape. She, in turn, is raped by three black youths after they lock her father up in the toilet. Her black, much older neighbour, Petrus, offers to marry her and look after her and the child, but in exchange she must cede her land to him.

'God, that's rough,' she said sleepily.

'Very. Not only is the daughter raped, she's gay. That echoes another atrocity: so-called corrective rape, except that those who "come out" in the townships are usually murdered for good measure. But the Supreme Leader and his ilk might have had a point in thinking the novel was racist because, if there is some nuance in the white characters, there is none amongst the blacks. They are, like the government itself, predatory, rabidly self-interested, contemptuous, detached. They don't ...'

Kayla was fast asleep so I let the fourth continue again, softly, looking at her perfect body and drifting back to David Lurie's daughter, Lucy. By accepting the arrangement, she more or less becomes a servant to her neighbour, and sacrifices her sexuality. If she has to come out under the patriarchal Petrus – ironically named after the disciple who insisted on being crucified upside down out of respect for his master, Jesus Christ – she is probably dead. All of this to continue working the land. She's a survivor, echoing Carla in Karel Schoeman's masterly *Promised Land*. The earthy, fundamental practicality of women. Lucy. She protects her privacy concerning the rape like a corolla protects the reproductive parts of a flower. David Lurie drives a Toyota Corolla, which is then stolen. His daughter's name also conjures up the primal skull found in another part of the continent, the Great Rift Valley, *Australopithecus afarensus*: good for trees and the plains. In other words, adaptable. Whether this was intentional or not is also not the point. *Disgrace*'s artistry lies in the fact that it can accommodate such a reading, much as one could make a case for Lucy being a nickname for Lucifer. Lucy. Named after a Beatles hit on the radio at the time: *Lucy in the Sky with Diamonds*. Picture yourself on the couch with a woman/who's sleeping just like your wife did. Music. Melody. That was much more comforting.

Round and around.

If we are not going to know more about Lucy than her sexual orientation, it leaves us with Lurie. Coetzee only gives his lead characters something approaching a personality, and we are mesmerised by this one, however suspiciously. Why are we hypnotised by him? Realistically he's a prick, a serial womaniser of young students and colleagues' wives as he gets older. He only stands by his daughter because blood is indeed thicker than water; the closest he can come to an endearment for her is to call her a very Victorian 'my dearest'. No Luce, Angel or Sweetheart. He is going to cling to his aloofness and never fully interact with mere black mortals. He clearly only judges 'them' politically. In a way, he represents most white South Africans, who have never bothered to take any interest in their fellow citizens, especially by learning one of their languages. Intellectually, he's seductive because his head is so *busy*. He thinks the South African story can no longer be told in English and that speech comes not from the need to communicate but to fill up our 'overlarge' and 'empty' souls with song. He does not dwell on the fact that original song might have come from our mothers, lulling us to sleep. And, to continue the musical line, he is composing an opera – on a banjo! – about an aristocratic woman pining for another literary lecher, Lord Byron. This has very little to do with the main story, if anything. The only way he will show any remorse for what he did to the student he raped is by prostrating himself in front of her mother and sister, touching their suburban carpet with his forehead, like a Muslim faithful. He is on his way to losing or giving up his predatory sexuality, as he does a three-legged dog, which will be put down, euthanased, killed. Soon he will be an aged man with a dead stick between his legs. The journey inward continues. David Lurie is as repulsive as any number of characters in the novels of Dostoyevsky, whose work is littered with the word 'disgrace'. This journey leads Lurie towards giving dignity to the very lowest of the low, dogs' corpses, for which he finally achieves a kind of Franciscan serenity. A deeply Christian novel, then, by an avowed atheist.

It was getting cold, late autumn, so I fetched two blankets and cursed myself for not getting a number for Judith, the most recent in a respectable line of prostitutes. The first had been in more exotic circumstances. I'd been heading to Greece, sunshine, and thought I'd pop into Venice. But no one had told me to change trains so I'd ended up in Rome, where I'd done that one thing the old man had never done, *ever*, not even in the flesh pots of Cairo, he'd assured me. I had bought a woman in the Eternal City, doing my best not to be like him, running away from him, but doing it with the money he'd sent me.

On Luck

Kayla slept until nine, by which time I wasn't going to get any sleep, or sex, so I made us an English breakfast. She loved that and looked much fresher and even wanted to get a little lovey-dovey as I started getting ready to leave for the old man's.

'Sorry,' she said. 'I forgot.'

'That's alright,' I lied. 'What are you doing tonight?'

'I've got a study group,' she play-moaned.

'Some other time,' I said.

'Did you make your ex-wife breakfast too?'

'I'd prefer not to talk about her.'

'Okay, sorry.'

'Shall we have some coffee?'

'*Good* idea,' the old man said, standing at the wash line and flattening a pair of pants with his large brown hands, as if he were still out in the desert.

I was hanging from the silver pole's crossbar and he asked me how many pull-ups I could do. I almost managed ten.

'Very good,' he said. 'I used to be able to do a hundred in college.'

'Then came the war.'

'Ja. But I was very lucky.'

'How come?' I said for about the three-hundred thousandth time, returning to *terra firma*.

'Well, out in the desert there was this thick line that ran through our camp, so I cut a piece out of it so that I can hang up my washing, like this. A few days later I hear it's the communication line to the front and someone's cut it and there's going to be hell to pay. So I quickly get rid of it, bury it.'

'What would have happened if they'd discovered it was you?' I said, propagating us towards the courtyard, the stoep and the kitchen.

'They would have shot me on the spot for treason!' he laughed, inviting me to share in his mischief, hazel eyes sparkling.

After the usual kitchen conversation we took our coffees and Lemon Creams out into the autumn light, sat down and I asked him how his week had been. His sister from Empangeni had called to tell him what to eat and there was this man from the church who was worried about the old man's soul, but he'd told 'the bastard' that *he* had a personal relationship with the Old Man and read the Good Book, every day, and had I read the latest *Reader's Digest*?

'No?'

A family had been stuck in a car on a muddy dirt road and, unbeknownst to them, a truck was hurtling towards them at full speed. It was night and its brakes had failed. But they prayed and tried one more time and drove out of the mud and took a turn-off just before the truck passed them.

'Hm?' I said, thinking about Kayla's body.

'Talking about trucks, the Stukas used to come flying over us and every time we'd have to jump off the back of those trucks and lie on the side of the road. But after a while I notice that the gaps between the rounds are so big that you can predict exactly where the next bullet will hit.'

'So?'

'I'm getting tired of jumping in and out of the trucks the whole time. So after a while I just stay on the truck and work out when to jump off, or not.'

'What did the others say?'

'They thought I was mad,' he said, laughing.

'Wow.'

'But do you know what?'

'No, Dad. What?'

He reiterated that he must be the luckiest guy in the world.

'Why's that,' I said, wondering whether Kayla was playing some sort of game with me.

'Because I only fired five shots in the war, and that was to test my sights.'

'And then?'

'We were captured at Tobruk and had to smash those beautiful .303s.'

A Week from Hell

That night I couldn't sleep, as usual, telling myself that I eventually would, but didn't. Butch and I went for a late walk and I made the further mistake of asking the Doberman handler with the mean black eyes how he was after all these months of walk-by greetings. Ask a stranger how they are and within five minutes they will tell you most of what you need to know about them, even with their silences, but this one wasn't that way inclined. Within seconds he was trying to convince me that the whole world was geared towards controlling our minds. The entire military was poised for takeover, the media wasn't (*weren't* you, idiot, media is plural) reporting on it because they was (were!) all in cahoots, and at least he wasn't that far gone to see that I didn't believe a word he was saying.

'It's all in the book I'm writing,' he said by way of authenticating it.

'Well, I'd like to read it when it comes out,' I lied.

'It should be done in about two months' time.'

'Cool,' I said.

'What do *you* do?' he ventured.

'I work in the media.'

He uttered a low, guttural gurgle that went for an ironic chuckle but felt more like he was about to order his two prize Dobermans to rip out my throat, and said maybe I'd like to review his book.

'But I'm part of the new military-media complex?'

'Ja, but there are still pockets of sanity,' he replied, his eyes looking quite insane.

I was sick of the whole anti-media thing. People bitched about politicians and the papers, but if it wasn't for the latter they wouldn't know what the former were up to, and if the politicians didn't get their way then it was either whites or the media's fault. Christ, if the country wasn't as oppressive and intellectually bankrupt enough as it was, you still had the Dobermen of this world to add to that claustrophobia in as open and supposedly free a space as this park. He might well have been right about the military-industrial complex, but if he was the alternative then I'd stick with the demons I knew.

'I'll see you,' I said and started walking away, taking in deep breaths of real and metaphorical fresh air.

'Maybe we can have a cup of coffee sometime,' he called after me.

'Sure,' I retorted. In your fucking dreams, sunshine, I thought.

That night I slept a little and could settle down to walking Butch, writing nothing and going to work again. Kayla called and apologised about falling asleep at my place, thanking me for being so understanding and promising she'd make up for it in a big way. I didn't say I'd believe that when I saw it, but I thought it and said let's see how things go.

I couldn't sleep again, so I finally put on the seventh quartet, the first of three commissioned by ambassador Andrey Razumovsky. It starts with a simple walk-along tune, the kind that might ease its way out of you as you take a brisk stroll. And, unusually, it's in the lower registers, starting off with a slightly melancholic cello. But soon it takes a darker hue, a more dangerous edge. There is always that potential for danger and excitement in Beethoven's work. Then back to the tune with all the improvisatory powers at its creator's command. The second movement is much slower, of course, much more stately. Or rather, that's how it starts out. But soon the maestro tires of such stasis, ignoring the fact that it's supposed to be the slow movement and the piece climbs out of its complacency into a kind of suspended excitement. Here comes the third now, the slower movement, all exquisite, rainy, winter's-day melancholy, art defeating death, even lending Mr Rossini a few notes for his much later *Barber of Seville* overture. Beethoven likes to go very slow and long when he's supposed to just go slow and longish (the same applies to speed and short). The piece goes on, never boring, always creating a what's-next expectation, though always logical in its argument, always innovative in its execution – note the almost jazz-like plucking of the cello – and who says that expectation isn't a bit of a tease? Who says it isn't erotic? Why not make deepest love to that music, I thought. Maybe such musical genius could awaken in the unconscious mind a sense of beauty, even if applied towards the political economy. There is no break between the third and last movement; they are one. This is also not 'allowed', but who's complaining? If anyone is, Beethoven certainly isn't losing any sleep about it. He's too busy working out the next argument. We are now supposed to be in an allegro, I think, but it isn't very fast, and it seems to have endless endings, like the film version of *Lord of the Rings*. It also has a Russian theme, though I'm too much of an ignoramus to hear that. But what is he doing? Is he solving a problem or playing a joke on us, or both? Here's another ending, but no, he has more to say. It's like this never-ending night. Off he goes again, building to an ultra-slow moment before the final push and Butch starts barking at the screeching hadedas at first light.

On Thursday night, after deadline and calling the old man, who thanked me *so* much, I went home like a good boy and did what legions of men do: I watched porn for too long, followed by the functional release that comes with it. On Friday morning I woke up too early, took Butch for a constitutional, saw and reviewed an okay film and kept to within the drink-drive limit afterwards. The next morning I did some shopping, went over to Jay and Veron's after lunch, watched a boring game of soccer and turned down the offer of supper.

'Why? Have you got a *skrop*?' Jay said.

'Maybe.'

'Well, whatever you do, use a condom.'

Kayla duly arrived and got Butch's spine undulating like a rope being twirled by a child, but she had even darker rings under her eyes, despite the make-up she had plastered over them and her blemishes. She seemed on edge and it looked like she had lost more weight, too.

'Would you like a drink?'

'Ja,' she said, distracted.

'Okay, hold what you're doing until I come back.'

I went to the kitchen and got the usual Grouse, glasses and ice. When I got back, she was still standing, looking at my lithos with her back to me.

'What makes you feel alive, Len?'

'Writing, Beethoven, sex, though not necessarily in that order.'

'Do you want a striptease, Mr Sub Man?'

'Sure,' I said, having given up on irony.

She slowly took off her shirt and dropped it.

'Undo my bra.'

I put down our drinks, went over and did so.

'Go and sit down.'

I did as ordered, seeing Butch outside cocking his head sideways and looking as dumb as my denim-constrained I.M.P.

She slowly pulled down her zip.

'God, I love that sound,' I said, wondering whether other atheists also used His name in vain when it came to sex.

'So do I,' she said, and we both laughed.

She kicked her shoes away.

'What do you think of my arse?' she said, reading my thoughts.

'I think it's a work of art,' I said. 'Enigmatic, but artistic nevertheless.'

'What do you mean?'

'I mean, judging by its shape you're a very sensual person. But you don't really take that sensuality all the way with me.'

'Some people think it's fat. Others, of course, think it's too...'

'Skinny?'

'Flat.'

'We really are expanding your vocab ...'

'Hm,' she said, turning to face me, standing there in her panties, walking towards me, putting her hands on my knees and sinking to hers. As aroused as I was, I couldn't help suspecting she was going through some kind of routine.

'Let's start with the shoes,' she said.

'You know, I've always believed in working one's way up from the bottom.'

'Good,' she said, removing my shoes and socks. 'Now let's get rid of these pesky jeans,' and she started busying herself with my buckle, then the button of my trousers, the zip, carefully.

'Lift yourself up,' she said.

I lifted my arse and she pulled my pants away, leaving me in my bulging boxers.

'And again,' she said.

Who was I to argue?

'That's good,' she said, staring at my very interested I.M.P.

'What would you like to do now?' she said.

'Well, I thought we could discuss Hegel's theory of history.'

'Tell me about it?'

'Not now, darling,' I joked. 'I have a headache.'

'But then you cannot possibly want sex.'

'The funny thing is,' I replied, 'it's the kind of headache that's *cured* by sex.'

'Really?'

'Yes, really!'

'Okay. But I first want a jay.'

'Fine! Let's have a jay.'

'But I've run out.'

'Well then let's *not* have a jay!'

'I know where we could get some more.'

'I'm sure it can wait,' I said.

'No,' she decided. 'I don't think it can.'

And with that she got up and sexily started getting dressed, an act that advertisers avoided because it started with nudity instead of leading to or suggesting it.

'Is this some kind of game?' I asked.

'No. Why would I do that?' she said impatiently. 'I just feel like a jay. It'll take us half an hour. Are you coming?'

The last thing I felt like doing was going out, but by then it could be safe to say I was compromised, and anyway, I suffered from that thing most writers do, even failed ones. I knew if I went along, I'd see something new and it could always be used as material. And I was very awake.

'Yes,' I said. 'I'm coming,' knowing that was the end of sex for the night, yet again.

On Captivity

Driving to Lyttelton, I listened to the E-minor, or eighth, which is an altogether different proposition to its predecessor. It starts off with a clear, sunny statement, but is then followed by an ultra-slow, church-like adagio that seems to go on forever. It reminded me of the impatience and restlessness I felt as a child while the minister droned on endlessly and the old man juddered and clicked away. Now I couldn't get enough of it, savouring it both in time and out of it, knowing there were further delights to be had.

The allegro didn't disappoint, conjuring up the image of a foal finding its feet, bursting with its own life, testing its legs, running and jumping for the sheer joy of it. The presto is full of Russian (as well as Italian, to my mind) exuberance. It is a virtuoso piece for the lead violinist to fly upon and the other three to support. A much sweeter quartet than the former, but it also plunges more depths. It is, as my mother would have said, too beautiful for words.

I took the Clubview turn-off, where the old man had dropped me off, freshly returned from Europe, with me running, him weeping. He was standing at the gates and looked the way I felt: not happy about something. When we got to the kitchen there was a lemon pie on the table, not the one he sometimes bought when it was a bargain at the local supermarket. This one looked like one of those home-industry types.

'I see you got us a lemon pie for a change, Dad.'

'No, I didn't,' he said, agitated. '*He* gave it to me,' he said, jerking his head in the direction of the neighbour's.

'He' was Uncle Vern, who had moved in next door with his wife and two sons when I was about, hell, very young and they were an almost handsome little family. Uncle Vern had had the prettiest Christian wife you ever did see. She used to wear such soft summer dresses and had such full pink cheeks and lips that I used to like her in ways that distantly puzzled me. The problem was that Uncle Vern had been (and still was) an atheist and Aunty Carrie wasn't. She was a Baptist or something and one fine day Ma told me that Carrie and the boys had moved out. Why, I wondered out aloud. The thing is that Carrie had met a nice Christian man and she and Uncle Vern, who was not exactly an oil painting, were going to get divorced. I was quietly outraged. How could this happen in our suburb, our street, right next to us, in fact? Weren't there rules against such things? And would I ever see Carrie again? Vernon Brown must have been pretty shocked too, because he never moved out of that house and he never got married again. The years would go by and Uncle Vern would always wear his check short-sleeve shirts, his baggy green shorts, long cream socks and ubiquitous Hush Puppies. When winter came, he would add a khaki pullover to his wardrobe and just get whiter and balder each year. He also had various back ops and was finally boarded for health reasons and paid a packet to not work for anyone else in the defence industry. He never went to see the rest of the world, never took up his hobby of sailing again, and always had a dry whistle as he pottered about a garden big enough for three families too. But then he was the one who was always helping the old man with an errand here, a meal there or just – God in his great absence help him – listening to him.

'That's nice of him,' I said.

'No, it's not,' the old man retorted.

'Why not?'

'Because I didn't *ask* for the pie.'

'But ...?'

'That bladdy man *irritates* me! The other day he takes me to the hairdresser ...'

'That's also quite nice of him.'

'But the bastard never cleans my neck properly. Look here!'

He showed me how long the silver strands were still in his neck, and he had a point, even though we'd had endless headbutts about hairlines as fashions had changed over the decades.

'So why don't you say so?'

'Agh!' he fumed, cornered and as coiled as a spring.

'Let's have some coffee and pie,' I said.

'*Good* idea,' he said for about the two-hundred-thousandth time and gradually calmed down as we went through the mug rite and he punctured two holes in a condensed milk tin and blew the thick, sticky milk into his coloured water. Then he did the same for my cup of pitch, which would kill me, and took a deep suck at the sweet whiteness.

'You know,' he said, 'when we got to Bari, it was raining and the women lined the streets. All I had was what I was wearing: my boots, a pair of shorts I'd made from some canvas in the desert, and my greatcoat. The women were weeping, but I'm not sure if they were crying because we looked so forlorn or because they thought we were the bastards who had killed their fathers, husbands and sons.'

'So the camp was in Bari?'

'No, it was about an hour's drive away, in a place called Gravina.'

'What was that like?'

'Easy. The guards used to sometimes give us their rifles to hold while they ate. Sometimes they'd give us some of their coarse bread too. But one day I noticed there was a foal in the field. *Beautiful* creature. So I started talking to her. Just getting her used to my voice. Talking to her. This went on for about two weeks. Then one day I filled my hand with condensed milk and let her catch its smell.'

'Where did you get the condensed milk?' I asked automatically, wondering how I was going to get through the rest of the day on no sleep.

'From our Red Cross parcels, obviously.'

'Of course. Sorry.'

'You could see she was scared, but her nostrils were quivering. She *had* to have this stuff. So I let her come towards me. 'Come on, my girl,' I said. 'Come.' I let her take a lick and pulled my hand away, but when she took a second lick, I grabbed her neck and started rubbing her gums with the stuff. Boy, did she go mad! She bolted this way and that! But I hung on to her neck for dear life! I ploughed a furrow in that sand as deep as my elbow! But she finally calmed down, and do you know what?'

'No, Dad. What?'

'After that, no Eyetie could come *near* her!'

A Jog Sans Dog

I struggled through that Sunday and by Thursday my corpse even told me it needed a walk, which got the perpetually optimistic Butch in a frenzy of excitement. By Saturday morning my body told me it needed more than just an impatient walk in the park, so off I went for a jog early that chilly morning, leaving Butch looking as forlorn as a cartoon character behind the security gate while I got the neighborhood's dogs behind theirs in a frothy again.

Despite the cold it was a refulgent day and I noticed Lukas was already there to catch the early folk, smoking a cigarette stub, accompanied by a little cough. On I went, past the notices and lost babies' booties and keys hanging on the spiky, newly installed palisades at the entrance, towards a grove, through the mud and in between all the plastic that washed down the street and into the park every time it rained.

After the grove I crossed the little stream that smelled of chemicals and ran into the main dam, next to which I'd had my audio satori. I was just wondering whether I might one day be doing this and keel over from a coronary when I heard a squeal. At first I thought it was children, but it was too early for people to have their kids in the park. Next I heard men's shouts and then three of them were running straight towards me. It took me a couple of seconds to work out what was going on. They had just robbed three women, who were screaming, which got the park's gardeners running to their aid with long machetes. That was all very commendable, but the trio running straight towards me had one outstanding feature about them. The man in the middle, a fine specimen, had his hand on a very large pistol sticking out of the top of his trousers. This could ruin my day forever. Fortunately, these men were not focused on me but on those behind them, one of whom was still in his civvies and shouting that he was a policeman – 'Poyisa!' – they must stop. He was lying, of course, and the trio just kept coming towards me, so I thought I might stop, change course, and go around them towards the women. I don't think the trio even saw me.

The man in civvies was on his cellphone and the women were all rattled, their border collie as enthusiastic as if they'd just suggested they were going to play fetch. The oldest woman told me they'd been walking along when the men passed them, seeing one of the other women's jewellery. The man had shown his pistol and demanded the woman's rings. She'd refused – one of them was an heirloom – and one of the unarmed men had wrestled her to the ground and tried to work the rings off her finger. That's when she'd started screaming.

By now we were at the gate and the women had to head to a parking lot that was in the same direction the thieves had run. So

I stopped a bakkie and asked the man to give us all a lift. He duly obliged, we turned a corner and saw that the place was crawling with cops. There were at least five police vehicles. One of the fleeing men had suddenly stopped and started loitering when the cop cars arrived, wailing. The other gardeners had seen him and, since they earned their daily pittance the hard way, they had no sympathy and pointed him out to the cops. So he was handcuffed and shoved into the back of a kwela van, scraping his shin bloody in the process. The robbed woman identified him as the man who had sat on top of her while the other cops poked around in the shrubs against the high suburban walls. Suddenly there were shouts, and another thief was found lying beneath some loose autumn leaves and branches, looking up at five pistols pointing at him. I thought they were going to shoot him, but they didn't and the man with the pistol was gone.

That afternoon I went to Jay and Veron's and, at halftime out in the garden, told Jay how reliable our cops were when it got to the really important things, like a white madam walking in a park with heavy jewellery. He said the women and I were 'fucking lucky' to be alive.

'I know. But don't you find it amazing that here we are, living our privileged little lives, while we know exactly what's going on – fifty murders a day, fifty reported rapes a day, a *day* – yet we carry on as if nothing's happening, just like our folks did during apartheid.'

'I know.'

'Have you ever thought of leaving?'

'Sure. But can you see Veron leaving?'

'Ja. Why not?'

'Not interested. She's told me. Are *you* thinking of leaving?'

'Ja.'

'What about your old man?'

'I don't know,' I said.

'Look, the teams are coming back on,' Jay said.

'Ja, like prize horses. What a bunch of paffs.'

So we went back inside, put the sound back on and Jay shout-asked Veron to bring us some more beers from the kitchen.

'Get them your fucken self,' came the reply.

'Who said it was going to be easy?' I said.

'And fuck you too. Go get the beer.'

'Okay. But I'm warning you: every time I leave a room a goal is scored. Usually against the host's team.'

Jay showed me a middle finger, so I went down their passage and into the kitchen, where Veron was eating a sandwich and asked whether we were getting 'shit-faced' again.

'No, Veron,' I said, taking two beers from the fridge. 'We've been discussing whether we're in the antithesis or synthesis part of Comrade Hegel's theory of history.'

'My fat Bushman's arse,' she said.

Veron had been a cadet at the *News*'s sister paper in Durban and Jay, who had fled the Free State to start off his career in that sub-tropical city, had taken one look at her soft brown skin and smouldering green eyes and that was it. Six months later they'd been secretly married. What most people, including Jay, didn't know at the time was that she was also an ANC operative. But as far as she was concerned, she didn't join the struggle to get rich but out of principle. Equally, she didn't believe in two girls being brought up with both parents absent – she'd seen how families were torn asunder by parents married to the struggle – so she worked from home but kept her main focus on the girls. She might have seemed all domesticated, but her opinions were published, known and respected, if not always liked, especially not by her erstwhile comrades. She and The Ex had been (and still were) friends and we'd all got on like a house on fire. The difference was that Jay and Veron had a roaring sex life and nothing else in common except their kids, one of whom wasn't even his, but he'd adopted her and that was their life. They were nuts about each other, but some or other domestic war was brewing and I didn't want to know anything about it.

When I got back to the living room, of course, The Scum had indeed scored, which put Jay in a particularly bad frame of mind. I always teased him that Liverpool were (sports teams and rock bands took the plural at the *News*) my second-favourite Spanish team. He didn't care who their coach or players were, as long as they won – and of late they hadn't.

After the match we slouched back into the yard again and I asked him what he thought of Kayla.

'A bit uptight, you know.'

'Ja, you're probably right,' I said.

'But she's got a great arse,' he added, sensing my disappointment. 'Why?'

'No, I was just wondering ...'

'Would you like to dick her?'

'If we were alone on a desert island? Sure. Wouldn't you?'

Of course he would, but he'd been hearing rumours.

'What kind of rumours?'

'That she's into nose candy.'

'As in coke?'

'Ja.'

'Interesting,' I said, adding that I thought I should go home.

Jay didn't protest that impulse and I looked forward to getting away from the acrimony in his home and flopping onto the bed in my empty one. But halfway there the phone rang and Kayla said she wanted to come and spend the night. She also wanted to come with me to see the old man tomorrow.

How about I come over to your place, I responded testily, inspired by Veron. But no, she said, her place was a terrible mess. I told her I thought she should get some sleep for a change, which she gratefully acknowledged, but she insisted on meeting the old man. I couldn't think of a quick enough reason for her not to come along – it might break the monotony of the drive – and acquiesced.

Refusing her to come over had been more contrariness than any kind of maturity. I wasn't going to allow her to call all the shots, but by about one that morning I still couldn't sleep, so I got into the Kitten and went looking for Judith again. I couldn't find her and most of the bars I knew were closing up, the last stragglers all fairly senseless, so I finally, predictably, settled for the PC screen with Aunt Hanna and her Four Daughters, wary of the links leading off to children, trying to comfort myself that at least I wasn't a rapist.

On Principle

I fell asleep just before Butch started barking at a pair of crack-of-dawn joggers, went through all the usual rituals and drove over to Kayla's block of flats because she'd insisted on driving; even that small change would be something. She met me downstairs and didn't look like she'd had much sleep either, and she'd attacked her face again.

'How're the studies going?' I said as we sped towards Midrand, the halfway mark to Pretoria.

'Exhausting,' she replied, sniffing. 'But I'm fine.'

'Of course you are,' I said, squinting at the Highveld glare.

'What's the matter?' she asked.

'Every time I go to Pretoria, I get pissed off about all these horrendous security villages going up. I used to play in this veld, which was then deemed to be too dolomitic for development. Now every second house is a pseudo-Tuscan nightmare.'

'It's amazing how much it's developed.'

'I don't know if that's the word, but my father predicted ages ago that Johannesburg and Pretoria would eventually become one.'

'Clever man. But how are you otherwise?'

'Oh, just dandy. Getting over my ex and trying to get some hussy almost half my age into bed.'

She slapped my leg playfully and wanted to know The Ex's name and I didn't want to tell her, so I continued bitching about how my beloved Highveld was being usurped by bad-taste capitalists and commies alike.

'Len, what' her name?'

'Jesus!' I yelled as a white minibus taxi scraped past us at speed. 'Where did that arsehole buy his licence?'

'Your ex.'

'Why do you want to know?'

'I'm ... curious.'

'Not good enough.'

Kayla put her hand on my leg.

'That's a much better reason.'

'I'm waiting.'

'Could you move your hand up a little, please.'

'First tell me.'

'Okay, what the hell. Shanti.'

She also thought it was a beautiful name, but that wasn't enough: she needed a surname.

'Govender,' I said.

'You don't mean *the* Shanti Govender?'

I said I didn't know what she meant, thinking of how I used to tease Shanti 'The People Shall' Govender.

'The deputy editor of the *Weekly Herald*?'

'The very same.'

Kayla was impressed, though whether it was because Shunt had an important position or was 'non-white' I couldn't fathom, nor did I care at that very moment.

'So she never took your name.'

'No, I wasn't famous enough,' I tried to say ironically, but wondered whether there wasn't a modicum of bitterness in the inflection.

'What do you mean?'

'I've heard of the most battle-hardened leftwing feminists realising their mate's got struggle credentials and suddenly becoming Mrs So and Fucking So. Now could you move your hand a little up, please?'

'No. It's not safe. How did your father respond to her?'

'Like he responds to any good-looking woman. His final word on the matter is that "all pretty women are pretty".'

We sped on in silence, apart from her sniffing.

'And your mother?'

'Couldn't stomach her. Saw right through her. Instant dislike. I should have gone with her mommy-knows-best instinct. I thought she was being a racist, but I was wrong.'

'What did she object to?'

'Her ambition, her heaviness. This was not the woman for her darling son.'

'How did you and your mother get on?'

'That's one hell of a question.'

'You had a pretty quick answer about you and your father.'

'It was normal,' I said for the sake of brevity.

'Okay. What did she call your father?'

'Son. As in child, not that shining thing above us.'

'Oh.'

Pause.

'Why?'

'From his surname. Sonnekus. *Sonnie* became Sonny became Son, as in male child. His sisters call him that. His wife called him that. Sometimes he's even *like* that.'

'It's an unusual surname ...'

'He thinks it was German. I don't. But if he's right I wonder if the original surname wasn't something like Schmidt, because the first Sonnekus arrived here in plus minus 1850, in George, according to the Cape archives. So I wonder if he wasn't causing *kak* on the ship and sentenced to fifty lashes. Now he had a choice. He could be flayed on board or take his chances over it. So he dived into the water, splashed about like mad and got washed out on that golden shore, that sunny coast, that coast kissed by the sun.'

'What a nice story.'

'One of the things that militates against it, of course, is the fact that the sun almost never shines in George. Not for nothing was its old registration number plate C.A.W., as in cold and wet.'

'How come you don't have the same surnames?'

'Long story.'

'Tell me.'

'Okay. I've taken the maternal one. Mommy's boy. And the Bezuidenhouts have been here longer. The first one was a master gardener at the Castle in 1668. Moreover, I'm convinced my mother had Spanish blood in her – she *looked* Spanish – and that's because Bezuidenhout means south of the woods, or forest. Some Spaniards settled south of the wood in The Hague after some war and no doubt intermarried with the locals. So, flamenco music, it stirs me. And if I'm correct then it means that those Spaniards had Moorish blood in them, too. All that whiny North African and Middle Eastern music; it's the original trance article. I can get off on it for hours. I really do understand it in my blood.'

'And Beethoven?'

'I suppose that's my Western side.'

This didn't interest her any further.

'Anyway, then the Bezuidenhouts came here and no doubt had a lot of hanky-panky with the locals, but always denied it. In fact, they were so patently anti-pom and darkies that they started a rebellion because of it, and got hanged for it. Not hung, by the way – that's for washing. Hanged.'

'So that's why you look the way you do …'

'What? Like a Puerto Rican pimp?'

'Yes. But didn't you and Shanti want children?'

Shun had never wanted children and I'd always thought it was a phase, an affectation. She'd change, I'd reasoned. She'd see that a career, her ego, wasn't everything. As in most things, I'd been perfectly deluded. People will hang on to their miserable little positions and possessions for all they're worth. But the folks had always thought we would eventually have kids and I never told them it wasn't going to happen, assuming they would either die before we could, or I'd make up a story about how one of us was infertile or barren. Or we'd get divorced, which we duly did.

'I never told them Shunt didn't want children.'

'"Shunt"?'

'The mouth, like the eye, is lazy. But also as in around. Later on it just became Shun.'

'Did *you* want children?'

'Ja. I like the sound of children playing. That, too, is a kind of music.'

'Would you still like to have children?'

'Well, it's getting a bit late in the day for that kind of thing.'

'No, it's not.'

Just then another minibus taxi swept by and I said: 'You say the sweetest things. But tell me, why don't you and Ed do an exposé on the taxi industry?'

At which point Kayla almost overturned the car.

'Hey!' I shouted. 'I'd like to die in a slightly more exotic manner than motoring to Pretoria, okay?'

She wanted to know how I knew they'd been asked to form an investigative unit and when I said I honestly didn't know what she was talking about, she said: 'If you tell anyone about it, I'll kill you.'

'Interesting how we use that term so often – and so easily – especially with kids.'

'Promise me you won't tell anyone,' she insisted, completely focused on state secrets as opposed to everyday usage.

'I promise,' I said, smiling.

'Why are you smiling?'

'I'll just write about it.'

'Len ...'

'Don't worry. I couldn't care less whether you start *three* special units. Your secret is perfectly safe with me.'

'Good.'

We took the Clubview turn-off and I asked whether her esteemed colleague had come up with any new pearls of wisdom. No he hadn't because he'd been in Xhosa Nostra country near Queenstown, again, for the last two weeks.

'What's he doing there?'

'Family, I suppose,' she sniffed. 'Is that your father?'

The old man was standing at the gates with his silver hair in his Sunday best, which he would wear nowhere except at home, but he looked confused. He didn't know Kayla's car and only let us through once he'd seen me. So we drove to the back yard and, after he'd closed the gate behind us, he came through to the back, smiled and said: 'Shanti, I'm so glad to see you again!'

Kayla found this highly amusing while I said: 'This is not Shanti, Dad. This is Kayla.'

'What do you mean?' he said, looking confused again.

'Kayla is my' – what was she? – 'colleague.'

'But aren't you ...?'

'No, Dad. I'm not married anymore. I'm divorced. Remember?'

'Of *course*,' he said. 'What a *fool* I am!' Then: 'Hello, my darling,' he said, took her damp white hand in his big, dry, brown ones and kissed it.

Obviously she was charmed and we proceeded to the kitchen and went through the coffee-mug routine, all of which delighted Kayla no end and got me in a mood at the opposite end of the spectrum.

Outside, we sat in the early winter light and the old man suddenly stopped juddering and clicking, asking Kayla whether she knew what. She obviously said no and he, for about the one hundred thousandth time said: 'I'm a poet / and I don't know it.'

'Really?' she smiled, charmed, while I wanted to kick a dog or something.

Now he went into a lyrical rendition of his favourite poem, *Piddlin' Pete*. It was his party trick and I wasn't going to spoil it. Truth is, he did it well and it was pretty impressive that he could remember it word-perfect after almost four score and ten.

> A farmer's dog once came to town
> Known to his friends as Pete
> His pedigree was ten yards long
> His looks were hard to beat

And as he trotted down the road
'Twas beautiful to see
His work at every corner
Every post and every tree

He never missed a landmark
He never missed a post
For piddling was his masterpiece
And piddling pleased him most

The city dogs stood looking on
In deep and jealous rage
To see this little country dog
The piddler of his age

They smelt his efforts one by one
They smelt him two by two
But noble Pete in high disdain
Stood still till they were through

Then when they'd smelt him everywhere
The praise for him ran high
But when one smelt him underneath
Pete piddled in his eye

And so he continued, delighting Kayla no end as Pete took up the city dogs' challenge and out-pissed them at every turn.

Then Pete an exhibition gave
Of all the ways to piddle

With double drips and fancy flips
And now and then a dribble

The city dogs said farewell Pete
Your piddling did defeat us
But no one ever put them wise
That Pete …. had diabetes.

Having ended it triumphantly, Kayla applauded and praised him, which of course he downplayed with an 'Agh'.

'I believe you were in the war,' Kayla probed.

I was waiting for one of the lucky speeches, but the story he chose to tell was in continuity with what we'd been talking about, and it also conveniently had great shock value.

'You know, in Italy,' he said, 'near a town called Gravina, we were told to clean the fields. Hay fields. They stretched for *miles* … right over the horizon.'

'Yes?' Kayla said.

'But I refused to work for them.'

'So what did they do?'

'The one sergeant said to me: 'Bravo, you don't work for the enemy.' But the captain told me I *had* to work, so the night before I was to start working, I took a hayfork and placed its middle prong on my foot.'

'And then?' Kayla said, captivated.

'I bashed it,' he said, smacking the side of his left fist with his open right palm, 'right through my foot.'

These Sporting Days

Jay was in a foul mood because Liverpool hadn't won the local or European championships and the season was now officially over. Television had spoilt us so much that we weren't interested in local soccer, which wasn't half as good as the northern hemisphere's, even though African players were infiltrating Europe very effectively on that score. Local soccer was as boring as the government's machinations, and the reason for that as far as I was concerned was because it was equally corrupt. So come winter – and it was here in all its hard, dry Highveld beauty – we would switch to local rugby instead of soccer. But that had become increasingly tedious too. The game had become a dull, kick-and-chase affair in which the forwards often became spectators as much as we were, except when it came to doing the hard work.

Jay was loyal to the Sharks because that's where he'd met Veron, who shouted for Province because that's where people thought she came from, and to give Jay a bit of opposition. I was supposed to shout for the Blue Bulls because I'd been born in Pretoria, but I'd been allergic to that place from the start and I'd fallen in love with the calming Free State flats on my way to the educated (but impoverished) east of the country, so that's who I 'shouted' for. Later I'd discovered that I had paternal roots in that province, which I might have sensed, but there were good dry jokes by and about the Free Staters too, so that was that. In matters of rugby, I was a Free State man.

We carried on with our office-sex talk as usual and Jay, of course, had picked up that there was something 'happening' between me and Kayla. I told him that we were merely flirting, so far.

'Nice,' he said.

'You don't like her, do you?'

'I think she's dangerous, bru.'

'You're probably right.'

'So why are you carrying on with it?'

'You know ...'

'Pass the fucking ball!'

One of the Sharks' wingers had run the ball dead again, which really got on Jay's tits. 'Just be careful.'

'In what sense?'

'In the sense – *Jesus! Can you believe it?* – mind your back.'

'Is there something you're hearing in the office?'

Jay, who got really excited when his team messed up, said there were murmurings.

'Are you going to tell me or not?'

'No. You of all people should know better than to get involved with a colleague.'

'Look who's talking.'

'Do I look happy?'

'You're still married.'

'I've got children, okay.'

'Fair enough.'

We carried on drinking once the game was over and started preparing for our ritualised braai, and much later I said if only the country could be run like our cricket instead of our soccer.

'Are you saying darkies can't organise themselves?' Veron said, heading towards her late-night, alcohol-fuelled aggression.

'I'm saying we've got world-class cricket, but crap soccer. The first has taken a gradualist approach, the latter has taken an absolutist approach. The government wants representative cricket, but doesn't give a toss that soccer isn't. That smacks to me of arrogance, if not downright reverse racism. All the funds the soccer bosses get for youth development, which is key, go into some very aged back pockets. The result is there for all to see: shit football.'

'There is another way of looking at all of this,' she said.

'I know,' I said, equally drunk and obstreperous. 'Start all over. Scrap everything. Fire all the European coaches you get across Africa for their alleged managerial skills. Get rid of all other whites and Indian entrepreneurs while you're about it too. And to hell with the so-called Coloureds, as usual. Start from ground zero. Who cares if it takes a generation or two before Africa is purely black and African again? Africa is patient, and who says it won't one day produce an all-black team with all-black coaching staff to win the World Cup?'

'Well, by then the English team will be completely black too,' Jay added.

'This is not what I meant by another way of looking at things,' Veron said.

I asked what she did mean.

'I was thinking more along the lines of banning *all* fucken sport,' she concluded.

She had a point. The older I got the less reason I saw to watch men (and, increasingly, women) chasing balls of different shapes and sizes. And why would anyone feel such loyalty to a team so far away that they would, as in one case in Kenya, hang themselves when their favourite European team lost? Then again, Jay would say, anyone stupid enough to shout for Arsenal deserved what they got.

Obviously these teams' managers could become as famous as their wards. If a team lost too often the manager would get the chop, but if it won and made a lot of money for its club he'd become almost as wealthy as his charges in the short term, but he could work into his seventies if he maintained his winning ways. The players could go on to become managers (or commentators, film stars, models or drugged-out nutcases after their relatively short spells of glory). But things were slightly different in South Africa. If your team lost you were fired but if your team won something as piffling as the Rugby World Cup you were fired too. It was such a constructive, generous culture.

Even less understandable was why anyone would be happy that their golfing or tennis heroes had just made more money in one tournament than any one of their fans would make in a lifetime. Was it a kind of sublimated desire in which the sporting god fulfils your failed dreams for you? Did people not want to be their own heroes? Obviously it was all the media's fault. Occasionally there'd be a moment of aesthetic beauty, usually in a five-day cricket match, for which no one had any time anymore, or thanks to Barcelona FC's chess-like cool, but most of the time it was just a slog and I watched because I liked socialising with Jay and Veron.

'Why do you support Barca anyway?' Jay had slurred.

'Because I once knew someone from Barcelona, and his name wasn't Manuel.'

'Ja?' Jay had said, shit-faced.

'He was a good friend and I was cruel to him and he died,' I said.

'What did he die of?'

'AIDS,' I said.

'How were you cruel to him?'

'I told him he'd been looking for it,' I said, remembering a terrible silence at the other end of the line.

'So I believe you're fucking Kayla Greenwood,' Veron, ever the diplomat, said.

'Where did you hear that?'

'Reliable sources,' she replied in a go-and-get-stuffed kind of way, at which point my cell started ringing.

'Talk of the devil,' I said.

'Guess what,' Kayla said, breathy with excitement.

'Are you at the airport?' I said, hearing familiar background noises.

'No, I'm at a hotel with Herman Sebogodi and Jack Weisz.'

Sebogodi was the chief of human resources and Weisz, as already mentioned, his suck-up.

'Okay. What are you doing there?'

'Guess.'

'You're having a *ménage* à *trois*,' I said jokily.

'No,' she said, too excited or ignorant to get the dig, 'I've just been offered a promotion. So I can't come over.'

'You've just been offered a promotion.' I said, for my drunk hosts' sake.

'Yes,' she laughed.

'To what? Senior political commentator?'
'No. Management.'

On Living

Someone – a driver, a pedestrian – had carelessly flicked a cigarette away and the butt had landed on a bone-dry tuft of yellow winter grass. It lay there smouldering for a while before a hint of Highveld breeze made the tuft's fringes touch the butt's heat and started smoking, then crackling into life. The small flame spread to the next tuft and soon the fire had a little life of its own, smoking blue, spreading rapidly under the distant sun. Soon the fire was a quarter of an acre big, then a hectare, roaring towards the highway, greedily licking at it and trying to reach across as I drove through a pungent black cloud on my way to the old man, who was standing at the gates with an equally dark cloud hanging over his silver head. I drove to the back and, after getting my hand squashed, asked him how things were going.

'Up to *shit* thanks.'

'Why, what's the matter?'

'They sent me a letter and said they want to take my pension away. I've been worried *sick*.'

'You're looking pretty good for someone who worries so much,' I mumbled.

'What?'

'Let's have a look,' I said.

He gave me the letter in the kitchen and said, 'I put the kettle on.'

'Good,' I replied, reminding him where he kept my coffee.

'Do you know how much I paid for this mug?'

'Let me just read this, Dad.'

'Sorry,' he said, looking lost.

'All they're saying,' I said, 'is that you have to prove to them that you're still alive.'

'Of *course* I'm still alive!'

'*I* know that, but they don't.'

'So what must I do?'

'We must just go to the cop shop and have you certified.'

'Let's go right away.'

'Do you know why they want this?' I said.

'No?'

'Because people claim against their dead relatives' pensions.'

'Bastards,' he said. '*Bastards.*'

'People are desperate.'

'No, they're just bladdy *dishonest*!'

'Get your ID,' I instructed him.

'I've got it here,' he said, feeling in his jacket pocket, then the other, then the inside pockets, his trouser pockets, becoming panicky.

'Now where the bladdy ...? I could have sworn ...'

'It's on the table, Dad.'

'You know,' he said gravely, 'sometimes I think I'm going out of my mind.'

'You're just getting a little forgetful, and that's at *your* age. I often walk into a room and wonder what the hell I'm doing there.'

He wasn't particularly interested in my ageing process so we drove down to the police station and got him certified as alive and, as we got back into the car, he said: 'Did you see that cop?'

'Which one, Dad?'

'That one standing there,' he said conspiratorially.

'What about him?'

'Look how fat the bastard is.'

The man was built like Lukas, the car guard, and wouldn't be much use in an on-foot chase.

'And he's smoking – in *uniform*!'

'Times have changed, Dad.'

'I have never smoked a single cigarette in my life! Not in uniform or out of it! Nor have I had a *single* drink!'

'And you didn't sleep with any other woman, except Ma.'

The old man looked slightly taken aback by that.

'Do you want to go to her grave?' I asked, the cemetery being just down the road.

'No. I'm not in the right frame of mind.'

'Fair enough,' I said. 'Let's go and have some coffee and pie.'

'That's a very good idea,' he said as we left the new station, which was opposite a vast old-age complex, situated on a piece of land that used to be an open expanse of Highveld where I'd been dive-bombed by plovers as a child.

'How'd you like to live there?'

'Over my dead body,' he said. 'If I die it'll be in my own house and they will carry me out of there, feet first.'

If he died, not when.

'But do you know what?' he continued.

'No, Dad,' I said, wondering what was coming. 'What?'

'I worked for *thutty*-six years to get a pension. Then I was declared medically unfit because of that horse.'

'What horse?'

'A horse threw me and I hurt my neck. It's been calcifying ever since.'

I remembered he'd had to stay at home for a year while the medical board decided on his fate. By then he'd been in his late fifties and he'd stayed within hearing distance of the telephone for a year of working-week days, but then he never went out anyway.

'So I was boarded, got my pension and left the police. And do you know what?'

'No, what?'

'The *day* after I left the cops, I started working for the State Tender Board and stayed there for another eighteen years. Do you know what that means?' he said, eyes glinting triumphantly.

'No?' I said, wondering about what Jay had said concerning Kayla.

'It means I get *two* pensions!' he laughed.

'Amazing,' I said flatly.

'One big and the other not so big. But all those bastards who smirked behind my back about what a menial job I was doing: where are they now? Dead, most of them. Or sick. Or broke. Or both!'

It was true that most people his age were not self-sufficient. In fact, everything he said was irritatingly true. We drove home, went through the whole panic of finding the keys for the security gate and back door, so that we could finally go through the coffee-mug business and end up in the warm winter sun outside.

'Are you still walking around the yard?'

'Ja. But I only managed going around once this morning.'

'Why's that?'

'I got this band of pain across my chest.'

'That'll be your heart.'

'Other days I can make up to ten times.'

'Well, you're not a chicken anymore.'

'No,' he said, that storm still hovering above his head.

'You used to walk around the perimeter of the concentration camp as well ...'

'Ja,' he said, juddering his left foot and clicking his right thumb nail.

The hayfork wound in Italy had given him malaria, somehow, and so he'd never worked for the Italians. But then he and his fellow POWs had been transported to Eastern Germany soon after, where they weren't required to work. The Germans had even given him some experimental medicine, which had cured him of the malaria.

'Didn't you get depressed – claustrophobic?'

'Not really. But others did. One night I was on toilet duty and someone said I better go and check on Rudolph Hendricks, who was a poet. He'd written a beautiful poem called *The Mountains of the Moon*.'

'So what did you say to him?'

'Nothing. He'd hanged himself.'

'Jeez!'

Click, click, click.

He had often told me about how he'd been the richest man in the camp, saving up all his cigarettes so that he could swap them for luxuries like condensed milk. Then one fine day he'd received a pipe in his Red Cross parcel and it had never left his mouth during his waking incarceration.

'But I never smoked. *Never...* Do *you* still smoke?'

'Ja,' I said guiltily.'

'It'll kill you,' he said.

'I know.'

He was somewhere else and I couldn't work out why, so I just continued asking him questions.

'But how did the Germans treat you in general?'

He stopped juddering his foot and worrying his nail.

'Generally, very well ...'

'But?'

He was quiet for a while and then said: 'We used to play sport every day, summer and winter. One day we were playing cricket and the ball rolled into one of the officer's yards, which were strictly *verboten*. Old Johnny van Heerden put his hand through the fence to retrieve the ball, the officer took out his Luger and ...'

'And?'

'He shot him through the head,' the old man said for the first and only time, his voice shaking. 'Like a dog.'

Flirting With the Foe

They awoke in the deepest recesses of a cave in the Waterberg, a cloud of velvety black moths, each one as big as a steelworker's hand. Then they made their way south in the cold, dry nights, laying low during the day, entering Pretoria and paying tribute at the grave of one their most famous victims, Eugene Marais. Onwards they went, towards Johannesburg, fluttering steadily parallel to the busy highway down below, then over the naked jacarandas and into our building, past the dozing security guard, up the stairs, into our open-plan floor with its cancerous neons, heading towards their target, sitting there in his Liverpool FC jersey, as if awaiting them. They came to rest on his head, his shoulders, and then started gnawing through his hair, skin, skull, nerves, blood, gristle and other matter, until they finally got to his soul. You could see Jay going elsewhere. He carried on functioning, but he became slightly glazed, very pale, his head sunk into his body, virtually paralysed by depression.

It was Thursday night and Kayla called just after I told the old man I'd see him that Sunday, having learnt not to specify a time anymore. She was calling me on my cell so I scuttled out on to the balcony, where the deputy editor was talking to her girlfriend. Kayla wanted to know whether she could see me on Saturday night.

'What for?'

'I'd like to make up to you for being such a – such a pain.'

'You don't have to make up for anything. It's fine.'

'You can come to my place,' she said.

'Okay,' I said, principled as ever, thinking about what Jay had told me. It made sense that she might very well be doing coke in the week to keep her multitasking self awake, then coming to me for comfort and some dope-induced sleep, though I suspected that wasn't the full story. Still, I wasn't going to confront her about it just yet; I wanted to see where the whole thing was going.

Driving there, I wondered what her one-bedroom flat looked like, expecting it to be as chaotic as her life seemed to be. But I was wrong. It wasn't so much minimalist as bare, functional. This was someone who was too busy carving a steep upward graph to collect fine art or colourful posters or wall hangings, though she had black-and-white photographs of unpeopled cityscapes and the prescribed books she needed for her MBA, nothing more.

'Welcome,' she said, looking a little less stressed out, dressed in comfortable clothes with the usual clashing colours.

'Thank you,' I said, migrating towards her ribbed heater. 'So what's it like being a suit?'

'Hectic,' she said.

I said I couldn't understand why they couldn't just wait until she'd finished her eternal MBA.

'Well, there's some urgent stuff that needs to be managed.'

'Stuff like what?'

'I can't talk about it.'

'Of course not. So have they created a special post for you?'

'Ja. Me and Ed.'

'The plot thins. Has he come up with any more nuggets?'

'Yes, he told me on the phone from PE that he now thinks *all* whites should be driven into the sea, women included.'

'Send him to me. I'll give him a piece of my mind.'

She said she still thought it was all talk and why didn't I pour us a drink?

'Okay,' I said, feeling distinctly ill at ease in that soulless apartment, pouring us two of her Johnnie (not Johnny, I couldn't help thinking) Black Labels and wondering why she wanted to see me.

'I don't know,' she said, sitting down and lighting a pre-rolled jay. 'I'm not good with expressing myself like you.'

'Then you must be an ideal candidate for business,' I replied.

'Can't you just accept me for what I am?' she asked, handing me the jay, exhaling a cloud of smoke.

'Well, I don't exactly know what you are,' I said, taking a long, crackling drag. 'You're someone who hangs out with me occasionally, mainly on a Saturday night. But you don't seem to want sex – or regular sex anyway – nor do you want anyone to know about 'us'. Why is that?'

'I don't know.'

'That's not very useful.'

She came back with an equally difficult question: 'Why have you never dropped me?'

'Well, I want sex, I'm at a loose end, and I suppose I'm a little intrigued.'

'And you're holding out for a little more ...'

'Probably.'

'Is it just my body?'

'I thought it was, but I'm finding I get confused between desire and an instinct to protect.'

'I like that.'

'I don't know whether I do. Am I supposed to be some kind of surrogate father figure? Would I be bad for your career if other people knew about "us"? Would you be embarrassed or ashamed to be publicly associated with me? I mean, if you get invited out to a function, who do you take with you? Me, that other arsehole, someone else, no one?'

'Are you being all ....?'

'Possessive? I hope not. But I know I'm starting to sound like a housewife who nags her husband because she thinks he's knobbing his secretary.'

'Well, that's partially why I wanted to see you.'

'You're fucking the secretary?'

'No,' she said, ignoring, if not missing, my jibe and taking the joint back. 'I've been invited to a dinner party next Saturday night. Do you want to come?'

'Who's going to be there?'

'Some people from management.'

'Great, a bunch of golf-playing, car-talking dickheads,' I said, letting the amber fluid luxuriate down my throat.

'There are some perks to it, you know.'

'Like what?'

'Come here,' she said.

So I did and she gave me the joint, hooked her fingers into my pants and pulled me closer.

'What are you doing?'

'Relax.'

'Wait a bit. Experience tells me this is going to go nowhere.'

'Don't worry. This time I'm well stocked up.'

'Okay. Do you want a smoke?'

'No thanks,' she said, undoing my belt, 'there's something else I want to put in my mouth.'

I was still feeling distinctly uneasy, but I was seriously compromised.

'Tell me a story,' she said.

'Again?'

'Yes.'

'My thoughts, if they can be called that, are elsewhere right now. But I'll tell you what. I'll play you a piece of music,' I said, producing a CD I'd brought along in my quest to educate and entertain first myself, then others. 'And if you give me a theme, I'm sure I could come up with a story.'

'Africa.'

'No less,' I replied, and put on the second movement of the C major quartet, half leaning over her with my crotch close to her face, the other immortal ninth. If the first movement started with a heavy, dusty, experimental air before it broke into light sunshine, then the second was very slow and very sensual and stayed that way for a very long time.

Kayla pulled my zip down and started kneading 'me'.

'You know,' I said, 'a cousin once gave me an album when I was fourteen and I didn't like it at all. It had a man on its cover in a spastic kind of pose. So I swapped it for another, *Benefit*, by Jethro Tull. I loved that album. It represented everything I was against. Rules, short hair, crap music. I loved its combination of rural English and electronic rock, which it combined in songs like *Son*, a nicely sarcastic piece about teens. But soon after that I started seeing films like *Woodstock* and *Mad Dogs and Englishmen*, and then I really liked the man who made those contorted moves.'

She unfurled my stiffening flag as I told her the man's name was Joe Cocker.

'What a coincidence.'

'Ja,' I laughed, as she put my I.M.P in her mouth.

'And I only realise now that he must have been a kind of bridge to what I'm about to tell you now.'

'Hm?'

'I mean, I'm still a great fan of his. He just keeps going, and I like that. I like it when people just … keep going.'

She too just kept going, which caused all kinds of micro-commuters to run up and down my spine. 'But let's get on with the story, shall we?'

She nodded as Mr Beethoven's strings almost sounded like woodwinds.

'Okay. I had just arrived at varsity, fresh from twelve years of Christian National education and two years of being an officer in the Air Force, bursting with my own self-importance. All I had was an instinct that something was wrong, though there had been plenty of glaring, neon indications along the road. But there was a band that was going to play at our Great Hall one night.'

'Hm?' she and the music continued as Ludwig and I did the shudder.

'There were three men on the stage. Black men. The middle man was a short guy with a huge guitar. He was wearing … running shoes, old jeans and a kaftan top. Sitting behind him was a man on a Yamaha or something.'

She removed the I.M.P. from her mouth and asked why there was a motorbike on stage before resuming her task. I told her it was an, ah, organ. Feeling her laugh that way just increased the number of commuters running amok along my spine.

'Sitting there was a man behind dark glasses and beneath a black beret. He was … he had a heavy, political air about him, but then we're talking late Seventies here. Those were heavy, heavy times … Biko had just been … Oh Jesus, that's nice.'

She took my cock out, said 'carry on' and put it back in her mouth.

'To his left was a man in a loin cloth,' I continued. 'The only other thing he was wearing was shakers around his ankles. He was surrounded by traditional Venda drums, he was shaven bald and he'd covered his whole … he'd covered his body in oil.'

'Cool,' she said, taking another breather, looking up at me through her specs. 'This is great music.'

'Jazz before there was jazz …'

'Yes,' she said, and carried on doing what women do in ice-cream ads for children's fathers.

'Take … your time. This piece still … has a way to go.'

She nodded.

'The … organ had started a floating kind of sound, creating a huge sense of expectation. Now the guitarist started playing a completely unrelated jazz riff … I was hooked, hanging, mesmerised. And then the drums came in, care of one Mabi Gabriel Thobejane. Deep, confident, proud, strong.'

Kayla made an encouraging sound.

'I felt as if my head had turned … three-hundred-and-sixty degrees. In fact, I didn't just … feel it. I knew it. But just as I was getting into a particular groove it felt like I'd been waiting for all my life, the guitarist … Philip Tabane, stopped and started playing something completely different.'

She mimicked him and took the I.M.P from her mouth.

'It was pure … theatre. He twisted his shoulders and face this way and that. He was saying we can't ... get complacent. Not in art, South Africa, life ...'

I was close to the point of no return and got the sense that she was trying to co-ordinate that with my story and the music, which still had a way to go.

'It took me a hell of a long time to realise that ... what he and his band, Malombo, were really saying was that black people ... aren't the sum ... or result of ... their political aspirations ... or white liberals' projections. They quite clearly have a ... life ... and culture ... and a universal one at that ... beyond ... the politics of the day.'

'What did it make you feel like?' she said before she resumed the task at hand and I waited for that long moment in which the four instruments breathe out to formulate everything into one desperate, grateful meaning and said exactly what I didn't feel right now: *'Home.'*

On Freedom

As usual, Kayla fell asleep and, satisfaction achieved, so did I, but only for about three hours. After another two of duvet boxing, I had to go for a pee and saw a rather bulky African necklace on the cistern, which dozily bothered me. I decided I was going to go and be sleepless in my own house, where I fretted. If I had failed to prove to my mother that I could succeed as an artist, then I was dead on track to do more of the same with the old man. Had I more or less ended up the same way as him, stuck in a job that employed about five percent of my potential? The confirmed question reminded me of seeing him on the train after work one late afternoon. It was during my second year at varsity and I'd been given a job as a student reporter at the *Capital News*. But what did I do? I hid behind a pillar and tried to write a novel. That month was the only time the old man and I ever worked in the same city, and occasionally we'd catch the same train in the afternoons, since he got up at five in the mornings, cursing, and I didn't, sulking. Then we'd pass the Fountains, stop at Kloofzicht and disembark at Sportpark. This he'd been doing for about forty years by then, every single working day.

That afternoon a typical Highveld storm broke out just as I got to the Herbert Baker-designed station, the rain hammering its high roof. I passed the mounted old coach in which Oom Paul Kruger had signed some or other declaration and entered the electric one. As the doors started closing a bunch of white, middle-aged men squeezed in, half wet, breathless, joking. Civil servants in their grey suits and Hush Puppies. The old man was one of them, laughing at their banter. As the train left the station the rain stopped and the sun burst through those dark storm clouds, beaming into that section where the old man was standing at the other end of the coach, unconscious of his son watching him, his son who never told him they'd been in the same coach that black-golden day, the old man enjoying his fellows' company, but somehow desperately separate, desperately alone.

And today I was driving towards him again, listening to the opening of the so-called harp quartet's first movement, conjuring someone waking up slowly, washing, getting dressed, locking up, getting into the car, driving through the suburbs and hitting the highway as the out-of-character adagio breaks and bursts into delighted pizzicatos for what is, after all, supposed to be a brisk movement. You're alive, you're moving and the man is cajoling you onwards, popping in and out of styles and eras, but always himself, always true to the centre of the piece, building up a good, complex head of steam. Now that you're fully awake you can indulge in the real adagio, a progressive sermon for what is, you recall, a Sunday, ending as it does on what could easily be the breathless departure of gentle Jesus' soul from this good earth.

But we've also been primed for the presto, bursting with comedic, cascading vim. There is a tiny break and we move on to some lusty, Bach-like hacking, giving the viola its mellow voice, then letting the cellist tap away as if he's a rock bassist. The final rush is frenetic before it ends with a polite, gently ironic conclusion.

The old man was standing at the gates of 123 Harry Smith and, after we've gone through the usual rituals, I said, 'What happened after the Russians liberated you from the camp?'

'A friend and I slipped away, walked through Europe, got to Brussels and flew to England. There I had to wait for the ship. I thought it'd take a few days but it went on for *weeks*. So every day I went for these long walks. And every day the dogs from the neighbourhood would join me and follow me until I had a whole bunch of them behind me. I'd do the circuit twice so that they could stop off at their houses, and I'd get back to the base without a single dog.'

'Is that it?'

'I saw a woman one day …'

'What, an English rose?'

'Ja.'

'And?'

'Nothing. The ship was leaving.'

'Were you glad to see Africa again?'

'I don't know.'

'Where did you stop?'

'Lagos. Walvis Bay.'

'How exotic.'

'We weren't allowed off in Nigeria but we got off at Walvis Bay. We were given train tickets home.'

'And when you got to Durban?'

'My mother, aunt and sisters were waiting for me.'

'Were you glad to see them?'

'My mother's hair, which used to be dark brown, had turned the colour of ash.'

'What did you do at home?'

'I don't know. I was there for a week or two and then I was posted to Springs.'

'What did you do there?'

He had worked in the state mortuary and had sometimes retrieved corpses from the lake.

'As you grabbed them their skin would come off,' he said.

'Charming'

'Someone had to do it.'

'And?'

'That lasted for about a year before I was posted back to the college in Pretoria as a PT instructor.'

'Is that when your nose got broken?'

'Ja,' the old man said.

'And the other guy?'

'I broke his jaw.'

'Why did you fight?'

'He insulted me.'

'What did he say?'

'I can't remember.'

'Did it have anything to do with Ma?'

'No.'

'Because that's where you met her, not so?

'Ja.'

One of his duties had been to work as a barman in the officers' mess.

'Even though you don't drink.'

'Not a drop. Ever.'

'And then?'

'She was standing by the piano, singing ...'

'Why are you pulling that face?'

'Because she had a drink on the piano, and a burning cigarette.'

'So why did you marry her?'

'Because her *mother* told me to.'

'Dad, that's not a very good reason to marry a woman!'

The old man just juddered his left foot and clicked his right thumb nail.

'So you got married and rented in Wonderboom South, where you met the De Freitases.'

'Ja.'

The old man had actually worked with Koos de Freitas, whom he said he couldn't stomach, like everyone else, but Ma and his wife Jasmine had remained friends forever. The young families had lived on the steep southern slopes of that white, working-class suburb, nestled beneath part of the Magaliesberg that separated the Highveld and the Bushveld proper, which stretched all the way up to Messina, followed by the then Rhodesia and, of course, Europe. The De Freitases had a son who became a Dutch Reformed minister and two daughters who had become teachers, typical Afrikaner aspirations of the time.

'Then you came here.'

'And I'm not moving again. *Ever.* People can go and see the world if they want to, but the only place I want to be is here. This place has the best weather in the world. This is *my* house and I'm staying here until I die.'

'And what if you can't look after yourself anymore?'

'Then I'll chase a bullet through my head.'

The Priorities of Power

Jack Weisz was hosting the dinner do and was his usual smooth, operating self in his double-breasted jacket, acting the generous, confident host, even though everyone knew his time at the corp was limited. The man had been offered numerous sweetheart deals before, according to Kayla, but now that I'd met his wife I knew why he wouldn't necessarily want to spend the rest of his days in a damp retirement village on the KwaZulu-Natal coast, sipping G&Ts and maintaining comms – if not consulting lucratively – with the office upcountry.

If it looked like a lump of old clay had been pasted on to his shoulders and painted deep maroon, then it looked like Chloe Weisz had been blessed with industrial-strength orange plastic for a hide. The look probably had to do with the fact that she'd had so many visits to the plastic surgeon that her forehead was, in fact, her back thigh. She wore a pair of dainty heels and an ultra-short-skirted outfit, adorned with considerate African themes, but it was the voice that would have driven me stark, raving bezonkers. It sounded like a glass rim being rubbed until it started squeaking, amplified, non-stop.

Meet the Weiszes, such a lovely couple.

They lived in one of the many 'park' suburbs, which used to consist of small properties containing mining houses with corrugated roofs on a rather dull, functional grid. But as the city's fortunes had moved north, Parkhurst had found itself bang in the middle of a boom that rendered its tiny properties worth more than the last vestiges of gold beneath them. Naturally every arty type with money who hadn't moved there yet did so now and converted those humble houses into artworks of one kind or another. Chloe had done a reasonable job of creating a 'flow' in the extended abode, which still retained its pressed ceilings and Oregon pine floors, complemented by early William Kentridges, which Jack couldn't help mentioning might be worth a fortune one day. Not that that was why he had bought them, mind you: he was just saying.

Next in attendance was Herman Sebogodi, high chief of HR and a one-time revolutionary journalist who was now in management, like Jack, because it obviously paid better. He, too, was stocky and only ever wore brown shoes, beige trousers and a button-up chocolate brown sweater to show that he was a township boykie from the Sixties. But if there'd been any mapantsula wit about the man it had deserted him years before; he was now as dour and impenetrable as a chunk of hardwood. All he seemed interested in was playing golf, usually with Jack. You could talk to him about anything and he would talk about Herman Sebogodi. You could threaten his life and he'd probably drone you into a lull. Nothing excited the man. But to think there was nothing happening behind that blank forehead would be certain folly. Herman also controlled the office purse strings and therefore knew everyone's movements, from Boeing to virtually bowel.

And, as is often the case with men like these, his wife, Noni, was quite a number. If her usage as a pre-subbed columnist was pathetic – one classic spoke about her living room being scatological with cushions – then her ideas weren't always that bad. At least she gave one some insight into what was happening across the racial divide, which was still as entrenched as ever. I would certainly not turn her down if she'd offered herself to me, but then I didn't even make a blip on her and her dickhead of a husband's radar. In fact, Jack and Herman greeted me as one might greet the Supreme Leader's driver, not because they wanted to but because they had to make a show of so doing.

Next there was Clive Copeland, a young foreskin who could even see the positive side to being biffed between the eyes with a cricket bat. I had instantly disliked this jock and made it quite clear to him before I realised his father had been a former editor of the national daily. That was when such people still had to find compromises between publishing the truth and keeping the paper afloat. So his son was liberal-to-left-leaning press royalty and I had burnt yet another bridge in my scorched-earth policy of annoying very important people. I innately distrusted such constantly chipper people, much as their persistently glum counterparts cheered me up no end. We always greeted each other cordially, but we knew we really had nothing to say to each other. He would always have a job and was looking to co-steer the ship, while I was on the starboard, talking to the chef during his smoke break.

But the first prize was on the right of him. There she sat in all her smug, serene glory, Shanti Govender, my ex-wife. In her turquoise sari, she looked like she'd just walked off a Bollywood set and I could already see the headlines for their power wedding: he, full of new-South Africa hey-ho; she, giving the kind of scheming smile that would be described as 'radiant' or 'mysterious'.

Stupid me for not asking who exactly would be coming to the party.

Penultimately, there was Edward Motshekga, wearing a shiny grey Mao suit, and his partner for the night, Melanie Davids. I had never met her incredible highness, but I had seen this sour, arrogant sow on television before she'd started wafting along our corridors like some toxic gas from a B-grade movie, holding her head as if she was the very queen of entitled pain itself. Her whole demeanour spoke of how *she* had been in the struggle and *she* had made sacrifices and *she* would always remind all and sundry that *she* was therefore political royalty. *She* would never date a white man, she had written in a 'feminist' column that was nothing more than self-promoting flatulence. *She* wasn't Coloured or Khoi-San, but black, proud of it and only wore African apparel, like the huge kaftan tent in which she was residing right now, graced with an ethnic necklace of no doubt deep significance. She had a very large face, which went with everything else of hers, and she was going grey, which she didn't mind showing to the world because *she*, after all, was a Woman.

'Hi Len,' Shunt said.

'Haven't I seen you somewhere before?' I joked, which seemed to put Clive at ease, after which I had to meet Ed and Mel. The former forced himself to shake my hand – I kept it Western just to annoy him – but the latter couldn't even be bothered to give me a three-way. In fact, she wouldn't *touch* me. I was white scum, she made it clear, which came as a bit of a relief: at least I didn't have to pretend that we had anything in common.

And so the night got started and the drunker Jack, Herman, Clive and their partners got, the quieter and more concentrated Ed's smirks became, as if everyone else was really just part of a sideshow while he waited in the wings with a certainty that was annoying socially and predictable politically. The evening was ostensibly to welcome him and Kayla to middle management, but once that little speech was out of the way we could all, bar two, get down to some serious self-mutilation and banter about anything from who was shtupping the editor to its parliamentary equivalent.

I was way out of my depth and kept my trap shut, as the old man would say, drank steadily and noticed after a while that Jack, 'Herm' and Clive would disappear and come back even more aggressively happy, which obviously meant they were snorting cocaine in a toilet Chloe Weisz had ensured smelled like a reservoir of synthetic strawberries. But what made me ice up was the fact that Kayla was holding on to me like a 'significant other'. Shunt instantly recognised signs of my rising temper and then relaxed, realising that it was no longer her problem. In fact, she started enjoying my discomfort as Kayla half hung over me and spoke office to Ed past me and the Empress of Bitch herself.

'Why don't the two of you go and have your chit-chat outside,' I finally suggested, which they thought was a 'brilliant' idea and duly did. Now I was alone with Mel and Shun, who discussed who they knew from the struggle days, until Mel made it quite clear that Indians were effectively as complicit as whites – why was she always involved with white men anyway, they were so useless – in oppressing blacks. Shanti carried on talking, but I could see her withdraw into herself and tick off a subject for her next editorial. In that rancid air I asked Mel whether she'd ever listened to one of my favourite Eighties bands, The Genuines.

'I was too busy fighting to listen to music,' she said dismissively, not even bothering to look at me and pulling her mouth as if I'd just eased out a silent but violent stinker.

'That's funny, my friend Veronica de Waal seemed to find time to listen to them *and* still work underground.'

'She's a spent force,' came the instant reply.

I burst out laughing and wanted to ask her whether she was actually a man in drag.

'By the way Len,' Shunt said. 'Is Beauty still with you?'

'Ja, I've just discovered Beethoven's String Quartets.'

Mel clicked her tongue at my deliberate Eurocentricity, still avoiding eye contact.

'I meant Beauty Motsepe.'

'Oh *Beauty*. Ja, she's still with me, if that's the word.'

'How is she?'

'Why don't you give her a call and ask her?' I said in a way that she knew accused her of being too busy caring for the masses via her weekly missives to bother about someone as real as Ms Motsepe.

Chloe came to the rescue and took 'the girls' to the kitchen to make coffee and share their gender-specific humanity, as signified by their near-hysterical, sisterly laughter, while 'the boys' drifted back in from their balcony smoke, from which I'd been excluded, followed by Ed and Kayla from the garden.

'So tell me Ed,' Jack said as the evening hit the witching hour, 'what do you think the digital age is going to do to publishing?'

'I think,' Ed replied, 'we must first get other priorities right.'

'Priorities like what?'

'The priorities of power.'

The room suddenly quietened, as if everything that had gone before was mere window dressing.

'Explain,' Jack said, sounding professorial rather than aggressive, even though he knew what was coming.

'The media are still in white hands,' Ed said.

'No they're not.'

'Yes they are. I know we have a black editor and even a black owner, but that is not real power.'

And now the man of the moment turned to look at me. 'We're still *acting* like a white paper, with white concerns.'

Chloe's cosmetically lifted eyebrows sagged with a certain weariness, Jack kept his poker face and Herm his usual one, which was the same thing, while Clive looked positively attentive and Noni seemed to imply that even this point of view could be incorporated into the broad church of the democratic doo-dah-day. Mel stared at the curlicued ceiling with the disinterested air of a dictator being asked to pardon the genuflecting corporals who had plotted to depose her, deliberating whether to feed them to the crocodiles or let them make a run for it across a field of African wild dogs with their cute big ears and nippy little teeth. Kayla squeezed my seething leg, warning me not to speak my mind and thus ruin her career or our relationship or both, such as they were.

'So how would you change the paper and still keep it profitable?' Jack said, as if he were calmly swallowing a puff adder.

'Profit is a white word. Why can't the government run the paper?'

'But then we lose all objectivity,' Clive interjected.

'Again, just another white word.'

To which Clive responded by saying 'But the Constitution ...'

'Can be changed with a two-thirds majority,' Mel interrupted without losing a beat, as if they'd been through this argument a thousand, tedious times before.

'So you're saying,' Jack shifted, as if to accommodate aforementioned viper in his very accommodating gut, 'that we must have a government-run paper.'

'Yes. It's the only way we can bring about a true people's democracy.'

There was one of those silences that occasionally befall a dinner party when it reaches a social or ideological stalemate, a moment to which Chloe rose admirably, asking if anyone wanted a liqueur. Everyone suddenly realised they had an early appointment the next day, Sunday or not, and the hugs, air kisses and three-way handshakes along a row of luxury German cars took as long as the drinks would have done. Kayla's old BM, of course, was a luxury model in training.

'What a bunch of fucking arseholes,' I slurred in the passenger seat.

'Why?'

'And thanks for telling me my ex-wife was going to be there.'

'But you're divorced. What does it matter?'

'So you *knew* she was coming?'

'Sorry, yes,' she said, feigning innocence. 'Why?'

'You obviously haven't been married before,' I said, fuming. 'And why the sudden open affection? Are we supposed to be an item now, or were you trying to show her something?'

'No, I was just in a good mood.'

'As for Ed and all his dated ideology ...'

'It's just talk,' she said.

'No it's not. He means every little syllable of what he said. If he could have a so-called people's democracy tomorrow, he would, as long as he could carry on wearing his fancy Mao suits, drive his Mercs, live in Sandton, fuck anything that moves and insult his hosts. Please don't invite me to one of these things again, unless you want me to completely ruin your career.'

'Okay,' she said, 'but I'm telling you, he's just a hothead. It'll pass. He's fresh out of varsity. He's still got all these ideals.'

'I've heard his degree wasn't exactly earned; more like bought.'

'I thought you were the one who said we deal with facts, not rumours.'

'Fuck him,' I said, which got her giggling. And you, I thought.

On Caring

As usual, it took me hours to fall asleep, so I overslept and was late and only thought of putting on a quartet, the 11th, halfway to the capital. This somehow helped me focus on the old man and got me thinking about a creature I'd once met. Uncle Oliver had also been a war survivor. He was the uncle of my first flame at varsity, B, and he'd been in an explosion. He'd decamped, walked into the Standard Bank for his first job interview after the war, turned around and gone home to spend the rest of his life having breakfast, lunch and supper with his mother. These rituals were interspersed with tea at ten and again at three. He would also go for two walks a day, one in the early morning and one in the late afternoon. All the small seaside town's dogs would follow Uncle Oliver on these walks. The rest of his day was spent reading the classics. That was it and at least *my* father wasn't like that, I'd thought, but I wasn't so sure anymore. All I knew was that he, too, would never stoop to talk to a therapist about himself because a) he would say there wasn't a problem and b) those people 'talk rubbish' anyway.

Right now, however, I had something else to worry about as I got to the old man's house at the end of the ultra-quiet second movement of the *serioso*: he wasn't standing at the gates. This got me fretting about his safety again. As a child I had spent sleepless nights worrying that he would die, but now I'd more or less accepted that he would 'go' with nothing being resolved between the two of us. Why should it be? If this hadn't happened between my mother and me, who were much closer, why then between him and me? But the thought of finding him dead in his back yard or kitchen was still not a pleasant one, so I parked outside, locked up, put a hand on one of the gates and swung my legs over. That's when I saw what had distracted him from waiting for me faithfully, worrying.

It came running towards me as soon as my feet touched the driveway: another canine nightmare, another dachshund, charging at me, tan ears flapping and barking as if I had just committed the most appalling crime imaginable. I shouted at the low bastard and took aim to kick its head through its delayed arse, whereupon it promptly lay down and proceeded to spray a neon-yellow fluid all over the paved bricks and itself. The old man came out through the middle door, looking as pleased as pie.

'What the *hell* is this?' I shouted, distantly aware of the fact that not only was I adjusting my curses, but I was doing so in a way that sounded scarily like him.

'I've decided to call him Howfy.'

'What kind of a name is that?'

'Listen to him when he barks. He's saying his name is Howfy!'

'Jesus,' I said, whereupon the creep jumped back on to its feet and started barking at me again, as passionate and hazel-eyed as its new owner.

'Howfy!' the old man shouted, and the pooch duly melted and crawled up to his new master's feet, one seriously traumatised quadripet.

The old man had changed in another way too. Instead of wearing the usual brown trousers, green golf shirt and beige check jacket, he had switched to a pair of baggy black woolen pants, a frayed black V-neck jersey and a grey baseball-style jacket, the inner lining of which hung down in raggedy strips. To top it all, he wore a red beanie that resembled a tea cosy, which kept his fine, silver hairs in place. The only thing that remained of the old, external costume was the well-polished HPs.

'That jacket looks like it's on its last legs,' I said.

He ignored that and, after we'd made the coffee and proceeded to the back courtyard, said: 'Can you believe it?'

'What, Dad?'

'I was at the doctor's and this bastard comes in and says he's going to have Howfy put down. "*I'll* take him," I said, right there and then. And now he's here with me, aren't you my dog?' the old man said, getting all gooey. And said canine looked up at his saviour with soulful eyes, his tail whipping my hungover leg so hard I could puke.

'You know, there's a special place in hell for people who abuse women, children and animals.'

'So you've said, Dad, but what were you doing at the doctor's?'

'Agh …'

'What does that mean?'

'Nothing …'

'Dad, what is it?'

'He wants me to have an eye operation,' he said, looking very uncomfortable.

'Why's that?'

'I've only got about fifteen per cent vision in it. Everything's milky. It feels like I'm seeing everything through cellophane.'

'This is news to me.'

He gave me his usual dead moment.

'Do you want me to take you to the hospital?'

'No, I'll just walk over.'

'Dad, this is serious.'

'They say there's only a small chance of it being successful. My eye'll be in a bandage for two weeks. I'm not allowed to bend or pick up anything heavy.'

'Then that's what you must do.'

'Bladdy optometrist gave me specs and they've helped bugger all.'

'I'll take you.'

'Don't worry,' he said. 'You've got to work.'

'I don't mind taking you, Dad. In fact, I'll be happy to.'

'No, you don't want to get into your bosses' bad books. They might fire you. And in any case, *he* said he'd take me,' the old man said, jerking his head in the direction of his kind neighbour, Vernon Brown.

'Are you sure?'

'Ja.'

Silence.

'So how have you been?' he suddenly said.

'Not good,' I said, surprised. 'Did you hear about that woman who was tortured to death with her own iron?'

He nodded bitterly and said: 'They don't want us here.'

'Who?'

'The kaffirs. Who do you think?'

'Dad, you can't talk like that. In fact, if you ever use that word again you won't see me. Okay? I fought hard to get blacks into power, and that was only in my head; it wasn't like I ran around in the bush with a gun for "them" or anything. I just happen to like their music, and just for that they employed me. I *like* working for them. And anyway, if it wasn't for this job, I wouldn't be able to come and visit you, okay?'

He didn't like it, but nodded grudgingly.

'This isn't something I learnt at university,' I continued. 'Do you remember how I used to hitchhike around the country, how I went to Zimbabwe?'

He nodded.

'Black people helped me as much as white people did. In fact, they helped me more because they didn't have any reason to. They didn't see me as representative of a race or an ideology, they saw me as a fellow human being and treated me accordingly. If anybody threatened my safety it was whites, because I didn't fit into their neat little compartments.'

He was silent.

'Do you think it's only whites who are being targeted?' I persisted.

'Yes.'

'Well, it's not true. That same day I read about a township girl who'd been raped and killed because she was too young to get a child grant. Both her parents were dead from AIDS. She was trying to parent her younger siblings.'

'Bastards. *Bastards.*'

'The point is, it's mostly blacks who are being targeted. I blame the people who allow this to happen,' I said. 'Their own leaders.'

'What about those who vote for them?'

'If you were black, would you vote for a white after everything that happened?'

He didn't like this either, so he said it wasn't going to get better.

'So what do we do?'

'You must get out of here. Go and start a new life somewhere else.'

'What about you?'

'I've got my dog, haven't I, Howfy?'

Whip, whip, whip.

A Mounting Need

Kayla had moved up a floor or two, so I didn't see her that often and when I did we greeted each other with something approximating amused embarrassment. It felt good to have her out of my life, but I couldn't go over to Jay and Veron's that Saturday because he'd been booked off sick and was only interested in staring at the wall. I was about to go out and watch some rugby at the local when there was a ring at my gate. It was that grim Afrikaans woman I occasionally saw in the park, looking particularly unattractive as Butch barked at her and/or the Alsatian she had in the back of her idling bakkie. I contemplated ignoring her, but I was curious as to why she would suddenly ring my bell.

Klara Groenewald had a strong, dry handshake, was in her mid-fifties, and had a horsy fringe, steel-grey eyes, a square schnoz, not much by the way of lips, and was still fairly trim, helped no doubt by the amount of daily exercise she got in the park.

She and her husband, partner, brother or tenant lived further up in the next suburb, I knew, because I often walked or drove past their house on my way to Jay and Veron's. He was a stocky, balding man with a broad ginger moustache who, according to the sticker on his Japanese generic, supported the Pretoria-based Blue Bulls. Occasionally I'd see her drive past my house or me on the street, either going to or returning from the park. Klara was terribly sorry to bother me but she had a very embarrassing thing to ask me and she didn't really know where to start but she had rearranged her entire living room but now that she had moved all the chairs seats side tables and coffee table she couldn't move the sofa it was just too heavy and she felt such a fool this was supposed to be a surprise for Dolfie her husband who was coming back early tomorrow after being away for a week and he was going away on Monday again and she'd wanted to give him a surprise but if I was too busy then it didn't matter and she was really very sorry for bothering me.

'Let's move your couch,' I said, leaving Butch looking abandoned and we drove to her house with her dog, Verdi, barking at me through the little connecting window and her telling it to shut up, jerking the window closed.

'Verdi?' I said.

'Yes, I love opera.'

'So did my mother,' I said. 'And your husband? Does he like it?'

'He hates it, so he calls the dog Ferdie. You've got to call them by roughly the same sounds apparently.'

'I know,' I said, taking note that the man was her husband and telling her about the old man's new darling.

Though this was a predominantly white English suburb, with an increasing number of Indian families moving in to be near the new mosque, her simple house was Calvinistically neat, done up in a way that aspired to be in 'good taste'. The living-room suite consisted of two heavy couches and chairs covered with chocolate-coloured faux leather and studs. The coffee table had a glass top and book of photographs depicting a soft-focus Cape, echoed by the bad but at least original oils on the walls, the kind of stuff you bought on Sunday afternoons at Zoo Lake. But my best was the three angels. There they stood on a side-kist from the days of Trekker yore, elongated and playing the violin, the flute and the trumpet. It was the kind of living room my long-suffering mother would have appreciated, since it was moteless.

Verdi wouldn't stop barking at me so Klara finally lost her temper with him and locked him in the back yard. I couldn't help noticing she had a flat arse, about which I had another theory: I was convinced such people were sexually dull.

'Geez,' I said in her language. 'Do they put lead in these sofas?'

'Do you see what I mean!' she laughed, still embarrassed that she'd imposed on me in such a way.

Once we'd finished, she offered me a cup of coffee or a beer and I settled for the latter. Man, she told me, her Dolfie (short for Adolf, as in Hitler, I couldn't help thinking) loved his beer as much as he loved his brandy and Coke, whereupon I asked whether I could have a shot of brandy too. I liked chasing it with cold beer and she said that was very German and did I like the Blue Bulls too? I replied that, for better or worse, I was a Free State supporter. Wasn't that a coincidence, she said, she also liked the Free Staters, and she didn't even know why!

You see, she was actually from South West (Africa) and half German and she was sorry that she was talking so much but sometimes she realised that she hadn't spoken for days and so talk she did. Dolfie had been a teacher and the only other employment he could manage after being retrenched – 'affirmative action, you know' – was a commission-only job as an agricultural rep. Did they have children? Ja, a 20-year-old daughter, but she had disowned them because they were too straight, apparently. She was living with some artistic type in Cape Town, Klara said with a bitter twist to her mouth, saying her daughter was actually supporting the man.

'Well, at least you've still got Dolfie,' I said.

'Ja, and I should be grateful he isn't like most men.

'What are most men like,' I enquired.

'Oh, they just want to mount each and everyone they see like randy dogs.'

I really don't know what she said after that, but I suppose I went through all the motions of polite society: making as if I was listening, saying I'd better go now, thanking her for the drinks, hoping Dolfie noticed the couch, walking home at dusk, feeding Butch and having quite a few more drinks to blot out waking consciousness. Maybe if I put on the rest of the 11th it would help, trying not to think of the effect the words 'mount' and 'randy' had had on me. I joined the third *serioso* movement in a masturbatory swoon, quickly and joyfully relieving myself. Then I listened to the calming first part of the fourth movement before it went all *agitato* again, like me, and I headed for a second, less speedy conclusion before I collapsed in a bathetic ending, because all I could think of – if think was the word – was mounting that older, seemingly unattractive woman in the next suburb.

On Sight

My grandfather was taken off the ship in Durban harbour because of his alleged German surname, had thus avoided becoming cannon fodder in the Great War and instead died in a motorcycle accident. His son had been captured before he could fight in World War Two and was going to live forever, and I had evaded war in my usual half-hearted manner and was neurotic about dying unpublished. I had volunteered to do two years of national service to avoid doing camps thereafter, and I'd get a nice payout that would put me through journalism school in a place that was as far away from Lyttelton as possible. Moreover, I was made a stores officer, which meant I had even less chance of seeing battle and got even more pay. Just to make double sure, I had enrolled for a distance course in criminology so that I could plead study time. But the military is nothing if inventive when it comes to shirkers and so I landed up on the Border for the last month of my two years because by then the academic year had ended. Once there, I refined my drinking habits as I saw what the bush could do to people, and returned a few days after New Year's and before clearing out for good. The old man was waiting for me at the air base, standing next to his yellow Valiant under a spinnaker sky, knowing his son wasn't going to take this excellent opportunity to have a secure income for the rest of his days.

'Well, that's the end of that,' he sighed.

Now he still wasn't standing at the gate, though his dog was charging, already picking up weight. I noticed that his master had forgotten to lock the gates so I opened them, drove the car in, closed them again and told the dog to bugger off. It rolled over, micturating itself, so I got back into the car again and drove around to the back yard, the lawn yellow, wondering whether I'd find the old man walking around the perimeter or lying dead on the courtyard cement. But he was nowhere to be seen. I walked towards the back stoep. Up the three steps. The bottom half of the door was closed and I called out, but there was no reply. I called again, a bit louder. Nothing. So I went in, shut out the barking sausage, my chest instantly closing up from the smell of dog, my mind running through all the possibilities the Afrikaans media presented us with on a daily basis. I looked in the main bedroom, the two other rooms, the toilet, bathroom, the airless living room with its mostly naked, olive-skinned, lips-parted, pseudo-Italian beauty lounging on a tree branch.

'Dad?'

Silence.

Maybe he was in the laundry. Sometimes he had an 'army bath' in there, just for a change. But he wasn't there either. Separated from the garage by a mere wall, however, I could hear something: a low hum. It was the Valiant in the garage. The engine was running, and then I was, remembering what the old man had said about doing himself in, pursued by the yapping canine. I jerked the garage door open, but after the bright light outside it took a few seconds before I could see whether a garden hose was leading from the exhaust pipe to the driver's window. As my eyes adjusted, I saw there wasn't, but the old man was sitting so still in the driver's seat that he could well be dead.

'Dad?'

He was either dead or just sitting deep in thought behind the steering wheel of his ship-like yellow automobile in a garage that reeked of old oil. The car was so wide it gave one very little room to move on the sides, so he'd nailed rubber bands along the walls to prevent us from accidentally denting the doors when we opened them.

'Dad?' I said a little louder.

'Ah,' he said in his new outfit of comfortable, old, dog-haired clothes. 'Hello my boy.'

'Are you okay?'

'Ja, I'm fine,' he said, switching the engine off and pulling the lever that released the hood. 'But I want to show you something.'

'Wait a bit. Let me see that thing on your eye.'

His eye was covered with cotton wool under a pink patch with an elastic band that made him look a little like a pirate.

'What does it feel like?'

'Gravelly,' he said.

'Remember not to bend or pick up anything heavy.'

'Look at this,' he said, ignoring me as usual, lifting a dusty, pink-and-white-checked bedspread off the Valiant, displaying the engine with its chromed parts to me.

'Wow,' I said, bored.

He carefully, almost reverently closed the hood again and

covered it with the bedspread Bella had sprayed with vomit outside Tembisa all those years ago. Next he opened an old briefcase full of pocket knives, silver Parker pen-and-pencil sets and a Montblanc beauty. Not only did he have good, strong hands, but he also had a beautiful handwriting and liked to show it off. He wanted me to take one of the sets we'd given him decades ago for Christmas, not knowing what else to buy a man who wanted '*nothing*' but wept copiously when he did receive them. So I took the set and, feeling a bit hemmed in, said: 'Let's go outside.'

'I've got something else here,' he said, putting the case next to the one that held his will, surrounded by a dozen two-litre Coke bottles he kept filled with water for 'just in case'. He opened a dusty bag, which had probably conveyed government tenders back in the day, but was now filled with piles of paper-clipped bank notes: plenty of them.

'What's that?' I said, knowing very well what it was.

'I want to give you a little something.'

'You don't have to do that anymore, Dad.'

'Here's ten thousand,' he said, ignoring my protestation. 'Count it.'

I counted it and it was correct.

'Thanks, Dad.'

'Don't tell *anyone* I gave it to you.'

Like I was going to tell the whole world he'd just given me a pile of money. Like the whole world was even *interested*.

'Shall we have a cup of coffee?' I asked.

'*Good* idea!'

It was a relief to stand out in the winter sun again and, as he locked up the garage, the dog started barking again. I cursed it and it rolled over and wet itself again, which was when I noticed that the paver had inserted a little hewn brick heart into my parents' driveway. Like so many things, I didn't mention this to the old man and, after we'd gone through the usual kitchen talk, I asked him whether the dog was sleeping inside.

'You know,' he laughed mischievously, 'sometimes I wake up in the middle of the night and he's sleeping on the pillow, right next to my head.'

'Well, hopefully he'll alert you if anyone tries to come into the house.'

'If anyone puts their *foot* on the property he barks.'

'Good,' I said, feeling my chest close up. 'Could we go outside now please?'

So we took our coffees and Lemon Creams to the courtyard and after a while he said the dog had almost gone berserk when those other two had been here.

'What other two?'

'Those bastards come here and ask me for work. I'm just sitting here and suddenly they're standing there.'

'What did you say?'

'I told them to bugger off.'

'Dad, you can't talk to people like that.'

'Do you think they really wanted work? They were looking for what could be stolen.'

'Still, you must be careful.'

'This is *my* property and those bastards can go to hell,' he said and gave the dog some of his coffee in a saucer, into which he broke half a Lemon Cream as a Boeing passed overhead. After a moment he looked up and, listening, said: 'I'll probably never see one of those again.'

My Full Attention

Jay was back at work that night, subdued but getting better, Judith was nowhere to be found on Oxford Street, and I couldn't wait for Monday night. That was when Dolf would be away selling cattle muti to farmers, who were being murdered liberally. When the time came to approach Klara, however, I wondered what the hell I was going to say by way of explanation. The solution, of course, was to have a couple of drinks after making sure Dolf's car was gone, so I did that and rang her bell under cover of the night. If he was there, I could always say I was drunk and had the wrong address or something: I'd had plenty of practice in my forty-two years on how to improvise, lie-wise.

'Hi,' she said enthusiastically, let me in and Verdi started barking. I said I hoped she didn't mind that I came round so late but I had just finished work and, since I didn't have her phone number, I was wondering whether her husband had appreciated the changes she had implemented. He hadn't even noticed them, she laughed, which was typical, but then he had other good qualities. 'Oh?' I said, encouragingly. Unlike most men he was as reliable and consistent as the sun – *'Verdi! Stil!'* – and there was something to be said for that. I agreed and told her how the old man had always stood watching me playing schoolboy rugby, first team, in my final two years. Every Saturday morning he would just stand there, smiling, unspeaking, apart.

The dog wouldn't stop barking, knowing full well that I was here to cuckold its master. She asked me whether I would like a drink and I said I would definitely like a drink and wasn't she going to have a drink.

'I don't really drink,' she said, 'but I think I'm going to have one.'

'What the hell: we can have a Monday-night party.'

So she poured herself one of those sweet, milky liqueurs and said she was about to watch such and such a film, but then she really didn't mind missing it; she could catch up on a rebroadcast. The dog would still not stop barking and she finally lost her rag and banished it out the back door. Returning, she said, 'That *effing* dog drives me crazy', whereupon the first melodramatic note of the 12th quartet was upon me, for my I.M.P. virtually flew to attention. Now I had to manage a semblance of civility, doubly standing up in her kitchen, and asked her what film she'd intended watching. She said it was a film I'd reviewed a while ago and I wondered how she'd known my name. No, someone in the park had told her who I was and I said I was glad to finally achieve my goal of being unspeakably famous and – like that mid-movement change in the allegro – told her to kiss me.

'But I'm married,' she said, shocked but practical.

'I know, but I want you to kiss me.'

'No. You must go.'

'Okay,' I said, taken aback by an erotic directness I never knew I had, 'but only if you kiss me.'

'No.'

'Yes.'

'All right, I'll give you a peck, just to thank you for helping me move the furniture, but then you must go.'

'Okay,' I said, and when she proceeded I gripped her and tried to kiss her much longer and deeper. She half responded, but then pulled away and said I must go now: what would the neighbours think.

'The neighbours are watching TV and have been doing so since five o'clock, even though the weather outside is glorious, if cold.'

'Go,' she said.

'What's your number?'

She gave it to me.

'One more kiss,' I said.

'You don't stop, do you?'

So she gave me a slightly longer kiss and I didn't even try to keep my pelvis away from her: I wanted her to know she had my full, canine attention.

On Falling

Contrary to the information I'd received, Dolfie returned home the next day and I had to content myself with getting off on every single little look, word, expression, hint of perfume and, of course, touch I'd experienced with his wife, Klara. I'd lie awake and hear the way she'd used the word 'mount'. What a magnificent word. Mount, as in mare (yes), mountain (no), mountebank (yes). I must have heard the way she'd used the word a thousand times, unable to sleep, regardless of whether I'd taken myself in hand or not. Talking of which, I'd get into a swoon about our first handshake and what she'd do with that firm, dry hand. Every pore on my body was receptive to that rough hand. Grip my left foot and I'd come a kilolitre. Christ, it was driving me completely, exultantly insane. I imagined fucking her in every conceivable position and state of dress in her house, with or without her husband (and a barking Verdi) watching, while out in the supposedly real world, people were still dying like flies or living like the turds upon which those flies feasted. All I could and wanted to think of was Klara's neck, or that word, or the faintest touch or flash of temper, or a smell, walking and sitting and talking with a perpetual hard-on, the bytes on my screen dissolving into that supposedly frigid middle-class woman, getting herself into a Teutonic fit about that absurd, narrow-eyed Alsatian representing every boring, responsible little clerk – except the old man – on the planet. I knew I hadn't fallen in love so I suppose you could say I was, in a word (or two, or possibly a hyphenated compound), cuntstruck.

Somehow the week passed and I finally drove through to Lyttelton on Sunday. The old man was still not standing at the gates, though when I opened them the dog came charging. After exchanging our usual pleasantries of threat and counter-threat, I drove down and around to the back and the old man's baggy black longs, frayed jersey and shredded windbreaker were hanging on the wash-line like ragged memories. He was busy sweeping the courtyard, wearing his usual HPs and a pair of suit socks, the calves pale and hairless from years of wearing suit pants, the flesh around the formerly athletic knees sagging and creased. He was wearing a torn and faded pair of PT shorts, and over his wrinkled torso an old white T-shirt that looked as if it had been holed by a German machine gun. You could do this of a Highveld winter's mid-morning, if the sun shone, which it usually did, and the wind didn't blow, which it usually didn't; it was pleasantly warm and still. Apart from the cotton wool and plaster that was still over his eye, he had an additional bit of bandaging around his shin. The red beanie was still keeping his fine hairs under control and I almost matched his grip as he asked what was that I had in my hand, though it was quite clear what it was.

'I bought you a nice warm winter jacket, Dad.'

'You *shouldn't* have,' he said, taking the bulky corduroy jacket with its blanket lining and looking extremely uncomfortable about it.

'Why not? It'll keep you nice and snug.'

'Ja,' he said, doubtful.

'Shall we have some coffee?'

'*Good* idea,' he said, relieved to change the subject.

So we went through the usual routine and I was about to comment on the house reeking of dog when I noticed that he'd opened all the windows. Very attentive, for such a deaf, seemingly selfish old man. Outside, I found a chewed old cricket ball and threw it to the bottom of the garden. Off the dog waddled at pace, and the old man looked particularly pleased. After a while he said he had a cupboard full of old clothes, didn't I want to have a look at any of them? I gently but firmly told him his clothes weren't my style and he accepted that, shaking his head slightly.

'So what is that bandage around your leg for?'

'Nothing,' he mumbled.

'Dad, what is it?'

'I fell the other day. I completely mis-judged the pavement,' he said, starting to unwind the bandage.

'Dad, I don't want to see it.'

He did it up again and I saw it was bloody and it transpired that this wasn't the first time he had fallen on his way to the bank or the supermarket, where he got his monthly pension and weekly groceries, respectively, respectfully.

'Alright, from now on I'm going to come a bit earlier and I'm going to get your groceries. When I call you on Thursday nights you can give me a list of what you need. Do you understand me?'

'I don't want to be a bother.'

You're not being a bother,' I muttered.

'What?'

I repeated myself a little louder, impatiently, which the dog, sitting on my foot, interpreted as aggression and started growling, whereupon the old man leant forwards and picked up the mutt, which was still imitating the universe and expanding rapidly.

'Dad, the doctors said you're not supposed to bend and pick up heavy things!'

'Man, doctors know *bugger* all!'

'Whaff!' the dog agreed, safe in its doting owner's arms now, after which we sank into one of our usual, awkward silences again, letting our differences simmer down while I tried hard not to think of Klara, which of course just got me thinking hard about her in that place that now seemed to be the permanent seat of my intelligence.

'Do you know what?' he finally said.

'No,' I said, expecting a set of stock stories, maybe even *Piddlin' Pete*.

'I saw a programme on TV the other night, about a man who was treated so badly on Robben Island that he'd lost an eye.'

'And?'

'That's not right.'

'No, it wasn't.'

'Bastards,' he said.

The Couch Lothario

Nothing happened that night because Judith was nowhere to be found and dear old Dolfie was at home so, thinking of ravishing his wife while he snored next to her, I went solo again. The next night I decided it was time to get back to the quartets, having completely lost my thread in that department too, and gave the first movement of the 12th a listen again. I wanted to hear how the master had built towards and constructed that change of pace when the phone rang. I put the music on pause, saw Uncle Ludwig swivel in a snit and answered. It was the old man, who never called me because he never knew what to say and didn't understand cellphones. The number of times he'd visited me could be counted on a butcher's hand – Johannesburg's traffic terrified him – but now he was calling me because he had some bad news for me.

'What is it, Dad?'

'Your aunt Esther has died,' he said matter-of-factly.

'You must go to the funeral,' I replied

'No,' he said habitually about anything that threatened the status quo.

'Dad, you need to go. I will book a flight immediately and I will take you to the airport and I don't want to hear any arguments about it.'

There was a slight pause on the other side of the line and, once again, I thought he might explode, but he thanked me, as subdued as the allegro's ending. I had the phone in my hand, so I might as well call Klara, just to make sure Dolf was gone. Yes, she said. Could I come over, I asked. Okay, she said, but only if you behave yourself. Of course I'm going to behave myself, I said, and put the phone down, my hand shaking.

She let me in as if I were a brother and we went through all the idle chatter of family members as Verdi barked at me incessantly and she told him to shut up and finally locked him out and asked whether I'd like something to drink. I said yes and followed her into the kitchen, where she told me about how depressed Dolfie had been.

'Why?' I said, leaning against a cupboard, half-blind and faint with desire.

'He's not used to sitting for so long in a car. His back is killing him.'

'How old is he?'

'Sixty,' she said, wearily.

He's impotent, I thought, can't get it up anymore, socially castrated, but then he's probably been smoking, drinking and eating so much meat it's no wonder he looks seventy.

'Ja, it must be hard,' I said, hard myself, wishing Dolf would die of a heart attack or in a car crash. Actually, no, I wanted him to carry on doing exactly what he was doing: going away often so that I could come and remind myself what it felt like to be a man in the most primal sense again. Beyond that I couldn't quite think right now.

'And you?' she said, taking a beer from the fridge.

'What about me?'

'How old are you?'

'I'm forty-two,' I said as she held the beer out to me and I put my hand on her breast.

'What are you doing?'

'I'm fondling your breast,' I said, not sure whether she was going hit me with the bottle or not.

'You can't do that,' she said.

'I know,' I replied, sliding my hand down and slipping it inside her blouse. 'But I am.'

'Len, this must stop.'

'I know,' I said again, moving my hand up to her sagging breast and realising that she wasn't wearing a bra and just had a light camisole on under her blouse, wondering whether that was a coincidence or not.

'Len, this is wrong.'

Now I had that full warm orb in my hand and could feel her responding.

'Then step away,' I said, but she didn't.

I slipped my other arm around her waist and pulled her pelvis towards me.

'You must go,' she said.

'All right, but then I want a decent kiss this time.'

'Okay. Then you go.'

'Right,' I said, feeling as if I was about to explode.

So she tried to brush my lips with hers but I wasn't going to have any of that and kissed her full on the mouth, cheeks and neck, moving my left hand down and gripping her flattish buttocks.

'Get out of here!' she commanded, though not very convincingly.

'Okay,' I said. 'I'll behave myself. Let's go and sit down and have a drink.'

'That's better,' she said, adjusted herself and we went back to the living room.

'Turn the lights down,' I said.

'The cheek of it,' she said, but did as requested.

'Can I play you something?' I said.

'Yes.'

I put on that churchy second movement of the twelfth, starting with its low, dark note. It felt like another Sunday in my youth, but at least the conversation here was more interesting. She was waiting for me to sit on the couch before she lowered herself onto a single chair opposite me.

'Come and sit next to me,' I said.

'No.'

'Okay,' I said, telling myself that I had to regroup. 'So tell me about yourself.'

'There isn't much to tell,' she said.

'I'm sure there is. How did you meet Dolf?'

She was from Windhoek and he was from the old Northern Transvaal and they had met at a party, an *opskop*, at the teacher's training college in Pretoria, where he was studying. She was studying bookkeeping at the technical college. He still had all his hair then, but the moustache was there already, had always been and, though they were very different, they'd instantly clicked.

'There's no end to life's riches,' I said.

He loved his rugby, his braaiing and his beer and did she replace the ones I drank, I wondered.

'Of course,' she said. 'I'm not stupid.'

I could just see him getting himself into a frothy about missing beers and not believing that she had suddenly felt like drinking one of his precious bloody ales. But what were her interests beyond opera, I asked.

'Not much, really. I'm quite involved with the church, helping the aged.'

But how come he'd been retrenched? I asked.

No, there'd been an incident.

'What kind of incident?'

Dolf had actually refused to teach black children.

'Why?'

'Because his brother was killed by a kaffir.'

It was on the tip of my tongue to say that that was ridiculous, but then I reminded myself that I was here for another reason. Lust, in a word.

'How?' I managed to squeeze out.

'In a car crash.'

It was getting more and more absurd, but then one forgot that there were still old-school idiots around and that when blacks said racism was still alive and well, Dolf and his dear wife were living proof of it.

'I'm sorry,' I lied.

'It's alright,' she said, getting up.

'Where're you going?'

'Somewhere,' she said.

She went to the toilet and I sat drinking my beer, realising I also needed to go and fantasised about barging in while she was on the seat, but told myself to think of something else. How was Jay, for example. It seemed he'd recovered from his depression, which Kayla had called the black dog. Talking of which, Butch.

Eternal optimist. The old man. How he'd disapprove of what I was doing.

The toilet flushed and I got up and walked in that direction, hoping for a bit of frottage with Klara.

'Where are you going?' she said, meeting me in the narrow passage.

'Somewhere,' I said, putting my hand on her clavicle.

'Are you starting again,' she said, mock angry.

'I'm sorry. I can't help it. Kiss?'

She gave me a peck and told me to go and do my business, which took quite a while because I was so aroused that I had to sit and fold myself double to squeeze out a few drops.

She wasn't sitting on her chair anymore but on the far end of the couch.

'So tell me about *you*,' she said.

'Well, I'm completely turned on by you,' I said.

'You hardly ever noticed me in the park.'

'I know, but I'm only recently divorced.'

'What happened?'

So I told her about how Shunt and I had lived our lie and that I'd been at least fifty per cent to blame, which got Klara saying she could understand why I might have been half the problem. But at least I had the balls to admit it, which of course got me all aroused again.

'Even though you're a liberal,' she said.

'Not really. If Frank Zappa could call himself a pragmatic conservative, then that's what I am too.'

'Who's Frank Zappa?'

'He's a musical genius and you're a sexual goddess.'

'You talk such nonsense,' she said.

'Come here.'

And lo and behold, she snuggled up under my left arm, saying Dolfie had become so cold towards her.

'That's probably because he feels threatened, isolated, castrated.'

'I know. I feel so sorry for him.'

'You're not a neo-Nazi or something, are you?'

'Would that be a problem?'

'Right now? No.'

'Actually, I'm just a German-Boer from South West Africa.'

'Namibia.'

'Whatever.'

'And you're absolutely desirable,' I said, meaning it and stroking her neck with my hand.

'You're lying.'

'Take off your clothes and see if I'm lying,' I said, barely able to articulate such a long – not to mention outrageous – sentence.

'You must be joking,' she said as I started kissing her neck and sliding my hand down to her stomach, under her blouse and up towards her breast again.

'Do it,' I said, as Verdi barked at someone passing in the street.

'The cheek,' she said again, getting up and doing exactly as I'd commanded, the movement ending on its ultra-quiet note. It was time for the comedy of the third movement and hacking of the fourth to begin, holding out for that clear, emphatic ending.

On Beauty

On Thursday morning my alarm clock went off before dawn because I'd managed to organise a mid-morning flight for the old man. This was so I could avoid the rush-hour traffic going to Pretoria in order to have a cup of coffee with him while that was in full swing, and to ensure that I'd have plenty of time to take him to the airport before the Joburg lunch crunch.

I put the key out for Ms Motsepe and decided that it really was the most lucid time of the day, no doubt because the old nut had had so much time not only to rest, but to work in another mode. Conscious thought is fed by unconscious thought, I thought, driving. The living are fed by the dead, which could mean that the reverse applied as I stopped in front of the old man's house. He and his four-legged friend were standing at the gate, the lawn still covered with frost, and he pointedly checked his watch.

'Let me see your eye,' I said.

Apart from a little redness, it looked fine, and I said so.

'I still can't see anything out of it.'

The dog put in its ten cents' worth of grumbling and the old man bent down, stroking its head, assuring it that there was nothing to worry about, 'See, my dog?'

'Who's going to feed it?' I said, having given up on any medical advice.

'*Him*,' the old man indicated with his head, having ensured Uncle Vern wasn't around.

We fetched the old man's suitcase and, after he'd shut the kitchen door with its Yale lock, he became convinced he'd left the keys in the kitchen and went through all his pockets – twice – in a complete panic before I found them on the wonky wire table outside.

'Shit!'

'Don't worry, Dad. We've still got plenty of time.'

I started the car and the old man walked to the gates to lock the chain and stroke his ward's warm brown head.

'Don't worry my dog, see?' he said, weeping unashamedly. 'I'll be back soon.'

He locked the gates, climbed in and again told me how the gasbag always waited for him, faithfully.

We drove down Harry Smith Avenue, through Irene and Olifantsfontein, past Tembisa. As a child I'd seen the township dozens of times on our way to the airport but had never asked a question like, why was it so different to where we lived? Yet the essential knowledge was there. It *was* different, clearly poorer, exclusively black. All one had to do was ask – why did black people live apart? – though at school that usually meant being ridiculed, and who wanted that? So the mind played tricks with itself, protected itself, carried on playing number-plate games.

But at the edge of its own awareness, it knew something was wrong about that mass of dull housing, and the only thing it couldn't delude itself about was that Tembisa was *there*. It was as there as your old man was there, absent yet always there.

As the air traffic control tower of O.R. Tambo came into view, we ran into the one thing we didn't need on the new highway that was being built to the airport: a traffic jam.

'Let's go home,' the old man said.

'Dad, I'm going to get you on that flight if it's the last thing I do.'

'If we're late I'm not going.'

'We won't be late,' I said, not entirely convinced.

A silence descended as we millimetred our way through the traffic, close to a route we had often taken to see Ma off on one of her overseas trips, so much so that at one stage I'd started resenting her for leaving him so often, siding with him. The silence became unbearable so I asked him whether he remembered my St Bernard, Bella.

'Of course I remember her.'

'Do you know what happened to her?'

'No.'

'One day I went on holiday and when I came back, she'd also had an eye operation. St Bernards have this genetic eye problem of in-grown eyelashes. Anyway, my fellow tenant's sister had come to visit, all the way from Botswana, and she'd fallen in love with Bella. So she paid for the op and said I could either repay her or Bella could go and live with her and her family in Maun. Our garden was too small and I was too broke, so I said 'take her'. She would be flown there in an Anglo American jet. I brought her here to the airport, gave her a fat, sentimental hug and she was taken away, and do you know what?'

Silence.

'She didn't even look back. Not once.'

Silence.

'Apparently she spent the rest of her days lying under a glass table.'

Silence.

'Dad?'

'We're not going to make it,' he said softly.

But we finally got through and at the airport the old man looked bewildered, frightened. I got him checked in and, after lugging his case on to the conveyor belt, saw him transfixed by something.

'What are you looking at?'

'Look at that girl,' he said.

Standing about two metres away from us was a particularly unattractive young woman with dirty hair, buck teeth and bad skin, which she'd tried to cover with too much foundation and rouge.

'What about her?'

'I've never seen such a beautiful woman in my life,' he said, gaping.

'Yes, Dad. They're saying you must go through that entrance over there.'

'Okay,' he said, sighing.

The traffic had eased by now and I drove home in a fairly good mood, partially because I'd have the coming Sunday off. Butch gave me his usual let's-go-for-a walk look and, as a break from her soul-deadening routine, Ms Motsepe was standing in the kitchen, ironing instead of vacuuming. I was determined to have a cup of coffee, which meant I had to stretch past and over her to put the kettle on with a 'sorry' here and an 'it's alright' there. As usual, we spoke Afrikaans, a habit that used to drive Shun mad because she'd never really been exposed to the language in the then Natal. But then she would have been very exposed to Zulu, which she'd also never learnt. What really drove her mad, though, was that we spoke a language she didn't understand, hated and, most importantly, excluded her.

Beauty, on the other hand, had grown up in the then Western Transvaal and had entered what was effectively an arranged marriage as a seventeen-year-old. She'd had seven years of schooling and was now a married woman who produced a daughter and son for her much older husband. He was a Sotho and she was a Tswana – and you can only push a Tswana woman so far. The man drank and wouldn't give her any money, so she divorced him, left the town of Lichtenburg and came to the City of Gold. Her children stayed with her mother and Beauty became a housemaid. Now she was working for a pittance and staying in a two-by-three-metre back room. She could send a little money home. Then she met Joe, who dazzled her and she gave him a daughter. Joe was a truck driver who travelled a lot and one day he just stayed away. Beauty was shattered. Occasionally he'd call her and say I still love you, baby. Beauty told him to *voetsek* in fast and furious Tswana, after which she was depressed for days. The daughter also stayed with Beauty's mother in Lichtenburg, getting the rudimentary rural education her mother's city money could afford. The years went by and her children grew up. The eldest, like her mother, was a true beauty. She had had that natural grace which artists like the much-maligned Tretchikoff had honoured in a way that had both conservatives and liberals pulling up their noses, though for very different reasons. Then she, too, married a much older man and gave him two daughters and a son before he disappeared into the blue yonder. She then worked as a kitchen maid on a farm and started drinking, but her youngest girl had a light about her. Maybe she would become a Member of Parliament one day.

Beauty's son had become a handyman and gardener around town, working an average two days a week. He'd married a Coloured woman and Beauty did not like Coloureds. They were dishonest. Gangsters. The pair had produced three lighter-skinned boys who would no doubt become good-for-nothings, even though the middle one showed some talent in maths.

The youngest girl, Joe's daughter, meanwhile, was also growing up. She had finished standard eight and Shanti had argued that it was not right that such a young girl grew up without her mother. I wasn't able to counter that argument, and Beauty's back room was an exception to apartheid's architectural legacy of live-in cells: it was a good seven-by-three metres. There was also a brick gardening shed in which a bed could fit – just. The teenager had moved in and finished her schooling so that she could go on study at university. Once that was done, she would get a job, start earning and move to a place where she could entertain the constant stream of young men already visiting her. Halfway through her degree I caught her with her fingers in my wallet and her mother called her in and shouted so loudly and hit her so hard that I had to step in and stop her. A few days later the daughter moved out anyway and went to live on the East Rand. One day she came to visit her mother and looked pregnant, but when I asked if she was she said 'No', laughing in that modest African way. She had also stopped studying.

On top of that, Beauty was getting at least one bad-news phone call a week. This brother and that cousin had died in such and such a town and could she have Friday off to attend the weekend funeral please. What did they die of? No, she did not know. Even the post-Joe boyfriend had eventually died in far-off Thabazimbi of some unidentified illness. Beauty herself often became ill, yet she somehow managed to maintain a capacity for laughter. One friend in particular would sometimes call her and tell her what a mutual enemy or stupid employer had done, and Beauty would be unable to talk or stand straight she laughed so much, her voice echoing up the stairs and down the passage, into my ears and my unwritten characters' lives.

Now, having made myself a cup of coffee and her a cup of tea, I regaled her with the story of getting the old man to the airport – the keys, the dog, the traffic jam, the ugly woman. She bent over the ironing board, her eyes streaming with laughter.

'He's such a difficult man,' I complained.

'Yes,' she replied, wiping away her tears and becoming serious again, the state doctor having accurately diagnosed Ms Beauty Motsepe's most serious condition as being that of an aching heart, 'but he's a *big* man!'

The Grape Escape

That night, after deadline and my first beer, I did what I'd been dreading the whole day: I called the old man in Empangeni, expecting a litany of complaints. But no, he'd had a *fantastic* flight and he'd sat next to *such* a nice young woman, whom he'd told *all* about the war, and do you know what?

'No, Dad. What?'

'I flew over Eshowe. I could see everything!'

'That's good. Are you okay otherwise?'

'I'm fine!' he laughed, forgetting that he was, in fact, there for a funeral. He thanked me passionately for organising his flight and God-blessed me as usual.

'It's a pleasure,' I said, and realised I had a free Sunday ahead. The only problem was that dear old Dolfie would be home so that avenue of release was out of the question. That meant everything returned to its usual masturbatory routine, ending at Jay and

Veron's that sporting Saturday. Now that he'd recovered from his depression, Jay drank with renewed vigour and Veron's bellicosity increased accordingly, even though she herself was letting rip and I saw no reason not to join in. After all, not only were we media people, we were South *Africans*.

Stumbling home in a very good mood and thinking about Klara's vagina, it occurred to me that if I wanted to go out looking for Judith or anyone else I would have to take a taxi, since I was smashed. That wasn't such a bad idea, I was thinking, when the phone rang.

'Hi,' a female voice said.

'Hello,' I said, 'who is this?'

'It's Kayla.'

It took me a full two seconds to realise who Kayla was.

'How are you?' I said a little too loudly.

She was okay, but not sounding it, and naturally I asked her what the matter was. She was feeling terrible about the dinner party. I told her to forget about it, for God's sake, adding that we might as well keep God out of it. But she wanted to come and say sorry to me personally and I said she didn't need to; I accepted her apology. But she was missing me, and Butch, and she wanted some advice; but if I was too busy she'd understand.

'Okay,' I said, drunkenly magnanimous and in lust, though not with her. 'Come over.'

I put on the second movement of the fourth quartet, the piece I'd introduced her to, hoping against hope that it might penetrate some recess, stimulate some continuity, but she probably thought it was good background music, perfect for a restaurant, perhaps, if she thought anything about it at all. She wasn't so much dressed as barely covering her nakedness. All she was wearing was a pair of sandals, a skirt that barely covered her panties, of which I got liberal glimpses, and a sleeveless top that managed to cover her cold-hard nipples, but only if she didn't breathe too hard. Butch, however, was so glad to see her that he did a series of three-hundred-and-sixty-three-degree swivels and, once I'd poured us a Grouse, she said she was sorry about 'the other night'.

'And as I said, it's fine. So what's up?'

'I've been like, what do I do?'

'Why've you been like that, *like*?'

'Sorry. I've been head-hunted.'

'What? In the Elizabethan sense?'

'You've lost me.'

'Never mind. By whom have you been head-hunted?'

'PrestonSmythe.'

'I take it they're not a folk duo, so they must be a pharmaceutical company.'

'They're international brokers,' she said in her usual quick-witted way.

'Ah, high finance. What are PressaPiss offering?'

'PrestonSmythe. Four times my present salary?' she said tentatively, as if I was finally going to snap and say how dare they fast-track her like this when the likes of me were hanging on to our jobs by the nails of our pinkies. But I said I thought it sounded like a damn fine idea and when could she start? There was a snag, though. Wasn't there always? I replied. I suppose so, she said. Did she, I wondered, now have to work twenty-*eight* hours a day?

'Very funny.'

'So what is it?'

'It's in Cape Town.'

'Oh shit,' I replied, eloquent as ever.

'What's the matter?' she said.

'That's far away.'

'How would you feel about my going there?'

'Does it matter what I think?'

'I thought we had something going,' she said.

Down the toilet, I thought.

'I mean,' she continued, 'I really started falling for you that night. I've been … I've been missing you.'

'Oh,' I said, by way of moving things along.

'Wouldn't you want me to stay?' she persisted.

'On the one hand I would, yes,' I lied. 'But then I also don't want to stand in the way of your career,' I said, wishing I had the gonads to tell her we should just call it a day, which would have been the sensible, let alone mature, thing to say and do. She was destined for great things in the world of business, no doubt. I was sure she could be very happy with her parents, brother and friend. Then, once she'd recovered from the first blush of media life, she could settle down with some nice balding bean counter who took their kids fishing on weekends at Noordhoek or wherever such things transpired according to the banking ads on TV. As for me, if I was going to leave the country, I was going to do it properly, not take the so-called grape escape down to the 'charming winelands' of the Western Cape, where whites could suffer the happy delusion that they were still in Europe.

'Have you told anyone else about this yet?' I said.

'Well, I went to management and told them about the offer and that I would really like to be back in Cape Town, so they made me a counter offer.'

'Which was what?'

'They'll pay me the same, but they'd also want me to go to Cape Town.'

'Are you going to take it?'

'No,' she said, looking deeply insecure, vulnerable even.

'Why not?'

'I like being close to you, Joburg. It's got a buzz.'

'Look,' I said, in a flash of inspiration, 'in my experience people who get transferred to the Cape usually end up spending half their time back here anyway, since this is where the business is. The Cape might have the beauty, but we've got the cash. It's like the whites who get fired and then get paid double to consult. Also, these migrant workers often spend a year or two there and then get promoted back here, because this is where the big decisions are made. So why don't you take the bucks, go to Cape Town and we can still see each other as much as we do anyway?'

'That's what I like about you older men,' she said, beaming.

Me too, I thought, rejoicing. Me too.

On Parole

But if I thought that was the end of it, I had another think coming. She wanted to stay the night, and when I said maybe it wasn't such a good idea, she burst into tears. Again I asked what the matter was, and it transpired that her father had cancer. When she finally told me what kind of cancer it was – prostate – I told her it wasn't necessarily a matter of life and death. But she carried on about how safe she felt with me and I finally acquiesced, hoping Klara wouldn't see her car in the driveway and that Kayla would leave early the following morning, as she usually did.

'So do you want to sleep now,' I asked.

'No, I actually want you to fuck me.'

'Come on Kayla, not everything can be cured with sex, wonderful as it is.'

'Does that mean we're not going to have sex?'

'Not necessarily.'

'Have you ever had coke before?'

'Once or twice, but I was too broke and disconnected in all directions when it was all the rage in the Eighties.'

'Well, I'm offering you some now. Free.'

So we started snorting away my time, after which she really felt like going out to a disco, but I probably didn't do that sort of thing anymore, did I, so off we went to a disco.

It took me a while to get going on a dance floor and, when I did, I didn't want to stop and I expected the DJ to have some kind of continuity, some sense of a dramatic arc, though lately the only criterion seemed to be to maintain the same beat, which was so fast that it killed all sensuality. There was lots of exhibitionism, but that had very little to do with sex. In fact, it probably served as a substitute for, if not destroyer of, sex. Obviously that beat – a kind of perpetual, masturbatory frenzy without the build-up or climax – also killed off any conversation. In other words, it was a kind of captivity, a kind of murder, a kind of death. In the meantime, we'd sneak off to some dark corner and snort pinches of the white stuff, get a drink after shouting our fluid desires to a free soul with a half-shorn head of dead black hair, go back on to the dance floor and act like we were being ultra-cool and energetic. The thing about the music was that it was so loud, so mechanised, so stupidly fascist, that after a while it became silent. It became conducive to thinking about other things, apart from the obvious goal of thinking what you were not supposed to be thinking, which was to bed the half-naked person in front of you. I finally got fully into the swing of things and even started feeling attracted to Kayla again, and she seemed to start feeling the same way and everything was heading towards a satisfactory consummation of the evening on the couch when she told me, in a fit of passion, real or performed, that she didn't want me to wear a condom. I said there was no way I was going to not wear a condom and she wanted to know why. I said I'd had some pretty dodgy affairs before I'd known her, and I didn't know who she had slept with before me, diplomatically avoiding the issue of whether she might be sleeping with – no, fucking – someone else while she was doing me on Saturday nights. Occasionally. Didn't I trust her? No, I mean, yes, I did. But I wasn't a hundred per cent sure about all the women I'd slept with before I'd met her. And I hadn't been for a test lately. But you were married then. No, I said, after that, as if I'd been bedding all and sundry. I don't like using a condom, she said. Well, I'm not taking the chance, I replied. Please? No. Okay, she said, saying it was almost dawn and she might as well go home and start studying. I wondered aloud how I was going to get through the day and she gave me a small roll of white paper with some powder in it.

'Try that. It works for me,' she said, and left.

I tried to sleep, but couldn't. This was no good. I had to *do* something to pass the gnawing time so I got up, went downstairs and put on the first of the trio of quartets ambassador Nikolai Galatzin had commissioned, which for me qualified as doing something. Maybe that would balance out the junk we'd been subjected to at the discotheque.

The B-flat major has a restless first movement, starting off portentously – as I paced back and forth, stopping every now and again to warm my hands on the heater in that dry Highveld cold – before bursting into a Bach-like cascade, of which we had some forebodings towards the end of the twelfth. But only for a while; then it's back to the doldrums. Another cascade. Still all very Germanic. But the man is moody, coming in from all directions. He's working towards a shift. Pausing. Wait for it. Shifting. Moving on to the snowy steppes. And here it comes now. Building towards the loveliest, briefest Russian melody against driving lower registers, before returning to those Bachian cascades. Back to the court in Moscow. Brooding again. Cascade. Darkness, followed by an upward, courtly ending.

The second movement was the one that had ripped me out of myself and was still as alive and vigorous as ever. It was also completely unrelated to its predecessor. Crisp, soaring, funny, brisk, business-like. I couldn't understand how people couldn't perceive its immensity and wondered what Beethoven did in his downtime. I did not believe he was only filled with music all the time. Surely he must have wanted human touch just like the rest of us, me, even if he was involved in that other race: conquering indifferent time in the little allotted to us?

The third movement returns to a courtly situation, nodding to a Haydn-like sweetness, with that dark undercurrent always there, however distantly. Its ending notes are just ever so sarcastic, followed by a sentimental start that might well have been heard in a Viennese tavern. It's verging on oompah singalong stuff, veers away, but comes back to it.

The quartet should be in its final movement now, but the man is only getting into his stride, returning to a slow, almost churchy, but more abstract, seriousness. If it echoes the starting portentousness, then that's its only relation to any of the rest of the pieces. Then again, they're all related because they're all bundled together, like family. Thinking of which, why couldn't the old man just listen to something like this at night when he lay worrying about his late wife, his dead and alive dogs, and, possibly, his son? Was he just worrying? Was he not perhaps mourning and, if so, about whom or what apart from the obvious?

Almost none of what has gone before prepares us for the fifth movement. Prince Galatzin probably wanted more Russian music than he might have heard in Razumovsky's triple commission and the first movement of the present quartet, so Beethoven gave him Russian alright. But it's the Russian of a century hence, after imperialism, so modern that it's Stravinsky's favourite piece because it's so primal, dissonant, fractured, desperate, half hysterical, displaced: a portrait of the Soviet century – in 1825! What were the listeners thinking of this Great Fugue, ears unbelieving, eyes widening? The near-hysteria ceases for a while, but the let-up isn't much of one, building towards a parody of the court, going beyond it, spitting out defiance, the cascades now cubist, jagged, industrial, the instruments sounding like they want to break, the notes falling down, going right down. Pause. Growl. Pause. Growl. Rebuild. Silence, before returning to a semblance of courtliness.

How could there be anything after this? There is nothing more to say. But that mighty fugue was just too real, too violent, too ugly, if you will, so give them a little cavatina, a merry tune as Butch started barking at the first early-morning joggers passing by, leaving me peeved beyond belief with myself for wasting my one day off from the old man, playing my pseudo-pa role for Kayla. Beethoven had wasted so much time trying to father his nephew, Karl, and the old man had spent so little fathering me.

Butch did his own little cavatina when I hauled out his chain and he dragged me down to the park, where the sound and sight of Lukas did nothing to improve matters: his cough had become worse and he'd lost quite a lot of weight.

A Small, Wet Place

Jay was late for work and reeked of alcohol, Desiree was in a snitty sulk, Black was being his usual cantankerous self, and I got by with a little help from the Colombian army. I only got to sleep at about two the next morning, and Ms Motsepe tip-tapped the back door five minutes later, or so it felt. I flew up in a rage and opened for her, couldn't go back to sleep again and was too exhausted to go see Klara on Monday night, but at least had a decent night's sleep. I was starting to feel half human by the time I went to work on Tuesday, where I had the privilege of subbing letters that were becoming increasingly telling. Apart from the usual whack-heads and old farts complaining about the waterworks, occasionally a black reader would write in and say whites didn't understand that until the land was restored to blacks there would be conflict. Then a white reader would respond and say that if blacks voted for idiots just because they were black then they had to suffer the consequences. So I went through the motions and finally got to the point where I called Klara on my cell to find out whether I could come over.

'Yes,' she said, sounding bored, but I knew her wiles by now and, standing in her kitchen, told her about the letters I'd been subbing, her mouth growing increasingly thin.

'Have you ever thought of leaving this country?' I said as she prepared our drinks, assuming that if she didn't say anything about Kayla's car in my driveway, she hadn't seen it.

'I see your girlfriend was over on Saturday night,' she said.

'She's not my girlfriend,' I replied.

'You don't have to lie to me. I'm married. I don't have a leg to stand on.'

'She's a friend.'

'I don't believe you.'

'We used to be lovers, but not anymore.'

'Why not?'

'Because you're so much better.'

'Why? Because older women don't swell and they don't tell?'

'I mean it.'

'Maybe you've got a problem,' she said.

'Well, if I do, I'm not having sleepless nights about it. Are you?'

'I've got better things to worry about.'

'Like what?'

'This country,' Klara said.

'Like I was saying: have you ever thought of leaving?'

'No. If it really comes to the crunch, we'll go and live in South-West.'

'But isn't Namibia just a short-term solution?'

'What else can we do? We don't have foreign passports. We're Afrikaners, not liberals like you.'

I reminded her again that I wasn't a liberal and she asked me where I would go to.

'I don't know.'

'Ja, fuck me and forget me,' she said with a little entitled bitterness, which of course got my nether regions all excited again.

'What about Botswana?' I wondered out aloud.

'What about it?' she sneered.

'Hey, I've been to Gaborone. It's a cool place.'

'What were you doing there?' she grimaced.

I had heard that the great exiles Abdullah Ibrahim and Hugh Masekela would be playing in that African city and I wanted to see them, and it. So I'd caught the train to Mafikeng to see a friend and then a bus to Gaborone, where I ended up on a balcony, drinking beer. After a few, I staggered into a photographic exhibition, got talking to a woman and ended up in bed with her. Later, her friend came into the shack and said she liked the contrast of our skins. The woman wanted money and I gave her a few notes, but I didn't tell Klara about any of this. I just told her I ended up staying in some or other nurses' hostel for the week, which got her pursing her lips again.

'I went to the Culture and Resistance Conference and rumours were flying that Ibrahim would be playing with Masekela. In the meantime, speeches and resolutions were made and Ibrahim ended up playing alone in a stifling hall, telling a white crew member to get his arse off the stage. All the South Africans burst out laughing, seeing a black man ticking a white one off for a change.'

Klara wasn't impressed.

'But the genius didn't play with Masekela and, when Bra Hugh's turn came on the final night, he played about being so near yet so far away from home, the stage getting progressively crammed with musicians elbowing their way on with a tacit nod from him.'

Standing in the wings was a man on an outrageously high pair of platform heels, his legs like pins in ultra-tight black jeans, a shirt as gaudy as a disco, and pink-rimmed shades the colour of a Kalahari sunset on a cheap postcard. In his hands he held a soprano saxophone, but it wasn't the usual straight one. It was curved, which made it even smaller, and gave it a plasticky, lucky-packety feeling.

'Jazz,' she said.

'Ja. Township jazz. Kwela.'

I had wondered whether my feeling for this music was enough to gain me any political credibility and decided it probably wasn't. Then again, I was here and not motorboating on the Vaal or something. There was, of course, the possibility that armed soldiers could burst in at any moment to capture or kill an activist, just for the hell of it.

'Why do you like that music?' she asked disapprovingly.

'Because it has a kind of ... holistic quality to it,' I said, moving in on her. 'It isn't all just head – you can understand it without knowing exactly what the words are all about. You can move to it, both mentally and physically. And there's no separation; in fact, there's a marriage of the two. So it's easy on the ear. It has a rhythm that makes you move, loosens you up, makes you feel good, gives you space to think whatever you want to. It amuses you, cleanses you, leaves you feeling healthy. Filled with goodwill towards others. And if that isn't intelligent – and democratic – what is?'

I was right up against her now, putting my arms around her, holding her shoulder blades. Then I turned her around, and started kissing her neck, massaging her hips.

'You and Dolf could apply to emigrate. Places like England and New Zealand are always keen on teachers, and bookkeepers are always in demand, anywhere.'

'Dolfie would never do it,' she said, breathing a little heavier.

I slipped my hands up under her jersey and vest, cupping her breasts, enjoying her instant response.

'And if I asked you to elope with me?'

'You wouldn't.'

'Sure?'

'Yes.'

'We could go to Gaborone.'

'Never.'

'New Zealand?'

'I couldn't live in a small wet place.'

By now my right hand had strayed down her stomach, teasing her pubes, letting her feel my hard jeans behind her.

'Never?'

'Tell me about the man with the saxophone,' she said breathily.

'Everybody in the crowd had been waiting to see what Masekela would do once he spotted the man with the platforms, shades and sax,' I said, a little breathless myself. 'Bra Hugh, the man with the angry-happy moon face who came from Witbank, which is about an hour's drive from where I come, but aeons away otherwise.'

'What happened next?' she said half irritably.

So I told her how Bra Hugh had finally given the Clintonite dresser his only chance to perform in front of a packed hall of smiling, sweating, pumping people, and how the man gave a perfectly cool solo on his tiny saxophone. When he finished the crowd almost collapsed with whooping, clapping, laughing applause, which was more or less how I felt as I took my hand all the way down and said I could easily live in a small, wet place.

On Ageing

That Saturday night I didn't get slammed with Jay and Veron but took a very soberly dressed Kayla out for her farewell dinner, where I very maturely declined to do drink, drugs or sex with her. When she cried, I teased her until she laughed, and later walked her to her car and kissed her on her cheeks, wondering what it was about her, apart from her wardrobe, that was different. Goodnight and goodbye. A company car would take her to the airport the next day.

The next morning I drove to the capital, thinking about Gaborone and how I hadn't told the old man anything about it, thinking he wouldn't have been able to relate to it in any way. But that was then; now I had to go shopping for him at his local supermarket in a town I refused to call anything but Lyttelton. He had given me the list that Thursday and it had been as basic as ever: milk, sugar, bread, instant coffee, condensed milk, butter

– 'not margarine!' – boerewors, potatoes, carrots, beans, onions, and miniature cabbages that looked like brains.

He wasn't at the gates, the dog didn't come charging, and when I fumbled with the chain I saw it was unlocked. I drove to the back, took out the supermarket bags and approached the back door, which was open. As I got to it, I tentatively said: 'Dad?'

The dog started barking, I went in and the old man was watching tennis on TV, his nose virtually touching the screen. The broken aerial had been replaced with a wire hanger, which still only produced blurry black-and-white images. This was in the spare room where we had once – and only once – had a tenant. She had broad shoulders that bore officer's pips and she had somehow been allowed to smoke inside the house. She arrived at a time when the usual cutting comments about Ma's useless father and her cooking had become too much, when the endless repetition of the same old good-luck war stories had palled, when Ma's good-natured rolling of the eyes had become a look of desperation, a film of sweat forming on her temples and beneath the snub nose I'd inherited from her. It was all very strange, with the old man now was back in his dark clothes and still wearing that tatty old wind-breaker of his.

'Hi, Dad. How're things going?'

'You know, I get so bladdy *irritated* with these players ...'

'Why?'

'Have you seen how many times they bounce the ball before they serve?'

'Maybe it's to give them balance or calm them down or something.'

The old man snorted with contempt.

'I'd happily watch with you, but I can't breathe in here,' I said, even though he'd kept all the windows and doors wide open.

'Let's go and sit outside,' he sighed.

I said let's first make some coffee, which he thought was a *hell* of a good idea and there was something different about him too, but I couldn't work out what it was as he grumbled about the fact that the players didn't wear white anymore, nor did they shave.

'And you've shaved every day of your life since you were seventeen?'

'That's right,' he said, soundly slightly whistly. 'Difficult as it is.'

'Why difficult?'

'I can't lift my bladdy arms above my shoulder anymore,' he complained.

'Maybe you should go for some physio,' I said.

'But do you know what really gets my goat?'

'No, Dad. What?'

'Bladdy soap operas.'

'Why? What about them?'

'These people are constantly stabbing each other in the back, and if they're not doing that they're sucking each other's faces!'

'I know,' I said. 'I avoid the stuff like the plague. But then I know some allegedly intelligent people who are completely addicted to them. But what gets *my* goat is that you have people out in the sticks who think this is normal. They can't read or write, but they've got the TV set, the antenna sticking out from their shack like a knife in Caesar's back. This is their education, this is what they aspire to.'

'That bladdy man from the church wants to sit here and talk to me about television programmes,' the old man continued.

'What did you say?'

'I told him I'm not interested. I pay my tithe and that's that.'

'Do you?'

'Yes. Every month. On the dot.'

'But you don't even go to church anymore.'

'What's the point? I can't *hear* anything. And the last time I went someone said it was good to see me *for a change*!'

'When was that?'

'You were about twelve or so.'

'Dad, that was thirty years ago!'

'So?'

'Maybe they just said it was good to see you again?' I said, knowing full that he'd again heard what wanted to hear.

After the usual speeches about the mugs we went outside and I hurled the ball for the dog, which was now so fat you could rest a tray on its back, but it still chased the ball with blubbery delight. The old man looked as pleased as pie.

'So what was it like being back in your home town?'

'Not bad,' he said, having lost all his enthusiasm for that particular adventure.

I wondered whether he realised it might be the last time he ever saw home again.

'There's something different about you,' I said as the dog eventually lay down, panting. 'What is it?'

'I don't know,' he said. 'But you know, I was wondering why that man from the church hadn't come round to pester me anymore, but he actually kicked the bucket.'

I laughed and asked where he'd heard that.

'At the dentist's.'

'What were you doing there?'

'Bastard tells me I can either have another bridge made, or he can pull the whole lot and give me dentures, so I said pull the bladdy lot.'

'*That's* what's different about you,' I exclaimed. 'You've had all your teeth pulled.'

He was too pissed off to even grace that with a comment, his cheeks sunken.

'And you still look good.'

Silence.

'When do you get your dentures?'

'In a week's time. If Lord *Muck* next door will deign to take me there.'

'He's very good to you, Dad.'

'Agh...'

'I mean, aren't you grateful he fetched you from the airport?'

'I can't see the planes anymore. The car's battery charger no longer works ...'

'How's the leg?'

'Oh, that's fine,' he said, starting to pull up a trouser leg.

'Dad, I don't want to see it.'

'But look here,' he said, showing me his thin white shank minus the bandage he'd been wearing. There was a jagged maroon scar there, but it was as healthy and shiny as that of a young man's.

'That's amazing,' I said.

'Do you know how I got rid of the scab?' he said, his eyes lighting up.

I didn't want to know but said, 'No?'

'Sandpaper,' he said.

Interpenetration

Dolfie was in for the rest of the week so it was all work and no sex with his deceptively hot wife. On Thursday night, after deadline and calling the old man from the office, the MD came downstairs and asked whether anyone had a corkscrew. Shunt had once bought me a Swiss army knife, taking her cue from one of the old man's boring knife-and-pen exhibitions in his garage, because she had no idea what I really wanted. At first I'd been mildly insulted, but I started carrying it around with me after realising it was very handy for things like, well, opening bottles of the alcoholic variety. It might even serve as a weapon with its lockable blade, I thought.

I couldn't conceive of any white MD inviting two lowly subs upstairs, so I was hugely impressed with this ex-unionist who always greeted me when he glided by in a BMW that resembled a glossy U-boat. But I instantly disliked his accountant, a short, big-headed, shrivelled-eared shit in a leather jacket expensive enough to buy me drinks for a year. He had been in exile, he soon informed us, and couldn't help mentioning that his parents wouldn't hire whites to do their housework in London; they just didn't clean properly. Jay was now hitting the bottle with a vengeance and telling the new MD about the general unhappiness on the work floor. I thought this was equally rude: the man invites you to have a drink with him as an equal and you start getting all workerist and maudlin. Jay's shin was too away for me to kick and the more I tried to divert the discussion, the more he dug in. The MD said, very reasonably, that he didn't mind dealing with the discontent, just like he wouldn't mind reverting to an old Toyota Corolla if he had to, but I could see he was mildly peeved. So I got us out of there as fast as possible and gave Jay a piece of my mind in the lift. He wasn't interested.

Friday passed in its usual way, as did Saturday, but stumbling back from Jay and Veron's I noticed Dolfie was out – so I stepped into his and his wife's living room and her arms. Something had changed. She was holding on to me with a kind of desperation and we went straight to the spare room. There was something she was trying to tell me as we tried to do everything simultaneously. I could feel there was some line she wanted to cross and asked her what it was.

'You don't understand that women see these things differently.'

'What things?'

'You're just here for sex.'

'What are you here for?'

But she wouldn't say, though it was clear to me that she was falling for me and she was right: I was just there for the sex and had always been very clear about it. But then I'd been thinking recently that maybe there was something like sexual love. You could want someone so desperately, so obsessively, all the time, that it became a kind of love. That was certainly the case for me. I wanted to fuck her from morning to noon, midday to midnight. I had never been so tuned to anyone sexually in my life before. She could talk about anything and I'd have an erection. Why couldn't that be love? I didn't care what she said and I wasn't interested in it. I had never been this predatory before and I probably never would be again. I was convinced we could screw ourselves beyond all social and emotional needs and sense. I could literally lose myself in her and come back wanting more. Obviously there was a degree of titillation in the fact that I was cuckholding her limp dick of a husband, but it went way, way beyond that. You got soul mates and you got sex mates and for me she was the latter. Pure, hot, sweaty, grunting fuck sex. She had no idea what I meant by the fact that my desire for her was purer than most kinds of love and neither did I, but I meant it. Obviously there was some kind of Freudian angle to the fact that she was more than a decade older than me, but I wasn't particularly interested in analysing it. I didn't care what might transpire ten years hence. Telling her I'd be the son she never had during coitus was enough of a turn-on in itself. Who cared what it meant? I didn't. She obviously wanted more than that, but I didn't. Was I supposed to go through her divorce, set up house like I had with The Ex and act like my love for her was anything but physical? What would we talk about? Her boring bookkeeping clients? I would have to liven things up with my subbing and cinematic stories, which also had their limitations. She knew – or sensed – that I wouldn't be able to live like that. But she couldn't bear the thought that she was cheating on her Dolfie or, perhaps, she wanted some kind of security or commitment, which I wasn't prepared to give. Straddling her, I said it wasn't only women who could be penetrated, you know, and, unlike Shunt or Kayla, she knew exactly what I meant and duly gave me a firm middle finger.

On God

The next morning I drove over to Lyttelton in a much better mood than my pre-Karla days, except that a certain restlessness had taken hold of me. Maybe I just needed a holiday, I told myself, which was true, but it felt like it was more than that. Much more. To add to my woes, there was a car in the old man's driveway. Once I'd negotiated his charging dog and its urinary ways, I found him and Koos de Freitas's minister son in the courtyard, finishing their plastic coffee. The old man was dressed in his Sunday best again. Gerhard was tall and bald like his father, and had bad skin like his tiny mother. He represented one of those obscure Afrikaans churches with a grim, sect-like feel about them, whereas we'd been working-class Methodists when we were anything. But his mother had sat with mine and held her hand and prayed for her as the cancer had methodically eaten away at her memory and bodily functions. Such people were angels and when I called her months after Ma was beyond caring to thank her, she'd said if I wasn't careful *she'd* start crying. Where do such people come from? Are these the 'sisters of mercy' Leonard Cohen sings about so exquisitely? It had always struck me that Ma, in her often-imperious way, had spoken down to Mrs de Freitas. Yet here was a woman who had helped someone step into the unknown and, in the old man's terminology, there must surely be a 'special place' for such people.

'Gerhard,' I said. 'How are you?'

'I rejoice in the grace of God,' he said calmly, standing up to shake my hand.

I don't, I felt like saying, but nodded and greeted the old man.

'Hello, my boy,' he said.

'How are *you*?' Gerhard said.

'I'm very well,' I lied under his gaze, sounding as two-faced as the old man to myself.

'Excellent,' Gerhard said softly. 'It's good to see you again.'

'Likewise,' I said falsely.

He was just about to leave, he said, and the old man, the dachshund and I accompanied him to his car. As he started reversing his dirty Nissan Skyline, of course, the dog went ballistic. The old man told it to shut up, which it did, whereafter the old man walked up to the gate and shook Gerhard's hand in that grovelling way he had. Then he closed the gates after him and came walking back to me.

'What was that all about?' I asked.

'Nothing,' he replied vaguely.

'That didn't look like a social visit.'

'I don't know why everyone's so worried about my soul,' the old man said. 'I may not go to church, but I pay my tithe and I read my Bible, every day, hard as it is with the magnifying glass. But do you know what?'

'No, Dad. What?'

'I talk to the Old Man, *all* the time!'

'Good,' I said. 'I'm taking you out for breakfast.'

'What for?'

'Because I'm sick and tired of sitting around here every Sunday.'

'No.'

'Dad, I'm taking you out for breakfast. That's it.'

'Can the dog come?'

'No, and we won't be long.'

He sighed, saw Uncle Vern approaching and said he'd go and lock up the house so long. Uncle Vern and I had a chat about his sons and their children – 'Gosh, how time flies' – and exchanged phone numbers in case something serious befell his neighbour. After that I joined the old man in what used to be the spare room, since he could no longer sleep in his and Ma's old one because 'It just doesn't feel right.' He was struggling to get his one arm into the sleeve – 'shit!' – so I helped him and asked him whether he didn't like the jacket I'd bought him. He became very uncomfortable about that and all it really boiled down to was that it was too bulky for him.

'That's fine, Dad. I'll take it. I like it.'

'I'll be *so* glad if you would. But don't you want to look in my cupboard and see if there isn't something you want?'

'Not really my style,' I said.

He nodded, and we went through the ritual of finding the keys, locking up, bidding the dog farewell as if he wouldn't see it again, *ever*, and headed towards the Irene Dairy Farm. Irene was a small village that had always thought of itself as English and even had a typical cricket oval. But it also had an Anglo-Boer War concentration camp cemetery, mentioning an unknown nurse, and, if you carried on with that road which ran parallel to the railway track, you could turn left at the village's only four-way stop, dip under the railway line, turn right immediately again and head towards General Jan Smuts's farm. The old man didn't seem to connect any of that with his personal experiences over fifty years ago, and let off steam about the usual stuff.

Apart from the smell of cow dung and milking sheds, the farm had changed. In the old days it was a large dairy with a small shop where you could bring your metal canisters or glass bottles and fill them with fresh Friesland milk. Now there was an additional balcony next to the shop where you could eat light stuff, and also a new, postmodern barn that echoed the original homestead, where you could eat a big Sunday meal. But there were so many people that we got a little flustered and ended up at the serious restaurant which, though open-air, was crowded and noisy. The old man suddenly looked lost, frail, half blind, with the loud music not helping either. I took his dog-smelling arm and led him away to the balcony, warning him of the stairs, sitting him down. It took him a while to calm down, and I expected him to rail against the service or the waste of money eating out, but when the poached eggs, bacon, toast and coffee arrived he ate with his new, uncomfortable false teeth as if this was the first square meal he's had since returning from the war.

'What's the food like, Dad?'

'This is the *best* breakfast I've ever had,' he said.

'Good,' I said, thinking of Klara, missing her in my highly evolved way, and the rest of the meal was civil.

But after coffee he was tetchy again, so we drove back via a lane of naked poplar trees, crossing a bucolic bridge, which was close enough to Johannesburg to feature in those car ads with their multi-cuts per second. Beyond that a golf estate had sprung up, with more pseudo-Tuscan nightmares, and further still, the Centurion Mall, living its last-bastion dream before becoming what it should have been in the first place: an African marketplace. So we took in a bit of highway, passed the cemetery where Ma lay, and for some reason made a small detour via Monument Avenue, so named because if you stood in the middle of it and looked north, you could see the Voortrekker Monument in the hazy bushveld distance. How clever, I'd thought a long time ago. And if you stand at a particular point on that tar between Cantonments and Langebrink streets, looking north, and turn right, you'd be facing the rough-brick Methodist church in which I'd been baptised and confirmed as a teen, affirming my faith in God loudly and clearly so the old man could hear, even though we all knew I was lying through my teeth.

Going Bush

The slow-motion nightmare that was the new South Africa hit home once again that night when I subbed a story about a family who'd been raped and tortured in front of each other before the intruders were interrupted and fled. The going comment, of course, was that at least they were still alive. I asked Jay if he'd read it and he nodded grimly. I typed one word into Google. co.za and saw there would be a seminar on emigration in some or other plush northern suburbs hotel and emailed that I would be attending.

That night I was sitting on Dolf and his wife's couch, getting aroused by her rattling on about something or other. She was wearing a creamy V-neck jersey, a charcoal skirt and black tights, and we went through the whole charade of chatting on the couch and exchanging pleasantries. Maybe she was so desperately lonely, I vaguely thought, that she needed to unload all that nonsense on to what was effectively a stranger, so I let her carry on for a while longer before I started stroking her face and neck. She liked that but kept her distance and carried on talking, which merely stoked my fires.

'Come here,' I said.

'Are you going to behave yourself?'

'Of course I am,' I said.

So she snuggled up with her back to me and carried on talking and I carried on stroking her cheeks and strangely erotic neck. After a while I slipped my finger into her mouth. She gave it a small suck before gently expelling it with her lean lips and carried on talking, so I simply put it back again.

'I thought you were going to behave yourself.'

'So did I.'

'Ha,' she smirked, then went on about how she'd gone down to the shops that morning and wasn't the price of everything just too awful?

'Terrible,' I said, letting my right arm stray down to her breast, then stroking her stomach.

She was virtually sitting on my lap and must have felt that my interest wasn't exactly intellectual, let alone economic, but on she went as I worked my hand under her jersey, stroking her stomach, then her soft breast. All the while I was nibbling her ear, kissing her neck.

'This is so wrong.'

'Why?' I said.

'Because it is.'

'Then why is it happening?'

'Because you're a monster,' she said.

Exactly, I said, and took my other hand right down to her small wet cunt.

'I can't believe what I'm doing,' she said.

'You were still talking about, uh, the price of things,' I said.

'Hm...'

'What exactly is it that is so expensive?'

'Food,' she said, moaning.

This was getting too uncomfortable, so I told her to move away so that I could stand up.

'What for?' she said.

'So that I can take my pants off.'

'You see. Here it starts.'

'Actually, it started quite a while ago. Take off your clothes.'

'Just like that?'

'Yes.'

'Ha!' she said again but duly obliged by taking off her jersey and vest and had to be told to take the rest off too in the unlit living room, with everything happening in silhouette, the light coming in from the adjacent dining room.

'Why don't you want the light on?' I said.

'I know you men,' she said. 'You go by what you see.'

I took off my shirt in her and Dolfie's warmed-up living room, kicked off my shoes and told her to undo my belt and jeans.

'You've got a cheek,' she said.

'Actually, I've got two,' I said. 'Do it.'

Again she obliged, struggling a little with the belt, but not the zip.

What would the old man, let alone Kayla or Shunt, think of what was happening, I distantly wondered.

'Put it in your mouth,' I said.

'No,' she said.

'Why not?'

'It's too intimate.'

'Have you done it to Dolfie?'

'That's none of your business.'

'Okay,' I said, and went down on my knees with my tumescent
I.M.P. bobbing about like a buoy and started kissing the insides of
her knees, parting them, heading north.

On Cars

I don't know if it was just my age, predisposition or geography, but I seemed to be going to at least one funeral a year. In this case it was another older friend who had died, another surrogate father, I suppose: Rob Amato. I got the news the next morning, and took Butch for a walk to the park, past a gaunt, wheezing Lukas.

Rob was the son of a Spanish Jew and I'd met him while in the careless ecstasy of student love with Alexandra. If this intense, compact man was shorter than me he felt much larger with those broad, powerful shoulders of a keen swimmer. He had burning black eyes and a mind as open (and sharp) as the ocean. His father had been an industrialist in the Congo until that collapsed and the family moved to East London, where Rob had come into the orbit of black and white Struggle royalty. When his father died Rob could have run the factory, but he chose to drop out even though he was a Rhodes scholar. He blew virtually his entire inheritance on funding a cultural magazine called *S'ketch*, which folded, and the Space Theatre, which gave a platform to the likes of Athol Fugard and Pieter-Dirk Uys. The theatre also later collapsed, but that wasn't the point as far as Rob was concerned.

'What about your children?' I'd asked him.

'There's enough for them to be educated,' he'd replied. 'What more do you need to inherit?'

Not for him the yarmulke but rather whatever came to hand, the shirt often skewly buttoned up. But always there was the matter of the domineering father, the man of action and industry, the provider, as opposed to the intellectual. And the questions. Was it *really* better to provide mental sustenance as opposed to food – and work – for people? My only claim to fame was that I could spin a yarn with some passion and maybe that's why we became friends. Like me, Rob had delighted in Alexandra and I'd admired him for managing to stay so young and alert, even though he was a good fifteen years older than us and had three children back in Cape Town. He and his wife had separated and he'd say he was missing his kids with a painful twist to his blackly bearded mouth, but there were also other problems to be solved – too many, we sometimes thought – and pleasures in which to delight. He had a great capacity for delight, did our Rob. And listening. You might toss off a casual line and he'd start interrogating you about it, boring into you, until you had to admit you're just being flippant, Rob. His guts and shoulders would start shaking, and he'd push air out through his clenched teeth, eyes twinkling with mirth, building towards the next brilliant idea. That was the one kind of laughter.

One night we'd all been sitting around and heard there was a new local band coming to campus. By that time, we were half paralysed on Western and African substances and too inert to go, but Rob got us all up and moving and we went to see an outfit called Juluka. Up on the stage there was a white man and a black man, which wasn't allowed at the time, and they were making their own music. Johnny Clegg had embraced and been accepted by Zulu culture without sacrificing his own. He was wearing African skins and dancing like a warrior, in unison with his friend and musical partner, Sipho Mchunu. We shouted our heads off and danced ourselves into sweaty sobriety.

'This is *so* important,' Rob said afterwards, analysing every cultural nuance of the evening as we started smoking and drinking afresh.

'Hm,' I said.

'What do you think Alex?' he said.

'If I'd been wearing panties,' she replied, 'I would have thrown them at him.'

That time Rob didn't laugh, he bellowed with Mediterranean joy.

After we'd finished varsity, he moved on to another campus and a year ago he called to say he'd migrated to Jozi. It was *so* dynamic, he said. He was living in a cottage behind his ex-wife's house, reading stuff like his good friend Don MacLennan's poetry, and writing an influential column about the separation of powers (his father had always said he'd make a good lawyer). We continued our conversations as if decades hadn't flown by in the interim. There was still that capacity for listening and laughter from this man who wanted to write a riposte to *Disgrace* and call it *Delight*. We diametrically disagreed on where the country was going – Rob always the optimist – and he had bought himself a Romeo-red, second-hand Alfa Junior. He had always wanted one and now he had it and came to visit me. There was a small painting of a mother and daughter he particularly liked, having lost a daughter in her infancy. So I gave it to him in the spirit that it had been given to me by my good friend Dick Reineke. Then one fine evening Rob went to a Cosatu meeting in his Junior, this man who took everybody's ideas so intensely seriously, and on his way home some moron had pulverised the Junior and him in a haze of Saturday-night auto testosterone.

I stopped the Civic outside the old man's local Checkers, got his groceries, resisted kicking the dog's head off as I tried to carry all the bags simultaneously from the car, helped the old man pack his goods away and told him we were going for a drive.

'No,' he said.

'Yes, Dad. We're going out.'

'Can the dog come?'

'No, it stinks.'

'Well then I'm not going.'

'We're going to be away for half an hour, Dad. It'll do you good.'

'What if those bastards try to rob me again?'

'What bastards?'

'There was a break-in here.'

'This is news to me. Tell me more.'

He seemed to regret having told me that and I had to drag it out of him. 'They' had come on to the back stoep and forced the bathroom's curly burglar bars back and taken Ma's old radio and some food.

'Did you report it?'

There was no point, he said. The police were useless. Anyway, Uncle Vern had welded the bars back into place and everything was fine again.

'If we leave the dog here, he'll protect the place,' I said.

'You don't know what you're doing to me,' he replied tearfully, the dog looking up at him with soulful eyes. I said I'd chuck the ball for the dog while he got dressed, so he went into the house.

Now he just had to find the 'goddamned keys' but it finally all came together like a film production and he shakily bade his canine farewell, looking up at him with its soft brown eyes on either side of its long, aquiline nose. He would soon be home again, 'see my dog?'

So we went for a spin on the highway and spoke about the cars, which he could barely see, though he was convinced the Volkswagen Jetta was the best car ever made. I wasn't even going to bother telling him about Rob, so all I said was, 'I can't believe you think that after the Chevy.'

'Don't even *talk* about the Chev.'

'Why not?'

'You know it's being used on a *farm* now?'

'No,' I lied, thinking the reason why my Kitten was always dirty was probably a reaction to his deification of first the Chev, then the Valiant. I also thought about the many, many near-heart attacks Ma had had with his furious driving, especially in the Chevy, during our annual holiday trips to the same small towns where his sisters lived, year in and tedious year out.

'Do you know what that Merc costs new?' I asked.

'No?'

'Three-quarters of a million.'

'*What?*'

'I know. It's criminal.'

'That's probably what my house is worth,' he said as we passed the cemetery next to the highway.

'Do you want to go to Ma's grave?'

But he still wasn't in the right frame of mind, meaning he was probably worried about his dog, but did I know what?

'No, Dad. What?'

'I'm really annoyed that we have to lie facing east.'

'Why?'

'How am I going to see the cars on the highway?'

As usual I couldn't think of a retort.

When we got back to the house, the dog was sitting at the gates.

'He waits for me, you know.'

'Really?'

'He sleeps on the pillow next to my head.'

'Hm?'

Pause.

'You mustn't think I don't appreciate this, hey.'

'Good,' I said, the Highveld light burnishing the white walls of the house.

'Don't bother coming in,' he said. 'You've wasted enough time already.'

'I'll just see you in, Dad.'

'Why?'

'I don't know. We might catch more robbers in the act or something.'

'Leave well alone,' he said.

'No.'

I thought he might create a scene, but he seemed impressed, so we got out, he finally found his keys, I unlocked the gates, and we entered the yard.

'Hello my dog,' the old man said, rubbing his loved one's head, almost in tears again as he comforted his piddling pup and apologized to it for having gone away, saying he would never do so again, 'Ever!'

I couldn't stomach the sop so I checked out the back yard for any intruders, my hand clutching my pocketed Swiss army knife, without which I'd begun to feel naked of late. Then I scoped the house thoroughly – behind doors, under beds, in cupboards – catching a glimpse of myself in the mirror at the end of the passage, where the phone was, where the old man had gone down on his knees and begged his wife to come back to him, saying he had banished that woman from our house and that he would forgive Ma for anything and everything.

Beware: Sociologist

The ants in my pants would not go and I thought it might be eased a bit if I told Kayla we had reached the end of our little affair. We had spoken to each other on the phone a few times, but it felt hollow, we both knew it and I wanted to have a stiff shot of Grouse before I called her and told her it – whatever 'it' had been – was over. When she answered the phone, it sounded as if she was in a pub.

'How are you?' she said all chummily.

'I'm fine,' I said, 'but I don't think we should see each other again.'

'What?' she said.

There was a slurred but good-natured political argument going on in the background as someone sang they didn't like reggae, they *loved* it, and I repeated myself.

'Just like that?' she said.

'Yes,' I said. 'I'm sorry, but I think it's for the better.'

'Okay,' she said breezily, and cut me off.

Butch looked at me as I called Klara to find out whether Dolf had gone for the week.

'Yes,' she said.

'So can I come and see you?'

'Ja, I suppose so.'

I should have known something ominous was brewing, but I still went and got her to tell me what I was doing to her in the most direct and vulgar way possible, which drove me to the kind of heights Shunt and Kayla, for all their savvy cocktail talk, couldn't even begin to imagine.

'What's the matter?' I said, still shuddering.

'I feel like a whore.'

'But we've got such a good thing going,' I said.

'*You've* got a good thing going.'

'Are you just a passive victim of this whole thing then?'

'No, but I am married.'

That was the first time I felt like sleeping with her, but she'd have none of it, and the next morning I woke up feeling good and asked Butch whether he was a closet dolphin or what. He started laughing like one, twisting this way and that. 'Yes, you are a dolphin,' I said. 'I know you are.' He may have been shaking his head in warbling loops, but it was all one-thousand-percent affirmation, so off we went, passing an increasingly emaciated, hacking Lukas. Further into the park, we passed a briefcase that had been forced open, its contents removed and flung aside.

The only thing that kept me here now was the old man, my writing, and Klara. He had told me to go, but I couldn't just leave him in the lurch, dog or no dog. As for the writing, which wasn't even happening these days, it was how I tried to make sense of what was going on around me, possibly even inside me, even if no one ever read it. Writing was like going on a big adventure: you discovered things you didn't know you knew. And then some. You also discovered that you knew considerably less than very little. I had always written about crime in one form or another, and realised I was continuing the old man and his father's legacy of policing. I also came to the conclusion that the ruling metaphor of rape wasn't the kind in which you survived, demeaned, disgraced, but the attempted murder of everything that meant something: love, art, dignity. We killed each other at the drop of a hat and, worst of all, most of us just looked away. If there had never been an overt revolution then there was a continuously covert war. The streets might not have been flowing with blood, but our living room carpets were soaked in it. On a purely expedient level, there was plenty to write about, but might it not be a good idea to write about my country from afar? Who said I had to write about my country at all? Who said it was my country anyway? Who said I could write? Who said it wasn't just my crutch, my delusion? Might it not be good for me, then, to walk right away from it all? Yes. Therefore, I could go, should go, stretch myself. Fly.

Which left Klara, who was married and therefore limited. But an addiction, like a country, is an addiction and it isn't easily cured. Ms Motsepe could find other work, and I could help her with that. Obviously I also loved Butch, but I didn't belong to that class of people whose lives are determined by their pets. Butch would easily fit in with others, much as I would miss him. And Jay and Veron? Well, I could access them via cybersphere, even though I would miss them still. In fact, I had come to the conclusion that they represented the only small ray of light in that dark hole of a geographic entity called South Africa. That is, people were doing what they always did. They were falling in love, but now they were doing so across racial lines – naturally. The Redlands were the perfect example, the real vanguard of change. Work, live and sleep with each other and you'll soon find out how boringly, predictably similar we all are, I'd discovered. After the intellectual and racial romance of being married to Shunt had petered out, it had just become another battle for power, the opposite to how Jay and Veron made things work. If Shun had broken away from everything that signified tradition in her culture, then she had replaced it with an ambition to override everything else, including sex, and it had left her a nervous wreck. She couldn't think about anything else except this new lover of hers, and I had been a jealous man – a very, very jealous man. If ten years of marriage had made me feel like a trapped diver whose oxygen supply was rapidly running out, then divorce felt like breaking that oceanic surface and taking in great lungfuls of fresh, life-affirming air. But that soon faded after I realised something else: there was no boat or land in sight. Nothing.

I went to work, couldn't find Judith on Thursday night and went to the emigration seminar at a Hilton hotel the evening after. Most of the people there were precisely the kind of people with whom I didn't want to be associated. But the presenter said he wasn't trying to bash our country; *his* country wasn't perfect either. In fact, there was at least one murder a week. Everyone burst out laughing.

On Saturday I went to Jay and Veron's and my friend was already pissed by the time I got there.

'Hey, don't you think you should cool it with the drinking?' I said.

'No, the girls have gone out.'

'Is that the point?'

'What are you trying to say?' he asked, voice rising.

'I'm not *trying* to say anything. I'm saying it's two o'clock in the afternoon and you're pissed already.'

'Are you telling me what to do in my own house?' he asked aggressively.

'No, I'm saying maybe you're drinking too much.'

'Listen here, I don't tell you how you've fucked up your life, okay, so don't tell me about mine.'

'Oh, have I fucked up my life?'

'Well, you fucked up your marriage; now you're fucking the office mattress.'

'And would you like to tell me how exactly I fucked up my marriage?'

'There must have been some fucking reason why Shanti left you,' he slurred bellicosely, opening another beer.

'Yes, there was. I told her I was tired of being married to a block of ice.'

'That's not what she told us.'

'This is news to me,' I said loudly. 'What exactly did she tell you?'

'She said you were a hyper-critical, prescriptive piece of shit!' he bellowed, mashing up all those esses and taking a drunken slug of beer.

'Well, you're turning out to be a fine friend!'

'At least I don't tell you what to do in your own house!' he said, spraying beer.

'That's because you never come to visit, you fucking dickhead!'

At which point Veron stormed into the room.

'Fuck you, you arsehole!' he shouted.

'No, fuck *you*, china!' I shouted back.

'Jay, you're pissed,' Veron said. 'Shut the fuck up. Len, get the hell out of here.'

'Thank you *very* fucking much!' I screamed at Jay over Veron's shoulder.

'It's only a pleasure!' he shouted, lifting his beer in a mock salute.

'What else did she say about me?' I demanded of Veron outside

'Nothing. He's talking shit. Go home. We'll talk when you're both sober. Goodbye.'

I stumbled to Emfuleni Road in a rage and the thought of facing that façade called home was too much, even with Beethoven, so I called a taxi and went to the disco Kayla and I had been to, not because I liked it (or her, or me) but because the others had closed or moved on, as is the nature of such grand institutions. I didn't want to dance or meet someone. I wanted my head to melt into some kind of numb neutrality, but what I got was something much worse: I became a sociologist. Worse, I came to the depressingly conservative conclusion that what a society needed to function was four interlinking elements. Irony of ironies, they formed the acronym NEWS: nurture, education, work, security.

If a child came from a secure family, it already had a massive advantage in life. One loving parent was better than none and two or more were even better. If the child then went to schools which integrated body, mind and soul it could start flying, but how did that happen? Teach children how to think rather than remember, or adhere to this religion or that ideology. Any society that could be that open would always have work for its people, and the petrol attendant would be as valued as the president. It wasn't the state's job to protect people, except insofar that it had to create conditions conducive to work. If people didn't have work, then neither should their leaders be paid. And if the down and outers did not want whatever work was provided, then they could starve. Basic services had to function. Cops needed an incentive to become cops, as did nurses and teachers. Obviously they had to love their jobs and subjects, but you can't eat love. They needed to be paid as well as middle managers because that was exactly what they were, which meant they had to take as much responsibility too. Mess up and you're out on your ear and have to start all over again. If your people are secure in themselves and their environs, that's all the security they need.

If those who didn't want to work became criminals, they were welcome to that as well. But what was to be done with them? Were they to be isolated and allowed to create what amounted to an alternative society? No. Were killers to be killed? That would be economical, but it would also be deeply irresponsible. Those people weren't animals; they were an insult to animals, the old man's people. Nor were they human, for they had decided to play God over others' lives. They were therefore gods. And gods have no claim to human rights. So, too, those soft-handed high-ups who steal money from the magnitudes. And if these prisoners want their rights back, they must earn them back by doing what we do. That is, they have to work. They have to learn that most of us roll a rock up a mountain with the full knowledge that as we sleep that rock rolls down the mountain again, and we have to roll it back up upon waking. For that we get paid. If they do not want that right, they can dig a hole every day and fill it up every day. If they want to carry on being gods, they can carry on digging and filling up the same hole for the rest of their days, or hang out in solitary confinement. If, however, they want to work they can acquire a skill, trade or degree. In short, they can become human again. Those who want to work must be separated from the hole diggers or the sol-cons. As soon as those who choose to work get their skill, they must do what we do. We work, we get paid, we pay taxes. We pay our debt to society. Why can't they, even in prison?

The secret, of course, lies in those who oversee these gods. Their fellow inmates, the warders, are merely enforcers. But the gods have to be taught what their parents or teachers did not teach them, which is that you cannot take another's life or property. There are consequences. They have to be taught by educators, not sadists. Only once they can understand what they've done and start making amends can they insist on that other human right, that other form of torture, that other death, television.

There is no greater security than a happy childhood, a good education and available work, but the ravages of AIDS had already left a million children parentless, and our Supreme Leader was still dawdling, creating a breeding ground for sociopaths and protecting his old Struggle pal, the chief of police. If apartheid had been a crime of commission, then the new lot were committing just the opposite: one of omission. If the structural violence of the old order had been the slow death of the soul, then the country post-Mandela was the quick murder of the helpless: the women, the children, the aged. Yet a great show was made of holding everybody's tender little hand at school, in the workplace and in prison, which was not the same as teaching them how to think. It was giving them a Disprin for a rotten tooth. Pension funds were being robbed by old capitalists and new socialists alike. The leaders pretended to lead, their friends the rich joined them at the top of the pile, the minority middle class paid punishing taxes to retain their dubious privileges, and the majority remained un-led, unread, and unloved.

In a word, fucked.

On Decay

The next Sunday I took a detour, driving up one street from Monument Avenue to my primary school on Pretorius Street. It was named after the poet and chef Louis Leipoldt and it was in *that* first-storey classroom that I had sung in the school choir. If I played rugby like my father then I sang like my mother. We would sing of the joys of the veld in Afrikaans, followed by the heavily accented *My Grandfather's Clock* in English. 'Ninety years without slumbering (tick, tock, tick, tock), his life's seconds numbering (tick, tock, tick, tock). It stopp'd – short – never to go again when the old man died.'

What was I doing? This didn't feel like nostalgia; it felt like some sort of farewell.

The old man was still nowhere to be seen and the dog, of course, went ballistic and came charging. The old man wasn't at the back either, but the security gate was open and I said: 'Dad?'

Nothing.

'Dad?' I said louder.

Still nothing.

'Dad!' I shouted.

'Ja!' he said and finally came to the door, squinting, as if from deep space.

'Hi,' I said, relieved.

'Hello my boy,' he said, sounding a little delicate, but taking my hand in his big one.

'What are you doing?'

'Oh, I've just been watching a bit of rugby, but it isn't rugby anymore.'

'I'll say.'

'What?'

Who the hell was this man, this stranger? Why had it never occurred to him to remarry? Why did he live his late life so stoically alone? He was so desperately lonely and craved company, and when he got it he just talked, poured out his heart and his soul and then went back to his hermitic life. I sometimes wondered whether he made the same negative statements about me to Uncle Vern as he did about him to me. And yet those who had crossed his path loved him, adored him, were fond of him, cared for him, as I tried to.

'I said I agree with you that it's just become a kick-and-charge bore,' I said.

'Why the hell haven't you shaved?'

'Because I didn't feel like it, Dad.'

'I shave every day of my life.'

'Shall we have some coffee?'

'*Good* idea,' he said.

After we'd run through the usual stuff he settled down with his coffee and Lemon Creams outside, but he'd acquired a new habit. He'd discovered that if he wore a pair of Ma's old sunglasses he could see much better in the glare and, as usual, he looked good in those too. But I couldn't sit anymore. I was all sat out, sensing that the old man wasn't going to move off his property that day, so I found the ball and chucked it for the dog, which duly chased it and returned it to its master.

'You're killing this dog,' I said, 'just like you killed the other one.'

He ignored that, juddered his left foot and picked at his right nail and said: 'Do you know what I did the other day?'

'No, Dad. What?'

'I handed in my service revolver.'

'So how're you going to commit suicide now?'

Ignoring that bit of flippancy, he said: 'They asked us to.'

'Well, that's very responsible of you, and I think it's better that you did.'

'Why?'

'People often get killed with their own weapons, or those weapons get stolen and used on others.'

'Well, I've got my little dog to protect me, haven't I, my dog?'

Pit-pat, pit-pat the fat slug's eager tail went as he sat on his master's foot.

'Won't you please reconsider going into an old age home?' I said.

'Never, never, *never.*'

'Then won't you at least let me put up palisades for you?'

'Leave it, Len. Just leave it.'

'Do you realise you could be killed?'

'Let them come. I've got my dog.'

'I can't exactly see him threatening a couple of thugs.'

'We're fine,' the old man said with some finality. 'Those other two came yesterday and I gave them some bread and tea when they asked for food. They thought I was very funny.'

'Still, be careful.'

A plane went overhead and he looked in its general direction, regretfully.

'Esther said I must go and live with her in Eshowe,' he said.

'So why don't you?'

'You people don't understand something.'

'What don't we understand, Dad?' I said, wondering who exactly fitted into that broad category of 'you people'.

'My *wife* is buried here.'

This was probably the closest he was going to get to admitting that he'd loved Ma and was missing her.

'Dad, I read about a family that was tortured and raped in front of each other the other day. That's *one* case. There are forty-nine others. A day. I'm telling you this because I'm worried about you.'

'Don't worry about me. Worry about yourself. You must get out of here.'

'You mean leave the country?'

'Yes. We're not wanted here anymore, if we ever were.'

'I couldn't do that and I don't believe it.'

'You must. Go to another country, start a new life.'

'I couldn't leave you alone.'

'I'll be fine,' he said. 'But do you know what?'

'No, Dad. What?'

'I'm bored. I'm tired. I want to die.'

'What the hell am I supposed to say to that?'

'I don't know.'

'Okay. Shall we go and wash the cups?'

'Good idea,' he said.

So we went inside and started washing the dishes and I realised he kept the Beethoven bust because it reminded him of Ma. He now told me how the cups and saucers should be washed, but his sight had deteriorated so badly that some of the cups were still dirty after he'd cleaned them. Halfway through, I had to go to the toilet. The passage was dark, the ceiling stained from a leak, and Ma's yellow woollen warmer on the seat was grubby. When I came out, I saw that the dog had crapped at the other end of the passage, right next to the phone stool and below the mirror where the old man had implored his wife to come home to him.

'Look,' he'd said, 'I'm on my knees. I'm begging you.'

She can't see you, my teen self had thought as I lay listening in the suburban dark.

A Shortish Holiday

Maybe if I took a break I'd get rid of this rat gnawing at my intestines. Maybe I just needed some respite from all the secondary violence, I thought. I was sick of it. It came at you from all angles. Whites knew they didn't have the law on their side anymore, but that didn't stop them from being downright rude. You didn't have to use racist language to prove you were a racist. There was the more refined and therefore nauseating weapon of tone. 'Things used to be so much *faster* in the old days,' a white housewife might say for all to hear in the supermarket queue as she inspected her nails. Blacks reciprocated by being as uncommunicative as possible. You asked an assistant for something in a shop and they just walked away without a word, leaving you wondering whether they were going to help you or not.

It was all good and well that we were allegedly equal now, with all our cultural differences, but it was almost impossible to make friends across the deeply embedded colour line without it feeling forced. If you tried too hard it seemed affected; if you didn't try at all you felt as if you weren't doing your duty, a word to which my mother had made me allergic for life. Once Shanti and I had parted our friends – bar Jay and Veron – had neatly fallen back into their respective social and racial camps. In the end I'd given up, being too lazy to do what the government should have done from the start: insist that every white person speak an indigenous language. It would have solved at least fifty percent of the problem.

The media were even worse. Public figures weren't criticised, reprimanded or castigated – they were lashed. They weren't fired or sacked or, worse, let go: they were axed. I couldn't help seeing people with axes deeply embedded in their heads. Daily. And I wasn't guiltless in providing those headlines. It was my job, as the saying goes. The violence came at you as you were driving, waiting at a red light, walking, or switching on the TV.

So that Monday I put in four days' leave without thinking too much about being the world's rankest amateur at taking holidays, possibly because the vacations of my youth had been such deadly dull affairs. But I had another reason why I took that particular week off. It was my birthday that Thursday, always a time that depressed me and made me shirty. The last thing I felt like was taking a cake to the office or having rah-rah drinks with colleagues and friends. Still, I found all kinds of excuses not to go away on the first, second or third days, though I did walk Butch a lot and saw Lukas had grown ever gaunter. I called the old man as per usual and he actually remembered and wished me many more and I told him I wasn't going to come over that Sunday. He understood, he said – did he sound relieved or was he hiding his disappointment? – and God bless you.

The next morning I told Ms Motsepe I was going away for two days, would she please put the lights on at night and feed the dog? Long face.

'I'll pay you extra, of course.'

Less longer face.

So I packed one of the tents and the sleeping bag Shunt had left behind, grabbed a couple of extra odds and sods, got into the car and drove towards the only thing that interested the bourgeoisie about Africa: the bush and its wonderful wildlife. I knew of a place that was only a few hours outside the city and gave you the illusion that you were far away from civilisation. At night you could lie and look at a sky almost as clear as the Karoo's in a range named after the rebellious Sotho leader Mogale. The camp was close to the Cradle of Mankind and equidistant to a dam being choked by hyacinth invaders and a visible ex-nuclear station, with power lines marching across the prehistoric hilltops like mutant King Kongs. But at least my week wouldn't be completely wasted, I thought. If anyone bothered to ask what I'd done in my time off, I'd be able to say I'd gone bush. It wasn't only a good place because of its proximity to the city but also because no music, TV or musical instruments were allowed. There would be no drunken singalongs around the campfire, thank you very much. No rumbling, window-rattling basses either.

I instantly felt better out there, of course, encouraging myself to do this more often, really. I went for a long walk through hardy bush, red soil and rough rock instead of putting up the tent, one of the many things at which the supremely organised Shunt had been particularly good. When I got back it was after dusk and I struggled to get the bloody thing to resemble any kind of shelter. In fact, it turned out to be our – her – provisions tent. In other words, it was a children's tent. Moreover, a wind had sprung up and come rushing over the hills and down into the valley as if ordered, turning my little fire into a joke of horizontal flames. I lay freezing in the mini-tent with my bagged feet sticking out, flame-side. This would not do, even though I did nothing about it. I finally lost my temper with myself and struggled out of the tent, accidentally tripped over and loosened the anchoring rope, which sent the thing billowing away like a tumbleweed. I chased after it, stepped into a nest of *duwweltjies*, hopping about while brushing the appropriately named little devils from my feet, and finally managed to wrestle the mangled mess of nylon into a ball, shove it into the boot and slam it shut. I didn't need to stomp out the fire because nature had already done so.

'Thank you!' I silently shouted at the sky. 'Thank you very fucking much!'

I opened the passenger door, eventually found the lever to push the seat back and wrestled my way into Shunt's sleeping bag. That was much better, except that I hadn't thought of bringing a pillow and could feel my neck heading towards spasm, so I couldn't sleep. Plus I could still feel a residue of her in there, smell her. For all our troubles, we had been able to talk, and laugh. We could have objective, even constructive, disagreements, as long as they were about ideas, art, politics, news, the country. In fact, we used to talk (and laugh) so much that we'd often arrive late at events as a result. It would be good just to have a normal natter – even disagreement – with her again.

But what now? After about an hour or so I knew. Beethoven. Listening to him build castles, no, much more, civilisation itself, in the air – with nothing. The first movement of the 14th is melancholic but never indulgent. If this work's predecessor is disjointed, restless, filled with silence and violence, then the 14th, his favourite, is filled with continuity, healing perhaps. Transcendence certainly. Beethoven in Africa. Why couldn't I feel perfectly at home in Africa while listening to Uncle Ludwig? Wasn't it, after all, a *black* radio host who'd introduced me to the quartets? But I had another, possibly more interesting question. Why did the eminently learned Professor Joseph Kerman say that a mature Beethoven piece, like this C-sharp minor, was 'a *person*'? Yes, Bach can talk to us, or himself, or God over the centuries as Bach and only Bach can, but you can hear Beethoven in so much modern stuff, good and bad. And if the music of Beethoven's two great predecessors, Haydn and Mozart, never spoke to us as people through their works, why does the good professor suddenly have this seemingly irrational moment in which he calls Beethoven's later work an italicised person? If it suited my personal needs that these works were people, beings one couldn't help but admire, and love, then I wasn't sure that I could rationally agree with the prof's assertion.

Naturally, I was looking at this music through that symbol so beloved of publishers to sum up the alleged romance of Africa – an acacia tree – while the music itself continued in its own fine, progressive way. Here came the brief but funereal sixth movement, flowing into the finale beyond death: assertive, powerful, affirmative, eternal.

Shanti.

The next morning I woke up with the early sun in my eyes, stiff in all departments, as usual, and discovered that my sole box of Lion matches had ended up in the flames the night before, a *whoosh* I had enjoyed causing as a child. But now I was fireless. The Crouching Kitten's lighter had long ago given up the ghost, which forced me to ask the neighbours for a light so I could boil some water and have a smoke. There were three of them, two men and a woman. They were about a decade younger than me, had all the accoutrements of camping, and the two men had a slightly smirking, messianic quality about them. Greenies. Vegheads. Cause junkies. The woman, however, a dark redhead, said she would bring me a cup of coffee and a box of matches after I'd done my ablutions. When she came over, I felt obliged to regale her with my heroics of the night before. When all else fails, make them laugh. Dance like a monkey. Entertain them. Except she wasn't laughing at me, just smiling, as if she was seeing and hearing something completely different to what I was saying. She was one of those open-faced beauties who didn't use make-up. She really wasn't my type: gentle, practical and, judging by her questions and silences, intelligent. We really had nothing in common, I told myself, but it turned out we lived a few blocks away from each other back in Joburg. The two men, however, were impatient to go on their hike. Neither of them seemed romantically attached to her, but I still felt irrationally jealous of them.

So I drove away from the camp, feeling guilty that I hadn't seen the old man, deeply reluctant to go to work on a Sunday (or any other day, for that matter), and intensely annoyed with myself that I hadn't asked that beautiful woman for her name or address, knowing she would have given both to me. The sum result was that it felt like I was driving in one direction but going in its direct opposite.

On Funerals

'Where are we going?' the old man said.

'To the cemetery,' I replied, steeling myself for the canine request and going through all the mug and lock-up dramas, then passing the high school and nearby hospital where he and I had signed off my mother's corpse. The nurse was a Zen-Buddhist in disguise, a woman who cheerfully told us to come and say goodbye to Ma. The old man burst into tears as he saw his late wife staring sightlessly at the ceiling with one eye. The nurse chatted away as he God-blessed Ma and the nurse closed that sightless eye. Women don't die, I'd always thought, and I'd been right. My mother wasn't dead, or gone. She had just changed. I kissed her waxen forehead – the candle extinguished – and consoled the old man that he'd had half a century with her, which he seemed to accept.

We passed Centurion City on the way to the cemetery, that

selfsame 'city' I'd taken my mother to for a cup of coffee. I told her I'd found that business of the tenant very confusing and that I thought her husband was a coward at life. She replied that nothing had happened between her and that woman, saying 'You're a full-grown man now. Leave us alone and don't you dare say a word against him.' That was the only other time I'd seen her cry.

The cemetery was a feast of heartfelt kitsch, ranging from sealed photographs of children to shared plots and biblical quotes, but time showed what it thought of such folly as damp crept into the photos, graves tilted, cracked, caved in or sank. I was quite impressed with a schoolfriend's grave, though, which had a cabbage tree growing out of his belly. I had left town by the time he had died at the age of twenty-three – how, I didn't know – and once again wondered at how we come into this life, leave a little smear, if that, die and are forgotten before a decade has passed.

We approached the grave of the old man's late wife, where part of the ritual was for me to clean the slab of granite above Ma's presumably indifferent bones, after which he always delivered his deep and penetrating rhyme:

'Here I stand where you used to be/ there you lie where I soon will be.'

Ma had seen two plots advertised for a discount in the local rag and had told me about it with a little chuckle, which was her way of saying she hated the thought, but certain things simply had to be done. That was twenty years ago; now it was almost ten years after her death and I still thought that, more than just 'Lovingly Remembered', she deserved the Nobel Peace Prize for having put up with the old man for so long. The only other time I'd seen her cry was when a criminal was tracked down to his mother's grave. He'd resisted arrest and was shot dead.

'He never knew his mother,' Ma had said to ten-year-old me, weeping.

Surrounding her were many of the people at whose funerals, weddings and baptisms she'd sung, along with all the Sunday services before and after the old man had decided the church was run by two-faces. A few graves away a man stood weeping silently over a daughter who had died twenty-five years ago.

By now I had filled a plastic bucket with water and started wiping down Ma's gravestone with one of the old man's ragged T-shirts, noticing that many of the brass letters on her neighbour's grave had been stolen, and saying so.

'Bastards,' the old man said.

The church had been packed with people I hadn't seen in decades. Lying in that box up front was my mother. The old man sat very straight, showing nothing and only once emitting a little squeak. A trio of friends sang 'How Great Thou Art' with voices that trembled more from age than grief. Sitting and standing next to me was a friend of Ma's, one of those old Methodist ducks who sees the good in everything and sings perfectly out of tune, loudly. I wanted to burst out laughing. It was the time of Halley's comet, and it rained for weeks on end, as if the very heavens were weeping for a woman who had stuck with a man through five very thin decades – and made something of it.

'I went to a funeral this week,' I proffered lamely, even though it hadn't been a funeral but a memorial for Robert Louis Amato: friend.

'I hate funerals,' the old man said. 'If I die I don't want any singing and I don't want any flowers.'

'Why not?'

'Flowers are meant to stay in the ground. And I want Gerhard to bury me.'

'Why him?'

'You know,' the old man said, having either not heard the question or ignoring it, 'something's been worrying me lately.'

'What's that, Dad?'

'I wonder if she was ever unfaithful to me on all those trips overseas.'

'You've only thought about that now?'

'Ja.'

'But what does it matter? She's dead.'

The old man nodded, saying they'd been very different, 'but we got on. When we were alone, we got on.'

'Are you saying I was a cause of friction?'

'Not you. Other people. We always fought in front of other people.'

'Even her father.'

'Oh, *him*. I couldn't stomach him.'

Oupa had been my only grandparent and the old man had poisoned me against him to such an extent that I'd been – to my eternal regret and shame – openly contemptuous of him. When he died, I was unable to console Ma or express any kind of sympathy to a woman who'd looked after *her* mother and then her 'useless' father while her siblings went on to varsity and professional careers. I hadn't even attended the old man's funeral, such was my acquired hatred of him.

'I feel really bad about him.'

'He was a coward. But worst of all, he was Ossewa-Brandwag. He was one of John Vorster's hangers-on, and Vorster was blowing up railway lines here in sympathy with those Nazi bastards while I was prepared to die fighting against them. But when the time came for Vorster to be interned, your Oupa was nowhere to be found. He denied ever having anything to do with the OBs.'

But he could have told me so many stories, I thought, he who'd lived in that residential hotel with its dim passages, its odours of limp cabbage and echoes of ignored voices. He was a large, besuited man in a small, dark room with a tiny basin and mirror inside a cupboard. And, just to add to the olfactory claustrophobia, every time we went to visit Oupa he'd produce a silver tin of Singleton's snuff from which he and the old man would take a pinch, inhale, and sneeze. The stuff was as dark as the panelled walls and I couldn't wait to get out of that close room, whose tenant nevertheless called me Napoleon. But stay we always did, and I was always convinced of Oupa's inferiority because, whenever he rubbed an itchy eye, his tongue went back and forth like a windscreen wiper across his chin. And if he did try to tell a good-time story, the old man would interrupt and start one of those mock-friendly arguments in which I happily participated, even though I could see Oupa and his daughter's discomfort. Thinking back on those family arguments made me cringe, especially after a dream had told me another story. Oupa was just a jaunty, good-time guy with a callipygous arse who took me to a rugby match at Ellis Park. He'd brought cushions for us and I was happy, excited.

He, who now lay a hundred metres from the daughter who had tended to him during his eight-point-eight idle decades. He, who had even ended up spoilt in the afterlife: his grave was one of the few resting in the shade of an acacia. It formed the apex of an imaginary triangle with Ma's grave and the equidistant Heroes' Acre with its pseudo-Nazi insignia of squared eagle wings, cement ox-wagon wheels and torches, their eternal plastic flames faded and cracked by the indifferent sun.

I silently said goodbye to Ma, emptied the muddy contents of the bucket and drove a roundabout route to the exit, stopping at my grandfather's headstone. The old man stayed put as I got out and gave Oupa's grave a quick wipe, remembering a rumour that he'd been a bit of a womaniser himself. Back in the car, the old man said it pleased him greatly that he was now officially older than that 'fat, lazy bastard'.

Symptoms of Morbidity

Jay took me out for a coffee on Friday, apologised for what he'd said about my marriage – he was preoccupied with his and Veron's troubles – and said he'd been clean for two weeks now.

'What do you mean?'

'I'm alcohol-free. I'm attending Alcoholics Anonymous.'

That night I was so impressed with Jay's resolve that I had a double Grouse on him before calling Klara and asking her whether I could come over.

'No.'

'Why not?' I said, flustered

'Because it's over.'

'Just like that?'

'Yes.'

'Why?'

'Because I can't live with myself.'

I wanted to say I needed her, but it would have sounded ridiculous because she was right: I only needed her for one thing and that was sex.

'Can I at least come and say goodbye to you?'

'No.'

'So that's it? We're just going to walk past each other on the street and in the park and make like nothing ever happened?'

'Yes.'

The end of another disaster and yet one less reason to stay. But my troubles were far from over – in fact, they were just beginning, for the telephone rang.

'How are you,' a female voice.

'Fine,' I said, instantly annoyed.

'It's Kayla.'

I modified my tone and asked how she was, though I didn't have the slightest interest in her answer. She responded equally civilly and said she was coming to 'town' on Wednesday and would like to end things face-to-face. Was this a good idea, I wondered, but she said I owed it to her. I said I didn't but was impressed when she quoted Wilde's dictum that laughter is a good way of ending things too. She probably picked up the Quote of the Day from her executive diary, I thought after I rang off.

She had traded in her old BM for a veritable ship of the same brand, the better, no doubt, to serve the stinking poor with her pearls of radical amateurism. At least Butch was happy to see her again and she looked exceptionally elegant in her black dress suit, her skin clear and her cheeks glowing with good health. Also, she was wearing a matching necklace that a magazine hack might describe as combining traditional African elegance with 21st century corporate realities, resting coolly above breasts that were either bigger or more propped up than usual.

'What's happened to you?' I said.

'What do you mean?'

'You're looking good.'

'Thank you,' she said. 'I'm in love.'

'That's nice,' I said. 'But there's something else that's changed.'

Loving the power she had, she asked me what I thought it might be.

'I don't – wait a bit. You're not wearing your specs. Have you got contact lenses?'

'Yes. Well spotted.'

'No pun intended, no doubt. So who's the lucky guy? Or gal?'

'You know who it is.'

'No, I don't. I wouldn't presume to know such things, though I've just realised something.'

'What?'

'That night I was in your flat, there was a woman's necklace in your bathroom. It was a traditional African woman's necklace, more so than the one you're wearing now, and I've just remembered where I'd seen it before – afterwards.'

'Where?'

'Around Melanie Davids's imperious neck at Jack Weisz's dinner do. Is she the new love in your life?'

Kayla played the mysterious femme fatale, sat down, then took a small, folded piece of white paper from her jacket pocket, proceeding with the noble art of preparing two lines of coke on Shunt's glass table.

'What is this all about? You call me about breaking off our relationship – such as it is, or was – you come here looking good and telling me you're in love but you won't say with whom?'

'I just thought we could break up on good terms.'

'Fair enough. But who is this lucky person?'

'First have a line,' she said.

'Okay,' I said, and duly snorted it.

'Why don't you pour us a drink and light us a smoke?'

'Sorry. I'm forgetting my manners here.'

'That's the Len I liked.'

'Now it's just "liked",' I said jokily. 'Past tense.'

'Hm,' she said, smiling.

So I went into the kitchen, looking at every object as if I were seeing it for the first time. Everything was heightened, hyper-real, like when someone dies, or is born, I imagined. All problems slipped away. Almost. I grabbed the bottle of Grouse and took a long, pleasantly burning slug before pouring us each a triple, vaguely aware that something was horribly wrong here.

Kayla had prepared another fat line for us and I gave her drink, sat down and lit two cigarettes.

'Can you play us something African?' she said.

'I'll play you some Moses Molelekwa.'

'Who's he?'

'A muso from Tembisa.'

'Cool,' she said.

'Pity he strangled the mother of his child and then hanged himself.'

'Eish.'

'So who is the lucky person?'

'"Lucky"?'

'Ja. You're a beautiful woman.'

'Then why did you break up with me? Is there someone else?'

'Isn't this academic? You say *you*'re in love with someone else.'

'Yes,' she smiled.

'So?'

'But are *you* in love with someone else?' she persisted.

'No. I'm a divorced man trying to get his life back. That's all. So are you going to tell me who it is or not?'

'Were you just on the rebound?'

'Kayla, who is it?' I demanded.

'You were right about Melanie. I mean, that it was her necklace. She was in my flat, almost every Saturday night. I was letting it out to Ed, who was doing her there, every Saturday night.'

'So you'd come and pass the time with an old fart who made you feel "safe"?'

Kayla nodded.

'Enjoying the fruits of our new democracy and all that.'

'Yes.'

'But why couldn't he just do it at his own place?'

'He was married.'

'Wonderful. So you weren't trying to make Shunt jealous at the dinner party. You were trying to make Melanie jealous?'

Kayla tried her enigmatic smile and I was so bored with this little game that I asked her how her father's cancer was doing.

'It's Ed,' she said.

'Ed?'

'Yes.'

I grunted cynically.

'What do you say to that?' she said.

'Well, I hope you'll be very happy.'

'Now you're being sarcastic.'

'No, I'm – well, personally I think he's a prick, as you know. So, honestly, I don't think it'll last.'

'And that's because he's black.'

'Not really. But if it makes you feel better, fine,' I said. 'But why are you telling me this? Have you come here to gloat?'

'No,' she said. 'I thought you might find it ironic that he's resigned and is now moving to the Department of Labour.'

'As what?'

'Speech writer for the minister. Spokesman. It's a logical step, he says.'

'And the money no doubt is much better, not to mention the power. But why are you really here?'

'I've come to say goodbye.'

'Goodbye,' I said for the second time that night. 'And well done, by the way, for conducting a conversation without having to like everything.'

At which point she stood up, but it wasn't to leave, it was to get undressed.

'I thought I'd give you a farewell gift,' she said, turning around and showing me her perfect young legs, buttocks and back, made all the more enticing because she'd put on a little weight, a bit of grip, as they say in certain circles. 'Show you what you'll be missing.'

'Okay,' I said, as high as a cloud and suddenly thinking about the woman I'd met in the bush, sensing her body through her soft green eyes, the way she'd smiled at me.

'You're not a bad lover,' Kayla said. 'But Ed is so much better, bigger, younger, stronger'

'Well, I'm very glad for you. And I'm very impressed at your ingenuity.'

'What do you mean?'

'I mean suddenly wanting me to come over to your place when he was away in Queenstown, as if to show you were being equitable. Giving me a blowjob just to get me to the dinner party in order to get him jealous. Actually, I'm impressed by the amount of *energy* you could spend on so much deception. Doesn't it get tiring, boring?'

She shrugged her naked shoulders, swaying to the music.

'And that's why you thought it was so funny when I said "fuck him" after the dinner party, because that's exactly what you were doing, or wanted him to do.'

'We never used a condom, you know,' she said over her shoulder.

'What's your point?'

'I suppose now you want to go for an Aids test?'

'Why would I want to do that?'

'Because you're nothing but an ageing, white, racist male. Look what you're going to miss,' she said, and bent over, her back to me, stark naked apart from her high heels.

'You're quite right,' I said, beyond ideology or morality, 'and therefore I'd better start licking management's arse.'

On Rage

The old man was buried deep inside his house, watching TV in his airless room of dog, the back door and security gate wide open. He was in a crappy mood because he hadn't heard me, couldn't see properly, his shoulders ached, as did the plantar wart on his foot, and his bossy sister had phoned again, and everybody wanted to tell him what he should do and the price of electricity was shooting through the bladdy roof.

I was in a pretty shitty mood myself because I had dreamt about Shanti again, falling in love anew with the idealised woman instead of the real one.

'You know,' the old man said out on the cement, his precious ton of dog leaning against his shin, 'people say they want to live there or there, but *this* is the only place in the world I want to be.'

'Good,' I said.

'This is the place they'll carry me out of after I've died.'

'Hm.'

Silence.

'So tell me, where's Shanti?'

'I don't know, Dad. We're divorced.'

'What?'

I didn't say anything.

'But wasn't she here the other day?'

'No, Dad. That was Kayla, a colleague.'

'I liked that girl, you know.'

'Which one?'

'Shanti.'

'So did I.'

'Then why did you divorce her?'

'I didn't. She divorced me.'

'Your mother stuck with me through thick and thin.'

'I don't think she had much choice,' I muttered.

'What's that?'

I repeated myself.

'What do you mean?'

'I mean she'd spent her life looking after her mother, then her father, then being your wife. She didn't have any qualifications. Where would she go to? What would she do on a dental assistant's salary?'

'People today get divorced at the drop of a hat.'

'Why don't you ask me why Shanti divorced me, Dad?'

'Do you think our marriage was easy?'

'Why don't you ask me?'

He stopped, looked at me.

'Why did she divorce you?'

'Because I spoke to her the way you spoke to Ma.'

'What do you mean?' he said, bristling.

'Nothing was ever good enough for you. The meals she cooked, the father she had – nothing was ever good enough. It was one long, half-a-century assault of venom and bile. And that's what I gave Shanti. I hammered her with your rage and my own. I may never have lifted a hand to her, but there are many other ways to torture someone, and I did. And guess who I learnt it from? You.'

'Bollocks.'

'Yes. *You.*'

The dog was up and barking.

'But then I even went one better,' I continued. 'I spoke to *everyone* like that, to their faces, thinking I was being very smart. Thinking I wouldn't be a two-face like you and crucify people behind their backs. Oh no, I went all the way. I told them what arseholes they were up front, to their faces, and in print. And do you know what I've got to show for it? Nothing. Sweet blow all!'

The old man was the colour of crushed shells and said we could all go to hell, he had his dog and that was all that mattered.

'Yes, and you're killing it with kindness, just like you killed all the others. Just like you tried to kill me, but I won't have it. If that's the only way you can show love, then shove it!'

I got into the Civic, started it, drove to the front gate, stopped, got out, opened the gates, walked back to the car, got in, slammed the door, and drove off. The traffic lights, of course, turned red and I sat there, seething. If he didn't want to take any security measures then he had to suffer the consequences, whatever they were. I lit a cigarette and didn't bother looking in the rear-view mirror. I didn't give a shit whether he was watching or not. Then I drove home and applied for my emigration papers before heading to work.

Headline Goes Hear

That Monday we had a new colleague and I'd more or less worked her out by the time deadline had passed. That she was black didn't matter, that she was as thin as a rake was concerning, and that she was determined not to learn a thing was more than worrying.

Caroline Witbooi had been a pre-school teacher, but obviously the money was no good and she'd decided to try her hand at journalism. Just like that. After all, she had a diploma in kindergarten teaching and therefore she knew how to become a sub. The editor of the associated paper in Kimberley had assured her father, a man who could claim Struggle royalty, that his granddaughter would fit in just fine. But Ms Witbooi had soon tired of that dry, thorny part of the world and its social limitations, and she'd requested a transfer to that place where the real action was: Egoli, City of Gold, Jozi, Johannesburg, Joburg, call it what you will. That was where the big bucks were. One time. But it soon became clear that Ms Witbooi didn't have the foggiest idea of how to spell or string a sentence together, and when we tried to show her how she seemed to have the memory of a goldfish. We thought Robert Black as revise sub would give her hell, just as he had us, but he swallowed her vacuous excuses to the point that we feared for his life. He looked like he was constantly on the verge of a heart attack. Jay made a call to an ex-colleague in the city of the Big Hole and it soon became clear what had happened. No one wanted her, but no one wanted to be seen blocking her, either. Therefore, she was passed on, with glowing references, to the next bunch of suckers. Jay made as if she didn't exist, Desiree was as blunt as a sledgehammer, I was fascinated, amused but mostly despairing, and Ms Witbooi was as impervious to it all as a tweety bird. The big joke was that she had neglected to write a headline for a story on deadline and, as these things happen, it slipped past everyone and there it was, top of the page, loudly proclaiming that 'Headline goes hear'.

It was for an obituary.

When she wasn't working, which was most of the time (Bob simply bypassed her and piled the pressure on us), she was openly reading celebrity magazines. Not local ones but international ones. There she sat in an anorexic daze, reading about Britney et al, chewing gum while flirting with the black heavies and clearly delighting some – though far from all – of them. Soon, no doubt, she would be promoted over us or invited to write for the social pages, which we'd have to edit, looking up various double-barrelled surnames like Gcugcwa-Brkic.

The next day I got a phone call at work. It was a certain Howard Nathan who asked whether it was a good time to talk. Ever the optimist, I thought he might want to offer me a job, even though I'd never heard of him in a profession where everybody knew about or was aware of almost everyone else, so I scurried out on to the balcony where I'd first shaken Kayla's clammy hand to hear what the man had to offer. What a pleasure it'd be to have a change of jobs, a change of scenery, a sea change, perhaps, but I should have recognised that fuck-you tone of certain Joburg lawyers. He said his client had laid charges against me.

'And who might your client be?'

'Kayla Greenwood.'

'What are the charges?'

'Rape,' Nathan said.

Was it my imagination or were people avoiding making eye contact with me as I returned to my desk? I went back to subbing something about 'levelling the playing field' in rugby, but I was thinking I'd been told off by Kayla as well as Klara, the old man and I weren't talking to each other, and now I had to deal with something that would probably end my brilliant career at the newspaper too.

I didn't sleep or listen to Beethoven that night and the next morning the chief of HR, Herman Sebogodi, called. He spoke circuitously when all he really meant to say was that, because I was up on charges I was being suspended from work, with – and here he sounded deeply regretful – full wages.

'Thank you,' I said, rang off and told Butch we were going for a walk, which got him delirious. We went down the road with its bare trees, electric fences, private guards, high walls and furious dogs, which, in the absence of a reachable quarry, turned on each other instead. Lukas wasn't in his usual spot, but then I saw the notice on the palisade that if anyone wanted to contribute towards his funeral they could put money into the following bank account.

There was an icy wind blowing off the 'Berg and across the

Free State plains, sweeping over the sweet Suikerbosrand, picking up more dust from the last mine dumps in the south, getting radioactive from the Brixton tower and screaming through the South African Broadcasting Corporation's skyscraper, down into the Melville bowl and over its ancient koppies, where it marched along the corridor of yellow grass between suburbia and the cemetery. This was where my maternal grandmother lay. We had gone there in the Chevy when I was a child, with Ma drying a tear at the graveside and the old man complaining that the jacarandas were messing up the car while I stuffed dead flowers into a concrete bin reeking of rotting vegetation.

That night I went to Jay and Veron's, told them most of what had happened and they were fully on my side. Veron said I needed a woman to defend me, made a call and I spoke to Aisha Mohammad, who said I could come see her in her chambers 'in town' first thing the next morning.

Jay and I watched a rugby final and, because he still wasn't drinking, I decided I wouldn't either and after a quiet, pleasant supper with him, Veron and the girls I went home.

Whether anyone else in the office knew what was happening to me I did not know, nor did I particularly care: the powers-that-be could gloat as much as they liked in their little political certitudes. The only thing that worried me was that the old man would find out about my situation. I needed Klara badly, too much probably, so after about an hour of pacing about I got into my car and went out looking for Judith. What was I going to do if I saw her? Repeat our sole exercise? Offer to take her away from her miserable life? Get some Nigerian pimps howling for my blood? She could be drugged, infected, dead, her children motherless, for all I knew. Well done, Mr Bezuidenhout. You really are the model of a modern major-general.

Having decided that I'd stop looking for her, I decided to cruise the strip one last time, as if I were going somewhere, away, keeping an eye out for some pedestrian who might come up to you while stationary at a traffic light, just to blow your brains out for your cellphone. Then it occurred to me that it was not beyond the realms of possibility that Kayla's fancy lawyer might have me tailed to get evidence of my moral character – or lack thereof – so I kept an eye on the rear-view mirror to see if anyone was tailing me. Or had I been reviewing too many thrillers lately? Whatever the case, so busy was I keeping eyes out for all these phantoms that it took me a while to realise that there was a familiar car not behind me but ahead of me. It had a Blue Bulls sticker on its rear bumper and I decided to follow Dolfie and see what he preferred to his wife. He headed to an area I wasn't familiar with and bartered with a man in a dress who, after a short exchange, gracefully entered his Toyota. So much for Dolfie's impotence and his agricultural products. I was grateful that Klara had always insisted on using a condom – was it because she knew or suspected what Dolf was up to? Should I warn her? Would she believe me? Would *I* believe me? Round and around.

Back at home I tried to listen to the A-minor, informed as it is by pain. But it wasn't getting through to me. I was drifting off on a tangent, wondering where that famous temper came from. Had it been something in the water or utensils in Bonn? And if it was true that the old man's genes came from that neck of the woods, had we inherited that temper? Possibly. Why exactly had the dying man lain shaking his fist at the heavens? His work was done, I thought, though I hadn't yet heard the allegedly more conventional sixteenth. All I knew was that he'd had difficult relationships with unreachable women because of their class, and that he'd failed to provide his suicidal nephew, Karl, with a moral upbringing. Was he in a rage because he'd failed to produce as much work as Herrn Haydn, Bach and Mozart as a result of his concerns with Karl? Possibly, but doubtful. So what was it? Maybe, just maybe, he lay there venting because that temper, that vehemence, that intensity, was his only other way of staying fully present and alive to the very last mortal moment.

When dawn came Butch and I went for a run before I showered, dressed and drove to the centre of the city. Ms Mohammad was wearing a chador and gave me a firm, hennaed handshake. After a couple of pleasantries about how she and Veron had been involved in the Struggle and endured such pleasures as solitary confinement (while I was trying to find my precious white soul at some country college), we got down to business.

'You're going to have to tell me everything.'

'Sure,' I said, feeling very small.

'What happened on the night in question?'

'We were drinking and coking it up. She was taunting me.'

'How?'

'Dancing with her back to me, naked except for a pair of high-heeled shoes.'

This woman from another world but the same country was writing assiduously, neatly, firing questions at me, questions that were only going to get more embarrassing.

'What was she taunting you about?'

'About how her black lover was so much better – and bigger – than me. You know, the usual insults: how I was just an old, white, male racist.'

Ms Mohammad did not show whether she agreed with that assessment or not.

'Did you notice anything unusual about her?'

'What do you mean?'

'Anything about her behaviour.'

'No. She'd done these strips for me before.'

'Was there anything about her appearance that was different?'

'Well, she'd certainly had a makeover. I mean, she'd always dressed really badly. But now she was wearing a smart black suit, and looked good for it. And she'd switched to contact lenses.'

'Nothing else?'

'No, unless putting on a little weight is unusual. I remember thinking I preferred her – physically – with a little extra weight.'

Scribble, scribble, scribble.

'What happened then?'

'Well, this is embarrassing …'

'Don't worry. I'm a lawyer.'

'You're also a woman and a …'

'… Muslim,' she completed my sentence. 'Does that change anything?'

'No. I'm sorry.'

'What happened next?'

'Well, I started kissing her … you know …'

'No, I don't.'

'Her buttocks.'

'Did she say anything?'

'Well, I was being quite rough, and … um, she seemed to be liking it. I mean, she said so.'

'Do you think she might have been acting?'

'I … hell, I don't know … I wouldn't put it past her.'

'Then you had anal sex with her.'

'Ja.'

'Were you still being rough and was she still encouraging you?'

'Yes to the first and … once I was nearing orgasm she started shouting that I must stop.'

'Did you?'

'No.'

She carried on writing, which I tried – and failed – to decipher, upside down.

'Okay,' Ms Mohammad said, anticlimactically.

'Is that it?'

'Ja.'

'So what now?'

'She doesn't have a leg to stand on, even if she did make a video or recording of it and cut out the encouraging part.'

'Oh Jesus …'

'I wouldn't put it past her,' Ms Mohammad said blankly.

'I'll say,' I said. 'But what makes you think she doesn't have a leg to stand on?'

'First of all, the fact that she only reported you five days after the alleged rape already blows her case out of the water, however traumatic it was – and she'll try to make it sound traumatic. Secondly, it's almost certain that she's pregnant, whether with Edward Motshekga or someone else, so she wants the world to know just how callous you are. But then taking drugs, alcohol and smoking while being pregnant isn't very responsible.

'How do you prove that in retrospect?'

'She's a known coke-head. I've been doing a bit of asking around.'

'I think we're on shaky ground.'

'Maybe. And I must warn you that she's going to try to play the media game. She'll try to blow it up out of proportion, and even when she loses she'll say she struck a blow for all abused women.'

'That sounds about right,' I said, feeling some very warm feelings for this woman. 'So what do I do now?'

'Nothing. You do not speak to the media. You do not speak

to your colleagues, no one. Not even Jay or Veron. You refer everything – and I mean everything – to me. The more time goes by and the more pregnant she is, the worse her case becomes.'

'Thank you,' I said. 'Thank you.'

After I'd shaken her hand vigorously and thanked her like the old man always embarrassingly thanked others, grovelling with gratitude, I walked out into the street and had the other feeling I'd had that day I walked out of the divorce lawyer's office, an allegedly free man. It was the lingering taste of what the old man would call the 'faint tang of es-aitch-one-tee.' Still, I was as elated that Aisha Mohammad could help me as I was livid with Kayla for having taken this vicious little route. Perhaps she'd suffered the delusion that her gender and not her behavior made her virtuous. But then I wasn't exactly feeling like a saint, either. I felt miserable that I'd have to tell the old man what I'd been up to. He would stand by me, I knew, but his unspoken disappointment would be as sharp as a knife to the liver. I felt equally miserable that I wanted to leave this country, whether he'd advised me to do so or not. If I did, I would miss this street, this light, this air, these people, as much as I didn't know what to do with this echoing solitude and restlessness I felt. Worst of all, I knew that leaving wouldn't shake off the sense that I had allowed myself to overlap with the type of creature who'd occasioned the news poster I now passed:

Girl, 5,
Raped.

On Edge

The so-called wheels of justice slowly ground away at my nerves as the days and weeks went by. I wasn't prepared to call or see the old man, but every time the phone rang I almost jumped out of my skin. Was it one of my former colleagues calling, asking my opinion on the rape charges against me? Was it the old man, asking what was this he'd heard? Was it Uncle Vern calling to say the old man had died? Was it the emigration people saying they couldn't accept me if I had a court case pending? But most of the calls were for Ms Motsepe, or someone trying to sell me something. I could have done a lot of reading and writing, but I did nothing of the sort. Most of the time I spent moping and walking Butch. I was in legal and living limbo and it was worse, much worse, than fiery hell. If it wasn't for Jay and Veron, I would have gone completely out of my mind.

It was August, that month which always brought bad news

for me. August, when winter won't let go of itself, even though it teases you with premature signs of spring. The wind blows and cartwheels around your hollow guts, aimless, acute, aching. September came and had no sense of renewal whatsoever, but at least the jacarandas bloomed in October. Towards the end of that month Butch and I were walking in the park – it was a Saturday – when I bumped into a trauma shrink I knew from the days when we'd all been young, fabulous and united in our opposition to the tedious horror of apartheid.

'How are you?' I said.

'I'm fine thanks, Len,' she said slowly. 'And you?'

'Just great, thank you.'

'Good. How is your father?' she asked in that methodical, interrogatory way of her profession, knowing I'd meant exactly the opposite about myself but was not prepared to indulge it.

'My father?'

'Ja. You told me about your father one night. On the jol.'

'What did I say?'

'You said he'd been in a concentration camp, that your family only went to one place for your holidays every year, that he never went out anywhere and that he was paranoid about little things like paying the bills on time.'

'Yes?'

'Do you know why that is?'

'No. I thought that's just how he is.'

'I'm only saying this because I met someone similar recently. He'd come back from the war and had lived in Pietermaritzburg ever since. He had taken a menial job at the municipal swimming pool, but do you know how many times he'd been to Durban in those intervening sixty years?'

'No?'

'Once. And then it was for his daughter's wedding. He could hardly sit through the reception afterwards because he wanted to get back home again.'

'Why?

'Because they're terrified. They truly think that if they trespass now, they'll still be punished, now, as prisoners in the camp. They generally tend to take menial jobs in order to remain as below the radar as possible. They stay at home, where they feel safe. Does that apply to your father?'

I could scarcely bring myself to nod, realising she was effectively telling me that in a sense the old man had never left the camp. I thanked her and went home, determined to call him. As I walked towards the phone it started ringing.

'Bezuidenhout,' I said, expecting the worst.

'It's me,' the old man said, sounding frail, breathless, embarrassed.

'Hello, Dad. How are you?'

'When are you going to come and visit me?'

That was as much of an admission of guilt as I was going to get and it was more than enough: I felt a complete shit for everything I'd said to the old man. No matter what he'd said or done, I was a big boy now and had to steer my own ship.

'I'll see you tomorrow at ten, Dad.'

Early the next morning I washed the Civic and felt so good that I remembered a song the old man sometimes played on Sundays. It wasn't the usual upbeat rhymes of his youth but 'Funiculi Funicula', sung by a woman called Melissa Gorgeous. Funny names Italians have, I thought. I pictured her as a short, dark, Latin beauty like my mother, like that woman in the print in our living room. Her voice was high to start with and would then go higher still and could surely not go higher but, good God, it did. After showering, I had a thought and typed the singer's name into Google. I discovered her real name was Melisa Korjus, she was blonde and Estonian, and someone had put that song onto YouTube. The scratchy old Decca record had not been recorded in Italy or Germany but *Europe*. I put it on loudly so that I could listen while I shaved and then got dressed.

Driving to Centurion, I thought again about the Sundays of my youth. The old man would get up early, as usual, and work in the garden. When his wife got back from having raised the church's roof with her forced soprano – for she was an alto at the opera – he philosophised that he'd probably live until he died. He often cooked a *potjiekos* stew in a three-legged, cast-iron pot, getting the mix of vegetables, potatoes and lamb just right. Once he made me a wooden horse. If visitors came by after lunch, he'd ruffle his combed-back silver hair, widen his eyes and mouth with matchsticks, curl his fingers, hunch up his shoulders, and chase us. We children would squeal with terrified glee. In the late afternoon we'd have his ginger beer in summer, his orange marmalade on fresh white bread in winter. At seven o'clock we'd listen to Dennis Smith read the news on Springbok Radio and, no matter how bad things were, all was nevertheless well in the world.

He still wasn't waiting for me at the gates, which were locked.

I left the car outside and hopped over the gates and got to the brick heart before the dog started barking. I told it to piss off and that is exactly what it did before it calmed down. Then it followed me past the garage, which was locked, and over the back lawn. I didn't have a good feeling. The old man wasn't at the wash line or walking around the perimeter of the yard; maybe he was in the washroom, garage or house. But he wasn't in any of the above. He was sitting on an old upright chair he'd brought out on to the cement, dressed in his Sunday best, dozing away in the sun, close to tilting over. This was how it was supposed to be, I thought: he had earned his right to nod off in the sun with his silver hair, leather skin, broken nose, wrinkles, sun moles and dog.

'Dad?'

'Ja,' he said, instantly awake and ready to deal with whatever presented itself, as he had been for four score plus, and rising.

'How are you,' I said awkwardly.

'I'm fine,' he said, unusually. 'Do you feel like some coffee?'

'*Good* idea,' I said, shaking his gnarly hand and hurting it a bit before we went up the sunny steps. I caught his elbow as he almost slipped, then we passed the flimsy security gate and bottom door into the cool kitchen, its windows wide open.

'Oh shit,' I said.

'What?'

'I forgot to get your groceries.'

'Well, I forgot that you'd get them and Vern got them for me.'

'That's nice of him.'

'You know, when I was young, our garden was full of avocados, figs, mangoes, *bunches* of bananas.

No wonder you've lived so long, I said.

But that wasn't the only reason, he replied.

'What else could it be.'

'It's because I've never smoked, drunk or slept with another woman.'

'I wish I could say the same for myself.'

'Do you know how much this mug cost me?'

'No?'

'*Two* ninety-five.'

'*What?*'

'Usually it costs *six* ninety-five,' he crowed.

'That's amazing.'

So which mug did I want to drink from, he asked. I said I wanted the one with the rings around it, and he said *everyone* chose that one.

'Really?'

'Ja.'

A triumphant smile.

'I wonder why,' I said.

'I don't know. But do you know that I miss my father every day of my life?'

'No, I don't.'

He proceeded to tell me the story of how he'd accompanied his father on a hunting trip, how his father had intended shooting a kudu, how he, his son had frightened it off, and how his father had never hunted again.

'Do you think he maybe sensed he'd die soon?'

'I don't know, but I knew he was dead when those two men came walking towards me across the rugby field.'

'How old were you?'

'Eighteen.'

'That's very young. And soon you were in the North African desert.'

'Ja.'

'Captured, held, seeing what they did to old Johnny van Heerden, shooting him in the head.'

There was a blank pause.

'I think something died in me that day.'

'But you've done well, Dad. You're still here.'

He seemed to be thinking about something.

'You know, one year I forgot my mother's birthday and I'll *never* forgive myself.'

'I'm sure she's forgiven you, Dad.'

'Do you think so?'

'Yes, I do.'

Not sure of that, he told me he'd got us some Lemon Creams to have with our coffee.

'Cool.'

'Let's go and have them outside,' he said. 'So you can breathe.'

We went outside and dunked our Lemon Creams in our respective coffees and looked at the back yard and he helped the dog onto his lap in the sun and we enjoyed the warmth on our skins and he said this was the *only* place on earth he wanted to be. I said it was a good place because the air was clean (and the clouds were magnificent), and he said it was also good because the shopping centre, schools and new hospital were within walking distance.

'True,' I said.

And he sat there behind Ma's cheap, silver-rimmed sunglasses and looked so good that I took a snap of him with my cellphone. And then he said something that shocked even me, because it was a word he had never used in front of me, ever.

'I'm fucked,' he said.

'*What?*'

'Have another biscuit,' he replied.

'Dad, is there something or someone who's bothering you?'

There was a pause that seemed to go on forever before he said, 'No.'

'You can tell me anything, Dad.'

Another pause.

'You know,' he finally said, 'I've got so many clothes in my cupboard just hanging there, don't you want to take some of them?

'Let's have a look,' I said.

We went into that dark passage and even darker room where his wife had lain disintegrating and he switched on the light instead of opening the curtains. There were two shirts there that suddenly appealed to me: a check brown Van Heusen (by Appointment to Her Majesty) and a white one with vertical blue stripes which I thought might go well with my Levi's. So I took them and he was delighted and said I must please take the jacket I brought because it wasn't his kind of jacket and I did because, as I'd said before, it was my kind of jacket and I'd wear it and the Van Heusen, thinking of him.

Then he wanted to show me something in the garage and I was glad to get out of that room, that passage with its mirror and phone at the end of it and into the light-filled kitchen, out into the sun before entering the gloom of the garage again. He showed me where his last will was and then opened the Valiant's expansive hood to show me the chromed engine, which didn't run anymore.

'That's fantastic,' I said.

He closed it very carefully and covered it with the bedspreads he and Ma used to have on their bed when I was a child and jumped in with them, saying he had something for me. What is it, I wondered. It was his thick black Montblanc pen and I thanked him and assured him I wouldn't tell *any*one he'd given it to me.

'Thanks, Dad.'

'It's a pleasure, my boy,' he said in that grim, claustrophobic space.

'Shall we have some more coffee?'

He said he'd been thinking *exactly* the same thing, smiling that sweet smile of his, and he locked up his sanctuary, which took a long time as I stared at the brick heart baking in the sun.

We went back into the kitchen and made his weak coffee and my extra-strong one, which would kill me. Once that was done, we went back out to the courtyard again and drank our second coffees and he said he couldn't see the planes overhead anymore.

'That must be very frustrating,' I said.

Pause.

'You should go to work now.'

'Ja,' I said, suddenly reluctant to leave and deciding I wasn't going to tell him about the trouble I was in. He didn't need to know right now and maybe he'd never find out about it. But I also knew that all it took was a quiet day at the newspaper for a nondescript story to catch, especially if there was something similar brewing in a film or TV series. You could be a zero the one day and a massive, neon zero the next. Well, if it looked like that might happen, I'd personally let him know before anyone else, but right now I'd take my chances: he'd had enough misery from me without having to know this as well.

I said I would first help him with the dishes, which worried him. But I told him I still had plenty of time and I wouldn't be late and I wouldn't lose my job, so he said okay and we went inside and he told me exactly how dishes needed to be washed and dried. First you washed them in soap, then you rinsed them in clear water, then you wiped them with a damp cloth, then with a dry-as-bone one.

Once that was over there was a silence and we both knew I had to go. It was the last thing I wanted to do but we shook hands and walked towards the Civic on the street. He opened the gates for me, his faithful dog by his side, and I got into the car, got out again and put my arms around him.

'You don't know how much we loved you,' he quaked, this old bag of hot skin and bones beneath his Sunday jacket, smelling of dog.

'Thank you, Dad.'

'Look after yourself, my darling.'

'You too, Dad.'

'Goodbye, my boy.'

I got into the car, started it and waved at the man with the silver hair, standing as upright as Charlie Chaplin, thinking I didn't mind coming here anymore. In fact, I looked forward to visiting again, even if he lived to be a hundred, and I hoped he did, no matter how much more difficult, deaf and helpless he became.

Late Spring

My living hell of waiting continued and the next Saturday I was in the park again when I bumped into that beautiful woman I'd met in the bush.

'Frauke,' she said, offering me her hand.

'Hi, Frauke. I'm Len.'

'Isn't it wonderful?'

I wondered if anything could be wonderful (apart from her eyes), but asked her what she meant by that.

'Weren't you here in winter?'

'Yes?'

'Didn't you see how the marsh was control-burnt so that it could renew itself in spring again?'

'Yes.'

'Didn't you see how the new shoots sprang up again?'

I *had* half-consciously noticed the strong green shoots pushing up through the burnt black stubs in passing, so 'Yes.'

'And look how tall the reeds are now.'

She was right. It was a miracle and I'd been too busy staring up my own rectum to acknowledge it.

'Would you like to go to a movie tonight?' I said.

'I'd love to go to a movie.'

'What's your address?'

She gave it to me as some friends of hers came along with their new-born child and she knelt to give it her full attention, instinctively covering its tiny chest. I inexplicably wanted to burst into tears and told her I'd see her at seven and left.

That night we went to see whatever the movie was called and I ended up spending the night at her garden cottage, telling her about my predicament. The next morning we made love again and I was too smitten to even call the old man, and so that Sunday melted into yet another long Monday of waiting.

On Death

The sun rose at 6.27am on November 13, 2007 over the municipality of Centurion. At 123 Harry Smith Avenue the old man whose wife and sisters had called him Son was awake already, for he was an old soldier, an old warrior, an old worrier. His dog, which had lain next to his head throughout the fitful night, needed to go out and relieve itself.

The old man got up, probably cursed as he had his whole life, and opened the kitchen door's two halves and the flimsy security gate. The sun streamed in from beyond the Waterkloof Air Base and the dog went outside and did its business. The old man put on the kettle and started preparing their oats for the day. Then he probably went to the toilet to relieve himself too.

When he came back into the kitchen the dog was done and the old man didn't close the doors or the gate; he liked the sun shining into his kitchen, even though the gate wouldn't really have blocked the sun. He and the dog had their porridge and tea and possibly watched the news on the scratchy black-and-white TV in the bedroom across the passage. At about 8.30 the phone rang down the dark passage and the old man probably cursed that too. Then he switched the TV off and went to answer the phone to talk to his Empangeni sister, with the dog faithfully following him.

Outside, the street was fairly empty, for school had just started. The old man had forgotten to lock the gates, which now opened. Feet started walking down the brick driveway, possibly two pairs, probably male. Their owners didn't know – nor care – that a black and white photograph had been taken on that driveway, long before the new bricks and their rough little heart were laid. The photograph was of an upright man and his smiling, scowling son. The man was handsome and his hair was combed straight back. He wore polished shoes, Oxford bags, a white shirt and a light-brown jacket. He was going grey already, but you could see he had the body of an athlete, a god. In his hand he held a stick which he would turn into a sword for his son, who had a big head and was squinting in the Highveld glare. The boy was leaning against his father's leg, feet turned inwards, wearing a bright-red cowboy shirt and blue jeans that were too big for him. They were rolled up at the bottom and rested on his veldskoens. The picture was taken by the boy's adoring mother, who also loved taking photographs on her many overseas excursions.

The old man assured his sister he was alright as the feet continued down the driveway, over the brick heart and past the garage where the lifeless Valiant now stood in place of the Chevy, the car in which the man in the photograph used to take the boy down to the military base every Saturday afternoon. This was the highlight of the boy's week and he loved the movies, but he desperately wanted his father to come with him. One day he'd thrown a colossal tantrum about how no one ever wanted to do anything with him, about how he had no friends, and the old man had gone into that bughouse with him. The old man had juddered his leg and clicked his nail and the boy liked to remember that the film they saw was the one in which a father and son are on the run from the Nazis. They hide in a concealed hollow in the forest and the soldiers come with long spikes, poking the earth to feel if there are any people hiding there. A soldier stops right above them and pushes the blade down and the only thing the father can do is put his hand in the way so that it feels like there's solid earth beneath the soldier. The father shudders with pain while he holds his other hand over his son's wide-eyed mouth. The soldier finally pulls the blade out, the earth wipes away the father's blood, and the soldier moves on as the feet passed the side of the garage and walked across the back lawn.

This is where the boy used to re-enact the films he'd seen, playing the role of cowboys *and* Indians, for without playmates he had to make do, dying a thousand deaths on both sides, but always keeping a spare bullet for that Indian who wanted to scalp him. Uncle Vern had once said if those deaths had been real the back lawn would have been a 'bloodbath, man'.

The feet now stepped onto the cement courtyard, passing the silver 45-gallon drum in which the man in the photograph had sometimes bathed the boy of a balmy summer's evening, when the boy had scraped his knees and elbows bloody from dying others' deaths, his eyes swollen and leaky from grass and dust allergies. Yet that dusky world had been timeless and filled with endless possibilities.

The old man felt slightly annoyed that his sister was worried about his diet as the feet approached the back stoep, passing the laundry on the left, which may have been locked, unless the old man had forgotten to close it, which was very likely of late. He had sometimes bathed his son in there too, standing him in one of the stone sinks and letting Len rub his feet over the bumpy part used for scrubbing clothes. The boy had once, and only once, painted a symbol on the washroom's wall with some Shoeshine. He'd seen that symbol in *The Sound of Music*, which the old man had only come along to see 'for the sake of the family'. Afterwards, he'd said the only part he liked was when Christopher Plummer tore that red-black-and-white flag in two, yet Len had gone and painted a Shoeshine swastika on the wall and the old man asked him whether he knew what it meant. Sensing something was terribly wrong, the boy said 'No.' The old man told his son that he'd been prepared to die fighting against everything that symbol represented, and the boy didn't understand but knew it was very important.

The feet went up the three steps and their owner or owners saw the back door was open, so the feet went into the kitchen where young Len had once walked in as well, but from his bedroom, yawning, as the dog started barking. His mother had made her husband bacon, eggs and toast. It was unusual for Len to be up so early, for he was a night person, but on that particular morning he'd stood up and entered the kitchen in his pyjamas. His father had sat him on his knee and held out a square-inch work of culinary art. On the prongs of that fork were a piece of hot toast, its salty butter still cold, some hot egg white with a dab of yellow yolk, topped with pepper and salt. It was a taste Len would never be able to replicate, much as he tried for the rest of his life. Then his father had finished his tea and Len and his mother had walked with his father to the front door, past the phone and the mirror, where he kissed his wife and son goodbye and started walking down to Sportpark station in the cool summer dawn, Len's hero.

Now the old man started shouting at the dog to shut up, said goodbye to his sister and came into the kitchen, where he was either attacked immediately or after he'd told the man or men to get the hell out of his house. Nothing much was taken, except a life, and afterwards the man or men rushed through Len's old bedroom, where he'd sometimes had terrible nightmares as a child. He'd lie whimpering until his father got into bed with him and told him it was all right, it was only a dream. 'Go to sleep now. It was just a bad dream.'

Dog Guards Master's Corpse

The hadedas cawed, a car alarm went off, a helicopter passed overhead and the traffic whined in the background. I got up, performed my ablutions and got dressed. Then, after putting out the key for Ms Motsepe, I told Butch we were going for a walk again.

A new, younger guard had replaced Lukas and had an ugly air about him. I avoided the Doberman jerk and the Rottweiler dragon and missed Klara. There was a dead duck in one of the dams. Further on and just off the track was an abandoned supermarket trolley, lying on its side.

We went home and I fed Butch but didn't feel like eating anything. So I made myself and Ms Motsepe some tea and started up my computer. Ms Motsepe came in and started drinking her tea in staring silence. I went upstairs and tried to write while I waited for the machinations of the law to take their course, but found it impossible to concentrate. There was no one I could call and nowhere I could go to. Wait a bit. There *was* someone I could call. I was still feeling guilty about not calling the old man after missing out on our usual Sunday visit, so I called to tell him I was thinking of him, but he wasn't answering. Occasionally I'd do that and he'd be *so* grateful. Probably out in the garden, I reasoned. Or the garage, dreaming of driving the Valiant or Chevy again. Or just ignoring the phone in a temper. Or really not hearing it.

I tried to write again. Still nothing. *Think*, I told myself. If you can't write one thing, write another. Start on that new story you've been thinking about. But it was all flat. Well then read a book or go see a film. Not interested. Ms Motsepe came struggling up the stairs with the vacuum cleaner and I passed her halfway down.

I wandered around in the back garden, which really was too big for a single man, let alone a large family, and picked the last lemon of winter. It was rotten. Was the old man near *his* lemon tree? Butch had joined me and I thought of the one time the old man and Ma had come to see our new house. Butch had taken to the old man like a duck to water. Animals instinctively knew there was safety and kindness there. And what's wrong with being attracted to kindness, comfort, food? A good curry smell – another thing Shanti had rejected – came wafting in from one of the neighbours as a Jumbo flew overhead. I'd call Uncle Vern and ask him to check up on the old man.

I couldn't go back to my study, my computer, my safety blanket, so I sat on the couch downstairs. I could always watch TV, but what for? The last thing I felt like watching was cheerful people selling anything from exercise machines to funeral plans. I'd go for another walk, this time alone. Butch could look after the house and Ms Motsepe, confusing any would-be burglars about any routine in my life. I could walk in such a way that I avoided the main road with its bloody headlines, so I did. Everything looked so orderly, so normal, yet the country was at war with itself. If it was open warfare in the neglected country townships, it was covert here. At night people walked or drove around, looking for ways to rob, rape, kill. There was a new minority ruling the country. And there was still a bit of a chill in the air. Strange how the seasons were changing. Every year winter came a little later and ended a little later. Nothing was how it used to be, you hear yourself thinking. How often you'd scoffed at those who said the very same thing. But it was true. In the past the summers had been as regular as clockwork. It was a rule that on the first day of spring it would rain. The day would start as bright and fresh as an apple blossom. By midday the air would start thickening, the sound of Maria's ironing board creaking in the heavy heat. By four the billowing clouds would have turned black, a wind whipped up before the first heavy drops of rain hit the tarmac, almost lazily stirring up the smell of the day's dust. The heavy clouds would release their load and the front lawn would be under water in minutes as you stood at the window, gaping. And, almost as soon as it had started, it was over. The air was clean. You ran barefoot in the sodden, splashing grass. But this was a confused, delayed spring. It was cold, warm, and the clouds didn't quite do their work. Maybe it was some sort of sign. Maybe I should take the whole thing of emigrating more seriously. Maybe I should go and live somewhere else not only because I found the local politics appalling, but because I found my*self* appalling. I had always fantasised about being a traveller. Now I could do that, once the trial – or jail time – was over. In fact, I decided right then I was going to leave. I would take myself to the airport and fly away. I needed to fight this fight from another angle. Yes. That was it.

I went home, timing it so that I could have lunch without having to negotiate my way around Ms Motsepe's current mood. But I couldn't eat. I was completely out of sync with the rest of the working world. Nothing would ever be the same again. If I won my case, I would always have that stigma of having been the accused. If I lost, I'd lose my job and I'd be back to square one: a failed writer, not to mention human being.

Would this goddamn day ever end? Is this what it's like to be old? You might be secure, but there's nothing to do. No one sees you or cares about you. You have seconds, minutes, hours, days, weeks, months, years and even decades in which nothing of any value whatsoever happens. You wait out your days as your body gets colder and more uncomfortable and your children deign to call you when it suits them – if you have children, if they bother to call – and some invisible clock ticks away, as coldly indifferent as the planets in that cold night sky that keeps you awake. You could write a *War and Peace* of regrets, but no one would buy it. *You* wouldn't buy it.

The phone rang and I almost jumped out of my skin. But it was, of all people, Shanti. She wanted to know how I was and I said I was fine, lying, knowing she'd know I was lying.

'How are *you*?'

'I'm fine thank you, Len.'

'Good,' I said, meaning it. 'I was just thinking about you and how you always refused to cook curry.'

A pause.

'Len, I know about Kayla.'

I grunted.

'She's trying to win a battle but she's going to lose the war,' she said in that sing-songy way I'd missed for so many months, weeks, nights.

'Thank you,' I said. 'How're things going with old whatshisname?'

'Oh, that's over,' she replied. 'Is there anyone else in your life?'

'No, but I want to say something to you.'

There was what seemed an expectant pause before she said, 'What is it?'

'I'm sorry about the way I used to speak to you.'

'That alright, Len. I wasn't exactly a colonial tea party, was I?'

'Maybe we could start an apologists' club,' I said.

'Oh, but it would much too crowded for you,' she lilted.

I chuckled and could hear her smiling and things could have gone back to the way they used to be in that silence, but instead I said: 'So what's up?'

'I just called to speak to Beauty too.'

Amazing what a little three-letter word can do for the spirits.

'Well, I don't know if she can be bothered during her lunch break,' I said, which got her laughing, as of old.

Another pause.

'I'll call her for you,' I said.

'Thank you, Len.'

'Bye, Shanti.'

The two of them had their conversation and I still didn't know what to do, so I went to my computer and saw that my application for emigration had been approved. Then I went out to Ms Motsepe's room and told her she could take the afternoon off. It was ridiculous that she had to clean this house every day. I told her she could stay on, but she only had to work here one day a week. I'd pay her the same as always so she could work for others and make more money. However, this would only be the case for the next year or two, unfortunately, because I'd be going away. Overseas. She didn't seem upset in any way – a lifetime of servitude didn't exactly encourage surprise – and we came to an agreement about what might be a reasonable payout for her.

I put on the 16th quartet, opened the front doors and sat on the front stoep, listening to that man whose quartets had become the soundtrack to my life. 'Must it be?' that great but fading work asks. 'Yes, it must!' it replies. Once that was over, I just sat there, listening to the city going home after a day's toil. There seemed to be a moment of universal stillness as I basked in the setting sun, having finally accepted what remained of the day and making some kind of peace with my ex-wife.

Then the phone rang.

On Farewell

The sea is utterly still. It is terrifyingly calm. There isn't a swell, a breeze – nothing. Even the accusing sky seems in cahoots with this vast mass. There are no satellites to show that man has been here before, but we know the little we know and this deck I stand on is real enough, as are the sleeping crew below decks. We are on a 21-footer in a vast ocean, heading towards the land of wiki, if we ever get there. We are more or less in the centre of the Ring of Fire, which was the whole idea. The others don't know or need to know that I have come out here to farewell you. I have to put an end to it all. I have to let you go and vice versa, but now that the moment has arrived, I hesitate.

If I were more superstitious, I might even see the first sign of movement as an omen, for the fog is moving in, like an army of ghosts. It soon envelops me and I might as well be the last man alive, if man be the word. I am sightless, unhearing. I am completely alone and must persuade myself that I am everything but. Apart from the sleeping sailors below, I could be surrounded by the spirits of a hundred thousand others. How many have rowed, sailed, flown past this point? Millions, thousands, hundreds, a few or none. It does not matter. It is time I learnt to be alone, and I am terrified.

How did I get here? I took your advice. I got out of that country. People told me they would also leave if 'that' happened to them. I gave up trying to convince them that the decision had been made before your murder, that I wasn't leaving to run, but to fight. You don't have to live in a country to help rebuild, subvert or continue loving it. But it's also true that there were other forces at work. My time at the *Daily News* had run its course. The trade unionist had been replaced by an accountant, who felt his salary had to be on par with those of other CEOs', so who better to get rid of than an ageing, opinionated white man who was more interested in the fact of Beethoven's genius than the accuracy of what some or other politician promised? And I still think, all evidence to the contrary, that it's better to be an optimist who is usually disappointed than a pessimist who is never surprised. I can't help it. I sit down and want to write about all the troubles of the world, but I feel *good* about the act. My spirits lift.

It is also true that I did not do this on my own. I married a beautiful woman and know that Frauke would have been your *favourite* daughter-in-law. She has borne you a grandson and of course you would have said that one day he'd grow a beard. At this stage, however, he is still getting used to the idea of exploring, and he doesn't sit still for one moment. They are safe in the house we bought in our new country. And, as these things happen, it's in an area where solid wooden houses were built for returning servicemen. The street names say it all: Tripoli, Al Alamein, Tobruk, where there has been trouble again. But then as soon as we got to this new country, an earthquake tore into it: Lyttelton was particularly hard hit. In the meantime, we've started all over again. We took menial jobs, grateful for that, for the day, for the fact that we were in a country where the elderly, women, children, animals and the dead are respected. Generally. We couldn't believe that the land is not merely a succession of bloody battles but also shaped by myths, love stories. Talking of which, I could also conjure up a good love story for you, thinking of that seductive beauty lounging on a tree trunk in our living room. Who says you didn't see this woman with her gleaming black hair, red lips, green eyes and olive skin on the rainy streets of Bari? Who says she didn't transfix you as a few did me in my youth? All I have to go on is a living-room print and the fact that she resembles my mother in her own youth, and the fact that you happily paid for her to keep her hair raven black in her later years – every Friday.

But I have subsequently read a local man's increasingly dark love letters from North Africa, Italy and then East Germany. Why did you never tell me about that desert pit you were kept in after being captured; the terror of crossing a sea crawling with submarines; the horror of Europe; the cold; the hard bunks; the torpor; the hunger (the never-ending hunger); the lice? Were the roads not lined with corpses when you left that camp? Why did you never talk about that? Equally as disturbing, why did I never ask you?

So here I am, effectively alone at sea, wearing that jacket you didn't want, accompanied by a smoker's cough. You were quite right about the jacket; it *is* too bulky, and at our age we need all the streamlining we can get, don't we? But did I ever tell you I wanted to run away to the sea? Of course I didn't. I never told you anything. I, who repaid your generosity with sullen ingratitude, sensing that you wanted to live your dreams through me. Even when I 'ran away' from home one school holiday you were delighted, even encouraged me. You, who would never go anywhere again, who would never the see world except through barbed wires. Well, on that particular adventure a man took me sailing on the Wild Coast and I discovered a sense of freedom, a sense of peace. Out there it was just me and the silent power of the wind. I have waited a very long time to recapture that feeling. So I thought I'd share it with you, finally. I thought I should sail out here and talk to you, farewell you – as they say in this new country – once and for all.

Still I hesitate.

This is not the first time I have tried to bid you goodbye; the previous attempt was a complete disaster. I had seen the name White Island and knew I had to go there. So I drove to that foreign coast and boarded the boat, heading out to the submarine volcano. What was I thinking, though? Was I going to ask the captain to cut the engines so I could do what I had to do in front of a bunch of day trippers, in broad daylight? Was I going to make a spectacle of myself, even in my most private moment? Couldn't I have done the deed while everyone was otherwise engaged, taking pictures of the approaching island, reputed to have been enveloped in a white cloud when Captain Cook first saw it? That island which Maori revere, and rightly fear. But it would have been too showy, too disrespectful. I tried to find a private corner on the roaring vessel, but someone joined me, a bald old fart with a beard who felt he had to talk. When that failed, he started whistling with a trill, which gave me the giggles, thinking of how you would have cut him to pieces – after the fact, of course. And then there were the boys, out on an educational trip. The kind of boys you'd like, boys full of normal, Dennis the Menace mischief. The fat boy sitting in the sun and spray, his white legs shaking like jelly. Another stealthily approaches and slaps the tender inner thigh – and runs – followed by a shrill curse.

But that trip wasn't entirely unsuccessful, because not only did I see my entire life in a tiny black bird, skimming the water, but I also discovered I wasn't some white man spewing sulphur over a personal affront as so many of our compatriots do in this new, far-distant country. I realised that I, too, am an African, shaped as much by the four-plus decades I lived on that continent as anyone else. After all, did I not learn lessons from the likes of Abdullah Ibrahim, Hugh Masekela, Lesley Makhene, 'Judith' and the incomparable Ms Beauty Motsepe? Was it not she who spoke the fundamental truth that you were a big man in years and therefore had to be respected, if for nothing else than that? Was it not ordinary people who taught me that Africa doesn't just consist of power-hungry morons, bloated babies and beautiful sunsets? Does that all fall away just because I left? I think not, much as I miss everyone, including Kayla Greenwood – such invention! – and Karla Groenewald – such *fortitude*. Surely that white cop who wept when she told us it would be better to remember you as you were than see what your killers had done to you is also an African? I tried to enter our kitchen after her tears, but the smell emanating from there was no longer that of Highveld air or dog. And that's all you ever smelled of: fresh air and dog. My youth was finally, irretrievably, belatedly and deservedly over. But surely that self-same cop was talking *African* sense when she said I should be grateful to have had such a good father for so long, considering what *her* father had called her and her sisters? Surely a part of her was also weeping for what could have happened if your wife, my mother, had still been alive?

As for those fools who killed you, singular or plural, they

could have been relatively rich. All they needed to have done was observe you going to your garage once a month, stacking away so much cash for your ungrateful son. Instead, they chose to walk into the kitchen of an old soldier who realised his time to fight had finally come. They chose to bash your head in with Ludwig van Beethoven's bust when you resisted them. They chose to tie you up when you carried on fighting, an old man driven mad by decades of loneliness, disappointment and shattered dreams. They chose to ignore you as you started choking on your own blood, your broken nose broken once again, the last seconds of your life as frantic as the song 'Son', alone, and ending as abruptly in mid-phrase.

I have to concede that I was wholly surprised by Gerhard de Freitas's sermon. I never thought I'd agree with a minister of religion, but this time I did. Well chosen, Dad. What insight from such a supposedly foolish old man. He seemed to transform in front of our very eyes, speaking not God's own Methodist English but that other African language, Afrikaans. If he perceptively and fondly described you as a 'beautiful curmudgeon' then he also perceived that your killers still had choices. They could repent or they could suffer the immense wrath of God. This was true beyond religious semantics. But you'd just done what an old soldier had to do, regardless of ideology. It is an ancient tale. You were the hero, are the hero, my hero. Not because you were prepared to die for your country, but simply because you were prepared to live with the daily disappointment of your long, terrified life. They do not inhabit my dreams as you do, nightly. So, long may they suffer the sentiment that five minutes of power can obliterate five decades, if not millennia, of love, service, influence. They are nothing until they start taking that dangerous first step of thinking about – and then acting upon – their actions. I have high hopes for such an eventuality. Equally contemptible are those bastards who came out here and never allowed themselves to be seduced by Africa on its own terms. You know, those pale parasites who pointed fingers there and point fingers here, too. They, who would never admit that they or their forebears put Africans in a rat trap and then expected them to act not only human but European, no less. They are as guilty of your death as the human flotsam who actually killed you, omitted to prevent it, and sometimes even wished it – guilty as charged.

But none of this really matters to you anymore, does it? What you'd really want to know is what happened to your friend, your companion. Well, after the police got a vet to sedate the dog who wouldn't leave your side (and which gave the newshounds their angle), he was put in a kennel for the night and I collected him the next day. My dog, Butch, was beside himself with joy. He played the poor thing back into shape, harassed it endlessly, kept it so busy that it didn't have time to miss you during the day. But the damage had been done long before you saved his life and at night he keened for you. When we left, he and Butch were taken over by Jay and Veronica Redland, and to this day they frolic in that most South African symbol of middle-class comfort, a swimming pool.

So you were right, Dad. All good stories do end happily.

As for justice, well, that's another story. That young woman I once brought home, Kayla, accused me of raping her and wanted to take me to court, which would have meant I wouldn't be standing here. But she made the mistake of telling our recently promoted deputy editor how she'd entrapped me, assuming that justice is determined by female solidarity instead of female intelligence. The new editor, though no friend of mine, told her in no uncertain terms that she would testify against her and fired her on the spot.

As for your killers, they are still as free as the living dead, thanks to your ex-colleagues, who botched the evidence.

But what is that shape in the fog? It cannot possibly be a coast guard. We're much too far out at sea. Is this what the good captain and his sailors saw after too many months on the water? Apparitions? I don't know, but if it is a ghost ship it has Japanese writing on its side, another bit of news out here on the quiet colossus, the rig starting to tap the mast softly. The lost ship slowly drifts by like a life, a race, a language, driven by the tides Māori could read like San do the desert. That is why I'm here. I need this terrifying immensity to remind myself of your wife's love for you and yours for her. And I can hear more than just the rig now, getting a little louder. For a while now I have heard your and Ma's laughter in those of the living. How could she laugh with such deep pleasure? How could you laugh with such intense mischief? But I also hear a school choir singing 'My Grandfather's Clock' in its second language. And I'm finally starting to understand the A-minor too, the 15th. Music that is out of this world, as Ma used to say. The music is saying, come. Look at your son, standing there on the boom with his back to us. What is he doing there in the dissipating fog at the end of the bow? Why is he putting his hand in his jacket pocket? What is he taking out of it? Is it a pistol? Let's go and look. Let's see how he chooses to farewell you and himself. Let's see what it is. Mind you don't slip, stumble and scrape your shin now. What does he have in his hand? It's not a pistol, in case you were worried, it's an envelope. Why does your son have an envelope in his hand? Well, as one storyteller to another, I was given this paper glove at your funeral – songless and flowerless, as you wished. It was given to me by the undertaker.

It is time to go now. I would have preferred to have a hundred warriors perform a haka to farewell you. If anyone deserves it, it is you and the millions of other nonentities whose lives are determined by those of ambition. But I am too new to this country. They do not care where we come from. They only care where we can take them. We cannot argue with that. It is right. So I will perform this act, make this gesture, born at my desk, for even there I tried to emulate you. If you were a fingerprints clerk and I a writer, were we not trying to deal with what makes each one of us so different, but human?

What is inside the envelope? Something even lighter and softer than that tiny bird's finest feather, something as heavy as this planet in the clearing, glittering sky. I must let you go and you must do the same. I have to go and live my own small life, die my own small death. I must tend to the insistent sail, for the wind is building, the ocean stirring. I am making this gesture in the hope that you have made peace with your God and your father and that you have forgiven yourself for forgetting your mother's birthday one year. I do so in the hope that you are with the woman who gave up her life for you, who did her best to protect your infinitely sensitive soul from this grinding, barbarous world. I do so in the hope that your death finally liberated you from the barbed wire of 1943 to 1945, that you are now free from whoever or whatever else it was that haunted you. I do so in the hope that whatever or whoever else it was that was torturing you has now left you in peace. I do so in the hope that you'll forgive me for being so angry with you over so little for so long, that I used that sad weapon of silence to deprive you of a life you could have lived by proxy. I do so out of gratitude for your giving me that one thing we fear more than anything else. I never knew freedom would be so hard. I do so in the hope that the great soul of that kudu you saved rests and abides with you, now and for evermore.

I'm sorry I never matched your generosity, which is greater

than all hatred and charity combined. I'm sorry that I was so wrapped up in myself that I never recognised your pain. I'm sorry that I wanted you to be something neither of us ever could be. I'm sorry about all the jagged things I said and wrote and thought. I'm sorry that I played a tiny part in your dying violently and alone, thinking what I thought, writing what I wrote, doing what I didn't. I truly think you were more sinned against than the old king himself, you old patron and piper of the canine kingdom. You old breaker of hearts and horses. You old maker of *potjiekos*, ginger beer and wooden steeds. You old judderer of the foot and clicker of the nail. You old soother of nightmares. You old charmer. You old young man. You gentle barbarian. You raver, you rager, you raconteur. You fearless warrior, you helpless babe. You sage, you frail old fool.

You free man.

The fates of the final movement have started, steady and sure and beyond any contradiction, the shroud slapping more urgently. I must go now, Father, not because I want to but to honour you, your wife, your daughter-in-law and your grandson. I have a story to tell and it's thanks to you, once again. I will try to do justice to the mystery you presented as yourself. I will try to tell your story as truthfully as possible, even if I lie wholesale about my own. I will sing your praises, for do we Africans not sing the praises of great souls? And so I open this envelope and hold its contents for the longest moment I have ever known. Then, with the help of Master Beethoven and the four winds, I open my fist and commit a tuft of your fine, silver hair to the mighty Pacific.